The Extra-Ordinary Princess

The Extra-Ordinary Princess

Carolyn Q. Ebbitt

BLOOMSBURY

NEW YORK BERLIN LONDON

First published in the United States of America in August 2009
by Bloomsbury Books for Young Readers
Paperback edition published in August 2010
www.bloomsburykids.com

For information about permission to reproduce selections from this book, write to
Permissions, Bloomsbury BFYR, 175 Fifth Avenue, New York, New York 10010

The Library of Congress has cataloged the hardcover edition as follows:
Ebbitt, Carolyn Q.
The extra-ordinary princess / Carolyn Q. Ebbitt. —1st U.S. ed.
p.   cm.
Summary: Although Amelia, the youngest of the four princesses in Gossling, seems in all ways
ordinary, she discovers that she has an important role to play in saving her kingdom from destruction.
ISBN-13: 978-1-59990-340-8 • ISBN-10: 1-59990-340-7 (hardcover)
[1. Fairy tales. 2. Princesses—Fiction. 3. Individuality—Fiction.] I. Title.
PZ8.E15Ex 2009   [Fic]—dc22   2008041101

ISBN 978-1-59990-484-9 (paperback)

Book design by Donna Mark
Typeset by Westchester Book Composition
Printed in the U.S.A. by Worldcolor Fairfield, Pennsylvania
1 3 5 7 9 10 8 6 4 2

For my mother, Marilyn S. Ebbitt,
with all of my love

Country of Reede

· Manderville

Fairy Grove

· City of Neeg

Western Mountains

Western Valleys

Gossling

NORTHERN

SUNFLOWER FOREST

· Golden City

Otter River

Jeweled Mountains of Nylorac

· Cramsie City

Southern

BRAMMIAN

The Extra-Ordinary Princess

PROLOGUE

ON THE SIXTH DAY, the queen lay dying. The afternoon was bright, and the sun peeking through the tightly drawn curtain was strong, though outside the heat of the past ten weeks had broken and it was finally fall.

For four months a terrible illness had spread through the small country of Gossling; it spread quickly through the tiny towns and villages, traveling down the long rivers and over high hills, through the country's dense forests and into its cities. No scientist, doctor, or scholar knew how the sickness spread or how it might be cured. For months, hundreds suffered and died, and in the palace the king and queen grew anxious and wept for their people. The royal advisors urged them to leave the palace, to go to the safety of the Blue Mountains that—ringed with snow—had not been touched with the sickness. But the king and queen would not leave, for they thought, *Who would rule? Who would give hope to the people?*

Poring over both modern and ancient books of medicine, surrounded by doctors studying the disease, the king and queen believed that a cure was not far from being found. Besides, in their hearts, the king and queen never believed the sickness would reach the capital or the castle that stood in its center.

Yet even the great stone walls of the city, the guardsmen, and the royal advisors could not keep out the disease, and soon it reached the palace. And on this bright afternoon, on this first day of fall, the sound of wailing filled the halls of the palace and the streets of the city. Only hours before, the good king had died. Now the queen held the wrinkled hand of her nursemaid, and the older woman knew that death was near.

Queen Charlotte opened her eyes and looked at her old friend. "Will you open the drapes so I can see the mountains?"

Dori moved quickly despite her age, pulling back the heavy green curtains and unlatching the windows—pushing them open to the light fall breeze. Below, the gardens were empty and the grounds oddly quiet; only the sounds of the nearby river tripping over rocks and moss filled the afternoon. Dori paused there, seeing what the queen saw. Her pale eyes looked beyond the palace walls, beyond the green hills, to the faraway Blue Mountains, covered in haze and snow.

Weakly, the queen sat up on the bed, her voice anxious. "The girls are safe there?"

"Yes." The older woman nodded, her voice confident and sure. "The sickness has not reached the mountains, I am certain."

"There is another danger . . ." The queen fell back against her pillows, exhausted, though still her eyes watched the mountains, as if she hoped to see the Winter Palace, where the four princesses were safe.

"Yes." Dori left the window, and walked toward the bed, "I sense it too. It is a danger that is not yet seen."

"I have seen it." The queen's voice was a whisper, and her body shook with fever.

Dori passed a cool hand over her forehead to soothe her, to try to draw the heat from her body, but the queen, knowing there was little time, pulled her friend's hand from her forehead and held it tightly in her own hands. "Listen to me, Dori, listen. There is danger, a danger that will do more than destroy the girls—it will destroy the kingdom, the country. It is a darkness and it fast approaches . . . promise me that you will try to stop it; that you will help the girls."

It is true that the queen was sick with fever, but her mind was clear, and she knew that the older woman had powers beyond her own. She remembered how, when she was a child, she had seen Dori's hands close over the broken body of a bird—and had seen the bird rise and lift from those hands, healed. Dori saw the memory of the bird in the queen's eyes, for that too was one of her powers, and she wanted to comfort the queen whom she had loved as her own daughter, but there was no comfort she could give, for her powers alone were not great enough to heal such a sickness.

"Promise me you will help them," the queen's voice was edged with urgency. "Promise!"

Dori nodded, but the queen's eyes were closing. "I promise," she said, squeezing the queen's hand. There was the faintest squeeze in return, and Dori pressed her lips against the queen's forehead, kissing her good-bye. From the valley below, she heard a church bell strike the hour. It was two o'clock and the queen was dead.

❧

In the mountains of Glacier, far beyond the White Mountains, beyond the Seven Ridges, on the basin of the Black Lake, in the cliff palace caves, something stirred and an old man rose to his feet. There was no one who saw the man rise. There was no human for a hundred miles. But if there had been people watching him, they might have gasped or cried out in fear, for he was frightening to look at. Under his black cloak, the man was very thin, almost gaunt, his body was hunched and bent, and though he moved as easily as a young man, his face was as old as the mountains around him—lined and pale as ice—only his black eyes burned. The man moved out of the dark palace onto the barren landscape, walking swiftly until he reached the shore of the Black Lake, its dark surface still as a mirror.

"The White Queen is dead," the man said, and around him the mountains seemed to hum and whisper as if in question. There was a swell of air, and the lake rippled and tossed waves onto the barren sand. The old man grimaced, his lips twisted into a tight imitation of a smile. "It's true. You have heard me correctly, the White Queen is dead."

In the trees that circled the lake a stir rose up, a ripple of sound, and one hundred ravens rose into the night—a dark, dark cloud.

"It's time," the man cried out, lifting his long fingers to the sky. With this gesture the birds began to fly, their wings furiously beating, their cries like icy laughter in the cold still air.

Amelia

I have learned that there are many ways to begin a story. When I first learned to read, my tutor Theo and I spent hours in the library reading the first lines of books. From Theo I learned that each book has a category: fiction, non-fiction, poetry, fantasy memoir. Here is where my beginning gets stuck because the story I'm about to tell falls into all of those categories and none.

Yet because I am a princess, I shall start my story this way: Once upon a time, in the small country of Gossling there was a good king and queen who had four daughters. The firstborn, Merrill, would one day be queen, and she was a serious princess—intelligent and hardworking, slow to anger, thoughtful and kind, and the king and queen were very pleased to have such a child. Two years later the queen gave birth to twins, and because they had the sweet faces of flowers, she named them Lily and Rose. The twins were great beauties, with long blond hair like the silk of new corn, and like their older sister, the twins were smart, graceful, and kind, and again, the king and queen were very pleased. Three years later, the queen gave birth to a fourth princess. But where her sisters were graceful, this princess was awkward; where her sisters were quiet, this princess was loud; where her sisters were clever in math and reading, this princess hated lessons. And the king and queen, being practical people, knew that a fourth princess would never be queen, so they let her be and loved her in spite of her non-princess ways.

So the fourth princess grew up happily unencumbered by the duties of a princess raised to rule a kingdom. The youngest princess spent most of her days trying to avoid her royal tutors, roaming the palace grounds with her best friend, Henry, swimming in the palace ponds, catching fish, and playing in the trees. In all, the princess grew up quite ordinary, and liked it like that.

The fourth princess of Gossling, the unlikely princess, is me, and the story I'm about to tell you is about Gossling's darkest and lightest days. It is a story of magic, wonder, mystery, adventure, great happiness, great sadness, and true friendship. But mostly this is the story of how even a fourth princess—even an ordinary, not-so-special, unlikely princess—can become queen.

So I begin.

CHAPTER 1

There Shall Be Four

WHEN MOTHER WAS MY AGE, twelve years old, something extraordinary happened to her. The story of the Extraordinary Happening was one of my sisters' favorite bedtime stories in the years before I was born, and they would beg her to tell them the story before they went to sleep, and so she would. Later, after I was born, my sisters liked the story less, but still we would ask. And on the evenings when she was able to sneak away from state meetings and royal dinners to visit the nursery, Mother would tell the story.

The nursery was really my room alone, although it still had my sisters' childhood beds in it. They had moved out years before, and slept now in the grand bedrooms of princesses—bedrooms with long heavy drapes, silver mirrors, and vases filled with flowers. Only I remained in the children's nursery. Mother had asked me a dozen times if I'd like to move into a more grown-up room, but I didn't want to; I preferred my room to theirs.

It's true that the nursery was a bit babyish, with four beds covered in powder blue quilts and yellow striped walls bordered with painted pink rabbits. Making things worse, it was filled with old toys that my sisters could not bear to part with, but were too grown-up to take to their new rooms: the twins' enormous dollhouse, Rose's worn stuffed animals, Lily's baby blanket, and all the books Merrill read at my age that I never opened. And, of course, there were my toys too. The room was cluttered and usually messy, which was just how I liked it.

Despite their grown-up rooms, on story nights my sisters gladly returned to the nursery, climbed back into their old beds, happy to have Mother to ourselves, even if only for an hour or so. And although outwardly I complained when they slept in my room—accusing them of tossing and turning, snoring and coughing, and keeping me awake— secretly, I loved it. Loved having them back. Loved all of us together in the nursery the way I remember us being when I was very little. The way we were before Merrill moved out, then Rose and Lily, leaving just their deserted toys and me.

The last night I remember Mother telling the story of the Extraordinary Happening she had stolen away from a state dance, happy for an opportunity to leave and hoping her absence would not be noticed. She whispered to Merrill at dinner that she would meet us in the nursery at half past eight, and indeed at eight thirty she swept into the room, her stiff gold dress rustling behind her. My sisters and I were tucked into our beds and Dori was showing us a magic trick, her old legs tucked under her like a girl's, her white hair a cloud around her face, her blue eyes snapping in amusement at our befuddlement.

"Do it again, Dori!" Rose called out from her bed, watching carefully as Dori made my favorite stuffed bear disappear and then reappear again. I watched, trying to seem nonchalant, trying not to look concerned, but secretly worrying that Dori would forget the magic mid-trick and my bear would be gone for good.

When Mother entered the room, Dori looked at her, beamed with pleasure, and asked, "Don't all my girls look lovely tonight?"

And it was true that Mother looked beautiful in her glittering dress, and the twins with their long gold hair and blue nightgowns, and Merrill in a pale pink dressing robe, her dark hair braided around her head like a crown, looked like true princesses. All lovely but me, my red hair stubbornly curling despite Dori's thick brush and my skinny arms scratched and scabbed from climbing the orchard trees. I wasn't even wearing proper nightclothes, just an outgrown pair of Henry's striped pajamas that I had rescued from a scrap box, much to Dori's sharp disapproval.

Mother smiled at each of us in turn. "I have the most beautiful princesses in the land, and the smartest!"

"The *only* princesses in the land!" Merrill pointed out, and we all giggled.

Mother smiled, "Technically, yes. But . . . well, still! What story will it be tonight? Or are you all too tired for stories? Or maybe too old?" And her eyes smiled, teasing us.

"Tell us the story of the Extraordinary Happening!" I shouted, before anyone else could choose a story.

Mother settled down on the bed next to me and put her warm hand on my back. Her hair, the same white gold of the twins, was pinned up in pink combs, catching the light from the fire. "Let's see if I can remember that story . . ."

"You remember!" Dori laughed and winked at us as she stood up. "I'm going to fetch some of that cake Cook was making."

"Wait! My bear!" I cried out, sounding younger than I meant to, and glaring at the twins who were rolling their eyes at me.

"Of course," Dori smiled, and with a wave of her hands, Bear appeared above me and dropped solidly into my lap. Then Dori went out the large doors, calling, "Good night, girls!"

"Good night," we sang out as the doors closed quietly behind her, then we turned back to Mother.

Mother cleared her throat and then began the story. "When I was eleven, my godmother gave me a set of bubbles and sent me to the garden to play with them. At first I spun around and around with the wand, trying to surround myself with a circle of bubbles, but then I decided that I would try to make the largest bubble I could. Well, after many tries, I made a bubble that was truly enormous, and when it suddenly popped, an envelope dropped from it, like a falling fortune from a cookie."

We leaned forward on our beds in anticipation. "Did you open it?" Merrill asked, though she knew the answer.

"At first," Mother continued, "I didn't want to open it. You see, the envelope was quite pretty, and made of heavy gold paper. And sealing it was a seal I had never seen before—of two swans flying before a sun or moon. Still, I was curious about what the envelope contained, and so finally I tore it open."

"What was inside?" Lily and Rose asked in one breath.

"A fortune, of course!" Mother laughed.

"What did it say?" I wondered.

"It said: *There shall be four*. Well, I was very confused and very curious, and I sat thinking four what? Four cakes with tea? Four spotted ponies for the carriage? Four new kittens in the kitchen? Then, without thinking, I said aloud: 'Four what?' And a voice whispered, 'Four princesses. There shall be four.' And though I searched and searched, I never found the owner of that voice, and though I waited, I did not find any answer.

"Years passed and I grew up. I became queen, and a few years after that I married your father, and we had one beautiful baby"—she smiled a special smile at Merrill—"and soon afterward twins—very lucky, double happiness." The twins grinned at each other and the luck of their double birth. "And all the kingdom believed there would be no more children, but I knew there would be one more. Two years passed, and though I was very happy with the three little princesses I had, I felt that one was missing, and I waited for her to come—waited for the fortune to prove true."

"Daddy didn't think there would be four!" I interrupted.

Mother smiled at me. "No, no one did. But I knew. Still another year passed, and I began to doubt myself. I thought perhaps I had made up the story of the envelope in the bubble. After all, I had been a lonely child with a good imagination.

"And then one spring morning eleven years ago, I was in the garden sewing and watching Merrill, Lily, and Rose play by the fountain. That morning Dori had given the girls each a bag of marbles, and somehow Lily had managed to drop her bag into the fountain. She was very upset, and so I put down my sewing and leaned over the fountain, ready to rescue the marble bag, when a fish leaped up, and although I know—of course!—that fish don't speak, he said quite clearly: *Where is the fourth princess?*"

"He reminded you!" I added.

Mother nodded gravely. "Yes, he did. He also just about scared me to death, but he certainly reminded me. Later, when it became known that I was with child, the doctors and the royal advisors and the astrologers said with great confidence, 'This child shall be a boy! There shall soon be a prince!' But I knew they were wrong; I knew that there were to be four princesses."

"But why, Mother? Why did you get a message in the bubble? Why did the fish talk to you?" Lily asked earnestly, her pretty face wrinkled with the question.

Mother laughed. "I don't know, I imagine my godmother was having some fun with me, or maybe she had her own reason for reminding me that our country should have four princesses."

"That may have been a mistake," Rose said doubtfully, looking at me.

I stuck out my tongue and threw a pillow toward her head, but Mother smiled and squeezed me close to her. "I don't think so."

Still, that night as I lay in bed, listening to the soft breathing of Merrill, Lily, and Rose, the fire crackling low in the fireplace, I couldn't help thinking that I was very different from my sisters, that maybe in some way I was a mistake. That if princesses were supposed to be so special, then there was something wrong with me.

❧

When we were younger, hide-and-seek was our favorite game. Henry, the twins, and I played it almost daily, spreading out to hide inside the palace. With many rooms to hide in, and endless possibilities for hiding places, the games could last for hours. One afternoon, I hid behind the heavy drapes in the sunroom waiting for Henry to find me, or waiting for the cry that the others had been found. Time passed slowly, and the sun filled the room and made the drapes hot. Warm, I drowsed into a light sleep. The sounds of voices woke me up and I instantly stiffened, thinking for a moment that it was Henry and the twins coming to find me. Instead it was the voices of two women—ladies-in-waiting who were searching for forgotten embroidery. I stayed quiet—still and hidden.

"I could have left it anywhere," the first woman sang out. "It seems I lose it twice a day! Anyway," she sighed, "I agree with what you were saying: the older princesses *are* lovely— so talented!"

"And bright," the other voice added.

"*Perfect* princesses," the first voice said. There was a pause and I heard the sound of pillows being moved on the couch. "It's a shame about the littlest one."

Behind the curtains, I felt my face blush a hot red. They were talking about me.

"It is! Not a thing about that child is special," the other woman laughed, a high tinkling sound.

"That's a fact," the first woman said. "But thankfully she's the fourth princess, so that ordinariness isn't noticed as much." She laughed. "Or even if it's noticed, it hardly matters. Oh look, here's my needlework, right under this chair!"

The voices faded as the women left the room, chattering about an upcoming dance, but I stayed hidden behind the curtains, my face burning and my eyes stinging with tears.

When Henry found me twenty minutes later, I was red-faced and silent. "What's the matter?" he asked.

I shook my head, pressed my lips into a thin, hard line, and crawled out from behind the curtain. "Nothing, it just took you a long time to find me and I got bored, that's all."

Henry tugged at his lip and looked at me, head cocked. "Are you sure?"

I nodded slowly, then asked haltingly, "Do you think I'm ordinary?"

"Ordinary?" His forehead wrinkled, as if thinking. "Ordinary how?"

"Just ordinary," I said impatiently.

He didn't answer, instead going over to the bookshelf and pulling out a dictionary. He sat down on the yellow rug of the sun porch and looked up the word "ordinary." "*Ordi-nary*," he read. "*Not remarkable or special in any way, and there-fore uninteresting and unimpressive. Of common, everyday kind, regular and average. Mundane.*"

I blinked back tears, thinking that the definition was a perfect fit. Before I could say so, though, Henry shut the dictionary with a hard snap, and said decisively, "I don't think you're *uninteresting* or *unimpressive* or *not remarkable*. You're just you." Then he looked at me squarely, his eyes sure and steady. "And I like you the way you are."

And even though I still felt ordinary, with Henry's voice confident and sure that I was not, I felt better.

☙

I should say now that the introduction of Henry is long overdue, and as he is very, very important to this story, it is time. On the night I was born, another child was born on the palace grounds, but as I was greeted with fireworks and one hundred chiming church bells, Henry was greeted only by grief. The story of our births is one that has been told countless times across our small country, but where it seemed thousands had heard this story told, those that should have known it, did not.

No matter how many times we begged to hear it, Mother—who loved to tell stories—would never tell us. Her face would become sharp and sad when we asked, and she would shoo us away or try to distract us with funny stories

15

about the time Father accidentally turned his boat over in the lake, or the time Rose ate half a bowl of clay on a dare. And when we asked Father, his face would cloud with sadness and he would grow quiet.

In the end, it was Dori who told us. We were nine years old, and had almost given up asking. Then one wet, rainy afternoon when Henry and I, with nothing to do, were sulking underfoot in the kitchen, Dori shooed the cooks from the room and dragged three stools over to a counter, handing us each a bowl of apples and a peeler.

Placing a green apple in each of our hands, she said briskly, "We'll make some pies for dinner, and I'll tell you a story you've been waiting to hear."

"The story from when we were born?" Henry asked, his voice thick with excitement, though he tried to keep his face neutral as he bent over the apples he was peeling.

"Yes." Dori nodded. "The story of how one begins is important. You must know where you're starting to know where you're going, and it's an important story—for there are journeys ahead of you two." Her eyes became sharp and bright for a moment. "A friendship is the most precious of gifts, and it is a lucky gift to be given. Your friendship began hours after your birth." Dori told the story simply, painting a picture so well with her words that we almost forgot that the two infants she spoke about were us.

❧

Henry began humbly, for as Princess Amelia was wrapped in silk cloth and handed howling to her mother, one of the palace's best doctors sadly placed Henry into the arms of his godmother as the infant's father—the queen's head gardener—knelt by his dying wife, sobbing with grief. An unhappy beginning.

In the palace, the queen also wept to hear of the motherless infant, and demanded the child be brought to her. It was an unusual request, and the head gardener, his eyes swollen with tears, the small infant pressed to his chest, entered the great room with hesitant steps.

The royal bedroom was brightly lit, and a sense of importance and excitement buzzed in the air. The attendants were gathered around the edges of the room awaiting instruction, nursemaids hovered in the corners folding delicately embroidered blankets and readying the princess's crib, while the doctors stood nearby congratulating themselves on delivering a healthy baby. It was a busy room, and on a bed stacked high with pillows rested the queen with baby Amelia before her.

When the head gardener entered the room, it was as if the rest of the room fell away, for the queen spoke only to him, her voice gentle. "I'm so sorry."

The head gardener nodded, his head low, and his throat too choked with sadness to speak. He cradled the baby closer to his chest.

"Let me see the child," the queen said gently, and Henry was lifted from his father's arms by one of the doctors and laid on the bed next to Princess Amelia.

It was clear to everyone in the room that the infant was unwell; he was small and cold. The doctor had already told his father that the boy would most likely die. The two babies lay before the queen, her own child with a rush of red curls and strong kicking legs and the other infant with his great gray eyes, his body small and pale, and still as a stone. Then Princess Amelia's hand reached out, and quite fiercely (she was a strong baby!) gripped his hand, and in that one gesture, in that slice of a moment, the queen made a decision that no queen had ever before made.

"They shall be milk twins. As he has no mother to feed him, he shall share the milk of the princess. There shall be enough." It was a command.

The court attendants gasped, and the nursemaids murmured in the corner, but the king nodded in agreement, and the head gardener wept his thanks. For months afterward, the advisors speculated on why the queen would save the life of a child of so little importance. "Perhaps," they whispered, "the king and queen wished the fourth princess had been a prince. Perhaps they wished to have a fifth child. Perhaps the queen has been bewitched!"

But the true reasons of the queen were much simpler, though Dori didn't share them then. Mother had seen the head gardener's eyes, had seen his sadness, had seen the child like a ghost before her, and felt pity. And in Henry, Mother saw herself, her own mother dead in childbirth, and the arms of Dori lifting her infant-self, just as she lifted Henry. And unlike the advisors, the queen believed all children were important, whether they were born under a thatched roof or a gold ceiling.

There was another part of the story that Dori did not

include because she did not know it. Still, it is important, and as we know it now, I'll tell it.

In that busy, bustling room filled with people, there was one who was unseen: Tiege, the godmother of Henry's own mother, stood in the shadow of the great door, and watched the queen choose life for an infant to whom she owed nothing. The older woman watched the queen lift the baby to her breast and watched him drink, watched color flood his face, and the woman made a promise that one day she would repay the queen's kindness.

And so Henry and I grew as twins. Not harmonious twins like Lily and Rose—who seemed to think, breathe, and act as a single person—no, we were difficult twins, hating each other one moment and loving each other the next. And in so many ways Henry was a brother to my sisters and me, a child to my parents. My mother, because she had saved him, loved Henry especially, and my father, who had no sons, loved him as much as he might have loved his own son. Because of this, Henry's life was much different than most of the other children who lived on the grounds of the palace. These children were the sons and daughters of staff and noblemen, and they attended school in the capital city and had little to do with the day-to-day life of the castle. Henry was different; he was educated with me and took most meals in the palace with us.

This did not mean that Henry wasn't loved and cherished by his own father and godmother, but his father had remarried and had small children to look after, and his godmother Tiege wisely believed that Henry knew himself well enough to come and go as he pleased between his house and the palace. The gossiping advisors were half right, the queen and king *did* have a fifth child, or perhaps—as he was shared—half a child, but a child whom they loved as a whole.

CHAPTER 2

An Ungraceful Princess

FOUR SISTERS ARE OFTEN VERY DIFFERENT, and there was almost no place that better highlighted the differences between my sisters and me than during our lessons: music, dance, and etiquette. Each day after our school lessons, we had one hour of instruction on the finer graces of what was becoming to a princess. While some of these lessons were private, others were not. On Wednesdays we danced the quadrille, and this was a group dance lesson—meaning that all the children who lived on the palace grounds were required to come and participate.

Thirty children gathered at four o'clock in the huge ballroom—the boys scrubbed clean, their hair wet and slicked back, the girls sparkling like jewels in the heavy gowns Mother had ordered; they moved carefully, as if they knew they were beautiful in this finery. The ballroom was one of my favorite rooms—huge painted panels adorned the walls, each telling a story of two lovers on a summer's day. An enormous chandelier hung from the ceiling, holding more than five hundred candles, and delicate sconces lit the rooms with pale light.

The quadrille is an old court dance, a formal series of short dances that come together to form one long dance. This elegant dance was to be performed in the late fall during a celebration to mark the country's birthday. The choreography of the dance was exact and depended on the precision of each dancer. Watching me, skinny, skinny Madame Needler would press her thin lips together in disapproval and clap her hands sharply, stopping the pianist again and again.

"Amelia, understand that this is a court dance. It has its own rules. You cannot turn when you wish to turn, or change partners at will." Exasperated, she waved her hands toward the stiff row of chairs that lined the back wall. "Sit out for now, and observe."

Reassigned to a chair, I would spent the rest of the hour happily watching my sisters dance with the other children of the court—their posture perfect, their steps measured and matched, all of the dancers moving together, spinning and stopping like the mechanical turnings of a wound clock.

Lily and Rose disapproved of me sitting out, however. One Wednesday at the end of the lesson, after our gowns had been carefully hung in our closets, I wandered into the Children's Library and I found myself confronted with my sisters' anger.

Lily and Rose sat together on the pink love seat, identical in creamy white sweaters, soft blue yarn on their laps, and knitting needles poised as they looked over a pattern.

Merrill slouched in a yellow chair, her legs dangling over the side, reading.

When I came into the room the twins both looked up, their eyes angry. "What kind of example are you setting for the younger children if you are allowed to sit out each week?" Lily demanded.

I shrugged, still standing in the door frame. "It's not my fault Madame Needler would prefer me to watch rather than participate."

Rose rolled her eyes. "Whose fault is it then? Honestly, Amelia! Everything is an excuse! You don't even try! It's like you're just waiting for her to send you to the chairs—it's embarrassing!" She punctuated her last word with her knitting needles.

"Leave her alone," Merrill said mildly, her eyes still on her book. "It's just a dance."

Lily shot Rose a look, and I knew their tactic was about to change. "We could help you learn," Lily offered nicely, and Rose nodded, her voice silky soft. "We could practice after dinner in the playroom. Maybe you just need more time to practice."

I snorted. "No thanks."

"Fine." Lily glared. "Just keep on being terrible at it then if it makes you happy."

It didn't make me happy to be terrible. But when I sat out of the dance, I didn't have to notice quite how bad I was compared to the twins. So for close to six weeks I was content to spend the hour watching the others practice and learn.

This all changed when Mother visited our class one afternoon.

"Amelia." Mother stepped into the ballroom and looked at me with a puzzled expression. "Are you hurt? Sick?"

"No." I shook my head.

"Are you in trouble?" Her eyebrows raised a little and she looked over to where Madame Needler was directing the rest of the children in dance.

"No, I'm just bad at it," I shrugged, "so I'm watching."

"I see." Mother pursed her lips together, thinking. "So if you're bad at something, you'd rather not do it?"

I shrugged, watching as Lily wove through a line of girls, her skirt rustling behind her. "It's not as if I'm ever going to be the best dancer."

Mother sat down on the chair next to me and watched as Madame Needler called out brisk instructions to the dancing children. For a few minutes we watched the dance in silence, and then she turned to me. "Amelia, when I was about twenty, I came to a terrible realization about myself."

I looked at her, interested. "What?"

Mother smiled slightly. "I realized that I would never, ever be the best at anything."

"What do you mean?"

"I mean just that. There is nothing that I will ever be best at—not dancing or painting or playing the piano or ruling the country. I won't even be the best mother!"

"But you're good at *all* those things," I protested.

Mother smiled. "Thank you, but I'm not the best in the world."

"But you're really good," I argued.

Mother arched one eyebrow. "Yes, but I'm not the *best*. And under your argument, people shouldn't try things they're not good at."

"I didn't say that," I protested.

"But that's what you meant, isn't it? You meant that if Merrill or Lily or Rose is good at something and you're not, that you shouldn't bother trying because you can't compete with them."

"I can't!" I exploded.

Mother's gray eyes looked grave. "Amelia, whoever said it was a competition?"

I shrugged miserably, and Mother's face softened slightly. "If people were only interested in doing things they could be assured they would be the best at, then no one would ever try anything." She put a hand gently on my back. "I'm not just talking about the quadrille, Amelia, I'm talking about everything. I'm not looking for you to *be* the best; I'm looking for you to *try* your best. And Amelia, I'm not asking you to do something you can't do."

"How do you know?"

Mother shrugged lightly. "I know."

I felt my eyes fill with tears. "But what if I just don't *want* to do it? I'm bad at it, just like I'm bad at everything."

"You're not bad at everything, Amelia," Mother said sharply.

"Fine, then I'm bad at some things and ordinary at everything else," I said hotly.

"Oh." Mother sighed and her voice became edged with

frustration. "When will you stop using the word 'ordinary' to describe yourself? There is nothing more ordinary about you than there is about any other person in the world! Everyone is ordinary in some way, just as everyone is special in some way."

I nodded. "I know, but I'm tired of being ordinary with just a little specialness, I want to be special with a little ordinariness. The way you, Merrill, and the twins are. But I'm not, I'm just regular old boring Amelia, and there's nothing special about me!"

Mother sighed again. "No matter how hard you work to convince yourself, you will never convince me that you are an ordinary girl. You are a little girl like any other little girl—you have talents and strengths, just the way you have weaknesses. And just like any other little girl in this kingdom—princess or not, extraordinary dancer or dreadful—I expect you to take part in the quadrille, and I expect you to do your very best." Her voice left no room for argument.

I stood up. "Fine," I growled, "but I hate the quadrille and I hate ballet and I hate school, and I'm bad at all of them!"

"Amelia." Mother's voice was sharp.

"I'm going," I took two steps toward the dancers across the room before twirling back to face my mother. "And I hate how ordinary I am at everything else!" Before she could answer I stormed over to Madame Needler, who clapped her hands to stop the dance, pointed to a spot for me to step into, and then clapped her hands again, indicating that we should begin again.

The music started and the dance began. I bumbled, trying to remember the steps, and felt my face flush with embarrassment when someone laughed, and again when I accidentally stepped on Lily's foot. Minutes passed slowly, and against my will I found my eyes sliding over to where I had sat on the chair, and saw that Mother was still sitting there, still watching. Even though I hated the dance, even though I frequently missed steps or turned right when I meant to turn left, I found myself trying, wanting to show Mother that even if I was bad, I would still try. When the lesson finally ended, Mother stood up to leave, and as she did she caught my eye and smiled broadly before stepping out the huge doors into the hall.

❧

The only lesson I had any interest in was sword instruction. When Henry turned twelve Father decided that it was time for him to learn to handle a sword. So it was decided that Father would give Henry fencing lessons before breakfast each day. For Henry's first lesson, I tagged along, still half-asleep, but interested. I sat in the cold clearing mist of the morning, perched on the stone wall of the sunken garden while my father and Henry adjusted their fencing costumes and lifted their swords. A fencing training sword does not have a sharp tip, it has a round ball—tiny, like a small cherry—so no one will accidentally be stabbed and hurt. This was a good thing, as Henry—so graceful in almost everything—was clumsy as a fencer.

I watched, fascinated, as my father showed Henry the first moves. One hand behind his back, Father moved forward quickly and with a deft stroke neatly knocked Henry's sword to the ground. I cheered from my place on the wall, and Henry lifted his face mask, grinning in surprise that he had so suddenly lost his weapon. Father lifted his mask as well, and picked up Henry's sword from the dew-covered grass and handed it back to him. "Fencing is a skill that requires intelligence and speed above all else. Like chess, to fence well you must know your opponent. More important, you must know yourself. Where are your weaknesses? Use them to your advantage—turn your weaknesses into strengths. Does that make sense?"

Henry nodded, though he looked confused. I thought I understood, though—it was like telling a joke about yourself before anyone else could. During ballet class I was always quick to laugh at my clumsy feet, awkward in ballet slippers. And rather than criticize me, my laughter usually made the others laugh as well.

For three mornings in a row I came down before breakfast to watch Henry's lessons with Father. I watched closely, careful not to distract them, trying to memorize the moves Father made, so that if I were ever given the opportunity to cradle a sword, I would know how to use it.

Finally, on the fourth morning, Father took pity on me. Lifting off the gray mask that covered his head, he squinted in the sudden light and looked to where I sat on the wall. "Amelia, do you wish only to watch, or do you wish to learn?"

"Learn!" I shouted hopefully.

Father smiled and pushed his damp dark hair from his forehead. "Come down off the wall then, and let's get you suited up."

Minutes later, dressed like Father and Henry in a fencing costume and heavy pads, I felt oddly invisible, anonymous, and it wasn't a bad feeling. Unlike dancing, where my mistakes were clear to any who watched, in the gray costume and dark head covering, I could be any young knight learning to fight. Clumsy or skilled, no one knew it was me.

When Mother found out over breakfast that I was learning to fence she looked doubtful. "She could be hurt."

Father shook his head. "It's only with the practice swords. Besides, I think this is teaching her grace far more successfully than the quadrille." Father knew about my ballroom troubles, and he winked at me over his eggs.

I winked back.

Lily wrinkled her nose and turned to Mother. "Isn't it unseemly for a princess to do swordplay?"

Mother laughed. "Of course not. The idea of a princess learning to defend herself and her country does not trouble me. As long as no one gets accidentally stabbed, of course."

Rose's nose wrinkled as if something smelled bad. "But shouldn't she have to change before coming to breakfast?"

"There's no time," Mother said, waving her oatmeal spoon. "She'll bathe or shower after breakfast and before school. Goodness, this is nothing to make a fuss over! I may take some sword lessons myself!"

෨ல

And so it was settled that my lessons could continue. My father was a good teacher, patient and kind. He did not yell his corrections or look to embarrass, he wanted only to teach us. Under his guidance, Henry and I quickly grew skilled at using swords. On mornings when Father was too busy to teach our lesson, we were taught by Maria, one of the tree pruners, who with three clean strokes could disable the sword of even the strongest swordsman. And so it was that almost every day Henry and I practiced our swordplay together. We were nearly matched as opponents, and without noticing it our feet grew swift, our strokes sure and fast, our swords confident.

"You're thinking like swordsmen," Father complimented us one morning at the end of a lesson. "You're both remarkable learners. If only you were a bit older, I would be honored for you to be knights in my court!"

Henry stood up straighter, and I felt myself flush with pride under the cover of my mask. Here was something— finally—that I wasn't just ordinary at, here was something I was actually *good* at. But whether just ordinary or very good, in a country like Gossling—peaceful and blessed—there isn't much use for a princess who handles a sword well.

❧

Two months after my lessons began, I realized I was better than Henry. I don't mean to be boastful, but Henry was such a natural athlete, so skilled at almost every sport he tried, that it felt strange to surpass him, even if it wasn't by much. The morning I realized this Father had ended our lesson early, and unchaperoned we chased each other out of the sunken garden, swords clashing as we leaped between the statues.

When Henry stumbled and fell, I pressed the round tip of my sword gently on his chest. "Beg for your life!"

"Never!" Henry rolled out from under my sword, and was on his feet in one deft movement.

Click-click-click. We chased each other across the courtyard until, red-faced with exhaustion, we called a truce and collapsed onto the grass.

"You know, I was going to beat you," Henry said lazily, looking through the trimmed grass for a four-leaf clover.

I arched one eyebrow at him, an art I had recently perfected. "Care to fight again?"

Henry groaned. "Not now."

I smiled at the clouds. "Because you know you'd lose."

Henry plucked a blade of grass and blew through it like it was a whistle. "You wish."

"Rematch tomorrow, then," I said, staring as the clouds drifted slowly across the morning sky.

"Deal," Henry replied, grinning at me.

Suddenly I sat up. "Dori's calling us!"

Henry sat up too, worried. "We're late to breakfast."

We half flew across the lawn, racing each other up the palace steps and into the dining room, sliding into our seats just as breakfast began.

Mother lifted her eyebrows at us, amused by our red faces. "And how was the morning's sword battle?"

"Amelia won," Henry said, reaching hungrily for the muffin

basket, but as he did the basket lifted into the air and danced just out of reach.

"Lily," Mother said sharply.

Lily looked up from her oatmeal, her eyes large and innocent. "Yes, Mother?"

"Please do not do this at the table." My mother's voice held a note of warning.

"It's not me, Mother."

Next to her, Rose smiled into her orange juice, and the muffin basket, still hovering in midair just beyond Henry's fingers, suddenly lurched forward, hitting Henry in the chest before falling to the floor, its contents spilling everywhere.

Mother looked darkly at Rose. "Rose, you will pick those up with your *hands*, and continue your breakfast alone in the kitchen."

Lily looked unhappy and asked quickly, "May I join her, Mother?"

"Are you also responsible for this little prank, Lillian?" Mother's voice was frosty.

Henry and I looked at each other quickly. When Mother used our full names, it was never a good sign.

"No," Lily whispered.

"Then you may not. Rose is eating in the kitchen as punishment, not as a social activity."

"But, Mother, I was only teasing." Rose looked sorry. "And Henry, I didn't mean for the basket to hit you. I was trying to make it go *to* you, not *on* you."

Mother held up one hand. "We have been through this too many times. Your powers are a secret. What if a maid

32

had walked in? And what of the fact that I have told you both time and time again that you are not to use your magic for pranks?"

Before they could respond, one of the cooks came into the dining room with a tray of french toast, and the discussion was over. Mother sighed. "Pick those muffins up, Rose, and then take your plate to the kitchen."

"Yes, Mother." Rose's face looked pinched, as if she were trying to keep from crying, and she picked up the muffins quickly, returning them to the basket.

"You may feed those to the birds after breakfast," Mother said.

Rose nodded and retreated to the kitchen with her plate and the muffin basket.

❧

As had Merrill's, the twins' magic arrived on their thirteenth birthday, the most wonderful present. When they concentrated hard on something, the twins could lift things into the air. Not heavy things like horses, but small things like books and baskets and sweaters. Dori had said that their power was still "young," which meant that they didn't have total control over it. (Hence, the muffin basket hitting Henry and tumbling to the floor.) And although it wasn't a power with much use, it was still a power. Once, while sitting in a chair, Lily had put all her schoolbooks back on the library shelves. And Rose had once cleared a small patch of leaves from the lawn. Impressive, but Merrill's power was greater. Although she used it less often: Merrill could make herself disappear. Not for very long, just for a minute, but it was unsettling—one moment she was standing next to you, and the next moment there was nothing there, just an empty space.

The powers were a secret, known only by my sisters, Henry, Dori, Mother, and Father. Soon after Merrill turned thirteen, Mother had gathered us all in her library, closing the heavy doors tightly behind her. We children had stood apprehensive in the center of the room, certain that we were about to be punished, and casting uneasy glances at each other, wondering what crimes had been committed. We might have stood like that all day, but Mother had impatiently gestured for us to sit. "For goodness' sake! No one is in trouble!"

We sat, and then for a very long while the room was quiet as Mother paced up and down the library, her long dress sweeping briskly behind her. Finally she had stopped before us, and with her face grave, told us that any magic we saw was to be kept a secret, never to be discussed with anyone outside the family. "No one outside of this room is ever to know. Is this understood?" And she had trained her sharp eyes on each of us, waiting for us to nod our understanding. And when we had, she sighed heavily and finally sat as if exhausted.

Dori had spoken then from the plump pink sofa, and in her cozy voice, she explained that most people did not understand magic. Magic either scared them or made them greedy.

"Greedy how?" Lily had asked.

Father had interjected then, smiling. "It makes them greedy thinking about all the ways in which magic could be useful to them!"

"Like the frog king capturing a fairy and asking for her gold!" I exclaimed.

And Rose had cast a disparaging look at me. "In fairy tales, maybe."

"It's a good example, though, Rose," Mother had said coolly, and Rose had hung her head and said nothing.

Father smiled at Rose. "Corruption is corruption—in people and in fairy-tale frogs. So for now, Merrill's magic is our secret."

The twins were only eleven during that meeting, and they had turned and looked with jealousy at Merrill. "Will we have magic too?" Lily asked.

Mother looked thoughtful, considering her answer. "Probably, but there is no guarantee. We won't know until you turn thirteen."

Like Merrill, when the twins turned thirteen their magic appeared—suddenly, as if a light had been switched on. But unlike Merrill, who guarded her power closely, the twins were sloppy with theirs. There had been many close calls— many instances when they were almost caught, and as a result there had been many lectures from Mother about secrecy, about guarding their magic for their own safety.

Soon after the twins' magic had appeared, I'd gone to talk to Mother about it. I found her in the library, writing letters at her desk.

"Mother?"

Mother looked up at me with surprise. "Amelia, is everything all right? Why aren't you outside playing?"

"I have to ask you something."

Mother put her pen down and leaned back a little in her chair. "Ask away."

I took a deep breath. "Does everyone have a secret power?"

Mother smiled. "Amelia, every girl—whether a princess or not—has her own power. Not necessarily a *magic* power, but power nonetheless. Each girl possesses strengths that define her character."

"What if I don't get a magic power?"

"If you don't, then it doesn't make you less special. As I just explained, every girl has power—magical or otherwise."

"But—"

Mother interrupted me, smiling slightly. "I don't think it's something we need to worry about now, Amelia. You're ten—three years from thirteen. I see no reason why it would be different for you."

I flushed slightly. "But I'm not like them."

Mother shook her head. "Amelia, it's true that you're not Merrill, or Lily or Rose. But has it ever occurred to you that they aren't Amelia either?"

In my head I thought darkly, *Why would they ever want to be like me?* I didn't say the words aloud, but Mother seemed to be reading my thoughts. "Amelia, although Rose and Lily sometimes try to be one person, they are two. Two *different* people, different from each other, and different from Merrill and different from you. Just as Merrill is different from the twins, and different from you. That's the way it should be, and that's the way it is! It's the wonder of the world, my dear, like fingerprints and snowflakes—everyone is unique."

I sighed and redirected my questioning. "Even if I don't get magic powers, why does our family have them? Is it because we're princesses?"

Mother looked thoughtful. "Both are good questions, but this is not the time for me to answer them. When all of you are older, I'll explain."

I was frustrated with half an answer. "But—"

Mother held up her hand and laughed. "No buts. It's a story for another day."

CHAPTER 3

School

IN EARLY MARCH in the year I was twelve, my tutor, Madame Bellow, quit in a huff. She called me ineducable and left without taking even her umbrella. At lunch when Father found out she was gone, he groaned and covered his face with his hands, and then when Lily announced that Madame Bellow found me ineducable, I saw my parents exchange a look I had seen before between the two of them when the troubles of my education were raised. And there had been quite a bit of trouble: before Madame Bellow, Madame Hohn had called me stubborn, Madame Calle had called me lazy, and now Madame Bellow had called me ineducable. A sort of grim silence grew around the table as Mother and Father considered what it meant to have a princess so difficult to teach that three tutors had left in two years. Lily flashed me a guilty smile, apologizing, and I glowered back. Dori broke the silence by bringing a bowl of Father's favorite pudding to the table. Spooning it into bowls, she smiled at me knowingly, and observed, "Children are like flowers; they bloom differently, and in their own time."

Cheered by pudding and Dori's sensible manner, my father nodded, but Mother frowned and shot a quick look at me. "At twelve years old, she reads like a five-year-old. She puts in no effort!"

I could feel myself blushing, and felt angry tears pricking the backs of my eyes. Henry squeezed my hand sympathetically under the table, but I shook him off, glaring into my pudding. Mother was right, and not right. I did read like a five-year-old, but it wasn't that I didn't try. Sometimes, I admit, I didn't try as hard as I should, but I always tried. The fact that I could barely read was made worse by the fact that my sisters were clever in everything: Merrill was truly brilliant and drank in books and numbers as easily as a bird flies, Lily and Rose were plenty smart and quick with math and clever at writing, and Henry, who was exactly my age, was reading textbooks that university students could read, while Madame Bellow brought me through elementary words again and again. I wanted to read, it just seemed that I couldn't.

Still, "ineducable" or not, a princess must at least try to be educated, and so Mother cleared her schedule of all kingdom duties and interviewed tutors for three days. By the third day, Mother had interviewed over forty tutors and none had met her approval. At lunch, her face dark and grim, she said, "I'll just have to teach you myself."

My sisters exchanged anxious looks; although they were

now taught separately from Henry and me, learning different lessons by specialized tutors, at one time or another all of them had experienced Mother as their teacher, and as skilled a scholar as she was, and as skilled students as they were, the experience had not gone well.

Father looked up from his soup. "Perhaps extend the search a bit longer, dear," he said mildly, winking to me.

Mother nodded, considering. "A few more days can't hurt," she agreed. "But," and she looked pointedly at Henry and me, "you shall take map-reading lessons with George in the map room tomorrow. The holiday is over."

By mid-afternoon every day, the children who lived on the palace grounds began to trickle in from the village school. It was a mix of children—they were the children of cooks and butlers, advisors, guards, knights, stablemen, noblemen, and so on; and outside of Henry and my sisters, they were my only friends. It may have been difficult for Merrill as the first princess and one-day-queen to play as easily with the palace children as I did. It's likely that everyone would have agreed with her, or that she would have been allowed to win every game. But as a fourth princess, this wasn't true for me. Almost every day Henry and I played with them in the gardens and on the long porches of the palace.

My father called us a pack of young wolves and was quite content with the company we kept, even though we often got too noisy. There was Poppy, the baker's son, who could hit a ball halfway across the great lawn, and ten-year-old Rosemary, the daughter of a nobleman, who could draw animals so well they seemed to quiver on the page. There was six-year-old Ralph, the son of one of the bravest knights in the land, who was scared of his own shadow and cried at the slightest thing, and twelve-year-old Sarah, the daughter of the Head Butler, who could imitate people so well that we would almost die from laughing at her. There was Julie, the child of an advisor, who could invent new games on the spot, and seven-year-old Kenny, the son of the tree pruner, who could climb anything. There was Bree, the thirteen-year-old daughter of the veterinarian, who always made sure that everyone was included, and eleven-year-old Patrick, the stable boy who could ride on the back of a horse like an acrobat. And that was just the beginning—when the village school was finished, the palace grounds were filled with children—Amy, Tom, Victoria, Nick . . . And finally there was Meg.

꽃

At eleven years old, Meg was the daughter of one of my mother's ladies-in-waiting and one of my father's most valued noblemen. Her mother, Lady Isabelle, was plump as a small bird and sweet, with a good-natured smile and practical manner. She had been a great beauty in her youth, and Meg had inherited her mother's golden hair and bright blue eyes. But where Lady Isabelle was kind, Meg was truly mean. I suppose there could be many reasons for this, but really there was only one: Meg was spoiled.

The only child of her parents, she was doted on and fussed over at every turn. Her parents told her every day how pretty she was, how smart, how special, and perhaps for another child such praise would have been welcomed through the filtering lens by which most children accept parents' praise. However, Meg took her parents' loving words as reinforcement of what she already knew. And the sad truth of it is that she *was* pretty, and she *was* smart. And—to be fair—she *was* special, but only because she was mean. She cheated during games, pretending that she hadn't been tagged when she had been, or pretending she was hurt to avoid being "it." When she won all of six-year-old Holly's marbles during a game, she kept them, despite our unwritten rule that marbles and jacks won from a younger child would be returned. When some of Cook's freshly baked cookies went missing, she accused Nick and Charlie, although neither had been near the kitchen.

Meg was uniformly despised by all of us, and if we had been allowed to exclude her from our games, we would have. To make matters worse, Meg's manners were as pretty as her face, and as a result most adults found her wonderful— perfectly behaved and lovely. Once I heard Sarah's mother ask her why she couldn't keep her clothes and hair as neat as Meg kept hers. "Really, Sarah," her mother had clucked, "it doesn't look right—you running around like a wild monkey—your dress dirty, your hair ribbons gone. Try to be more like Meg, she looks like she's spent the afternoon reading a book!" And I had heard Amy's mother tell Lady Isabelle that Meg was a jewel, and that she wished her Amy could have half the poise that Meg did. It made my blood boil.

While my father was not immune to Meg's charms and always smiled at her pretty curtseys and chirping hellos, my mother did not. I once overheard her tell Lady Isabelle that it would do Meg good to get dirty sometimes, and I heard her tell Dori that it was a shame that such kind people raised such a dreadful child.

Meanwhile, although we were forced to include her, we had all but given up trying to break Meg of her meanness and cheating. One wintry afternoon, after Meg had "accidentally" upset a checkerboard during a game she was losing, Poppy had pointed out through a mouthful of cookies, "A zebra doesn't change its stripes."

Still, sometimes one of us would try to change those stripes, explaining to Meg what she already knew: that the first person found during hide-and-seek is the next person to be it, or that throwing a ball directly at a person as he or she ran the bases was dangerous and against the rules. But Meg was slippery, evasive—and she would pout and look hurt and bewildered, as if she were the one wronged.

On this day, in the hour before dinner we gathered on the veranda, where we were holding a jacks tournament. With children partnered everywhere, the veranda was filled with the buzz of chatter and bouncing red balls. Two games away from me, Meg was playing against tiny Ralph, and she had just won, her voice crowing out her victory, as Ralph's eyes filled with tears. "Now they all belong to me!" Meg's voice sang out across the crowd of children. Hearing her, I could feel my face flush, and felt my temper rising. I stomped over to where Meg was collecting all of his jacks.

"Give them back," I growled at her. "The rule is that older doesn't take from younger."

Ralph looked up at me gratefully, and I noticed that

other games had grown suddenly hushed; the veranda was silent, everyone waiting to see what would happen next.

Meg flushed slightly, but then recovered quickly, her voice honey-sweet. "Really, Princess Amelia, I know you're the princess, and that, of course, you must be right, but if you were to read the instructions, I think you'd see that the winner of jacks gets to keep the loser's jacks." She looked up at me, her blue eyes innocent. "Why don't you get the instructions and read them to all of us aloud. I'm sure many of us could do with a reminder." It was a direct challenge. Meg knew my secret, knew that I could barely read, and she meant to embarrass me. "Would you like me to go find the directions so you can read them to us all?" she asked, her voice smooth.

I saw Henry, usually so calm, jump up as if he meant to fight her, and with that I could feel some of my anger drain away. A fight would mean trouble for all of us.

"You know the older-younger rule," Poppy snorted. "It might not be written down in the rule book, but it's how we've played it for as long as I can remember. So you're either stupid or you're a cheat, and I happen to think it's the latter."

There was a ripple of laughter and nodding from the group, and Meg stood up, shaking with anger, her golden curls quivering. "Keep your stupid jacks, then," she said as she shook the jacks out of her petticoat pocket so they rained on Ralph like sharp falling stars. And with that, she flounced from the porch, slamming the huge double doors behind her.

The games resumed, but I was troubled. I knew that she would seek revenge. Meg would wait, wait until the moment was right, and then she would punish—first Ralph and then me. I thought that she would try again to expose that I couldn't read, and thought how unfortunate that she was the one Cook had chosen to send to our palace classroom three months before.

It had happened on a school holiday. Mother agreed that since the palace children were on holiday, we could also have a half-day holiday. Madame Bellow was less amenable to a half-day schedule, and she was reluctant to let us go down for the special children's tea party the cooks had prepared. However, Cook would not allow tea to start without us, and with children looking longingly at the frosted cakes and warm scones, Cook had ordered Meg to go to our classroom and fetch us.

I was reading aloud when she entered the room. Madame Bellow held up one hand at Meg as if to silence her, although she had not spoken. So Meg stood, listening politely while I stumbled over words in a book that even four-year-old Nick could have easily read. I could feel my body grow warm with embarrassment, and felt my face burn as it flushed a deeper and deeper shade of red. Meg's face, though, was neutral, carefully arranged to show no expression, as she prettily asked Madame Bellow if we could come down to tea a bit early.

But at the tea party she sidled up to me, her voice as sugared as the cookie in my hand. "If you ever need me to read anything for you, Amelia, I'd be happy to. You know, I'm the top reader at school."

Before I could respond, Henry answered shortly, his voice cool. "I don't know what you think you're talking about.

Amelia doesn't need anyone to read for her, and if she did, you would be the last person she would ask."

Now with Ralph carefully collecting his jacks, I felt my stomach anxiously churning. It was silly, I knew, that with so much going on in the kingdom that I would be worried about how the palace children saw me, but I did.

❧

Before I fell asleep that night, Mother sat on the edge of my bed, her face serious. "Amelia, when I find a new tutor for you, I want you to work harder than you did with Madame Bellow."

"But—" I started to protest, ready to argue that I *had* worked hard.

Mother held up her hand, stopping me before I could continue. "I'm not saying you didn't work hard, I'm saying I want you to work harder."

I could feel tears beginning to smart in my eyes.

"Amelia, things worth having rarely come easily. They must be worked for. Better to learn that now."

"They come easily to everyone else," I said stubbornly.

Mother looked thoughtful. "Amelia, you possess gifts that do not come easily to others."

"Like what?"

Mother stretched out a little bit on the bed. "Let me tell you a story. When you were six years old, Lily and Henry, of all people, put bath soap into the fountain. It was a child's prank, not terribly original, but annoying nevertheless. Predictably, the fountain became a bubble bath, and bubbles spilled out onto the courtyard. As funny as you children thought it was, the cleanup would be work for others. Dori and I decided that the guilty parties would help the maids clean the courtyard of soap, as well as write an essay about their prank and why it was wrong. The problem was that no one would admit a role in it. With Merrill gone and the palace children at school in the village, that left four potentially guilty children: Rose, Lily, Henry, and you. We questioned you first. I admit that we assumed that you had some hand in it, and as you were always quick to take responsibility for your wrongs, I believed that you were the quickest route to confession. However, you said that you hadn't done it, and because you were always honest we believed you. I asked you if you knew who had done it, and you nodded yes. Patiently, I asked you who was responsible, and then— with your eyes as big as saucers—you shook your head and said *I'm not telling*. Dori encouraged you to tell us, but you wouldn't. You said you would rather clean the stones yourself than tell. It was a grand statement from such a young child. Your refusal to name names led, of course, to Henry and Lily confessing. Still, it impressed me. Even at a very young age there was a loyalty and truthfulness in you that is rare, and they are gifts."

I shrugged. Although I did not say it aloud, I thought I would happily trade loyalty and honesty for intelligence and grace.

Mother was not through, however. "You're stubborn, Amelia. That's another strength, and one I believe you inherited from me. If you want something badly enough, you don't stop until you've gotten it. You take the time to figure it out. This is what has always baffled me about you and school—I can see that you want to learn, Amelia, but you don't approach school the way you approach, say, fencing; you don't try in the same way. With this new tutor—whoever she or he is—promise me that you will try with everything you have."

She waited, but I said nothing. I couldn't promise, and I wouldn't lie and say I would.

Mother kissed my forehead, and brushed back my hair with one smooth hand. "Think about it, Amelia."

CHAPTER 4

The Education of the Fourth Princess

DIRECTLY AFTER BREAKFAST the next morning we reported to George outside the map room. George was my
parents' very top advisor, as well as my father's oldest friend.
As the top advisor, he was an expert on almost every topic,
and was especially well versed in history and geography.

George smiled at us when we approached, and waved us
into the room. "This is the map room, of course."

The map room was one of the rooms we—as children—
were not permitted to enter. There were only a few forbidden rooms in the palace, and although Henry and I had
longed to enter the forbidden sword room, we had never
been temped to creep into the map room. The room was really a colossal library of maps—maps papered the walls and
were laid out across long tables, covering nearly every surface of the room. There were brightly colored maps, and
faded older maps, and strange textured maps that showed
the topography of the mountains, there were small maps
and large maps, and maps of countries with names we had

never heard. It was extraordinary. Henry and I drank in the room for a long moment.

"Come and sit, children." George pulled two chairs over to a long table that stretched across the back of the room. We obediently sat and watched, fascinated, as George unrolled a large map. The map was yellowed with age and brittle, yet it had been brilliantly painted, and even with its paint fading it was still magnificent.

"This is one of the earlier maps of our kingdom, and a favorite of mine because, as you can see, almost every creek is drawn, every mountain peak labeled and identified." George smiled at the map, as if pleased by it. "This is also the perfect map to start our lessons with because it has so many details, and because it shows our whole kingdom—our whole beautiful country." George adjusted his glasses, and placed one finger delicately down near the center of the map. "Here is the palace."

We looked at where his finger had landed and saw the palace painted the very faintest gold. "Now watch," he ordered. "Follow the main road north, and what will you find?" His fingers traced a path to the faraway Blue Mountains, where a small drawing revealed the Winter Palace nestled among white peaks, the huge lake painted in front of it.

"The Winter Palace," I said.

"Correct," George nodded, and handed me a large magnifying glass. "If you look very closely, you'll see that the artist painted waves in the lake."

I looked at the tiny crested waves through the magnifying glass, and then handed it to Henry.

"What's this?" Henry held the magnifying glass over one of the mountains, pointing to what looked like a small bell tower.

George peered down and then straightened again. "That's one of the four towers. The first was built on the top of the Southern Mountains as both a lighthouse and a lookout point. Beyond the Southern Mountains is the Brammian Sea, and the light was meant to help steer ships safely through the fog to the shore. It was also used as a lookout tower. Hundreds of years ago, our country was invaded by armies from across the ocean. They were defeated, however for years afterward soldiers were stationed there to keep watch over the water, so they might sound an alarm should invaders once again approach by sea. Later, three more towers were built— to the north, east, and west."

"But isn't the country of Reede in the west?" I pointed to Reede on the map.

George nodded. "It is."

"But the people of Reede are our friends, so why would we need a watchtower to the west?"

George smiled. "The other three watchtowers aren't really watchtowers, they were built more for show than anything. The tower to the west is a shared tower between the countries of Reede and Gossling. Once it was a place to exchange messages between the kingdoms. Usually these messages were written and exchanged by messengers from each country.

One signal was very clear, however: if the tower light was lit, it was a signal for help."

Henry tugged at his lip, thinking. "Isn't there some sort of trouble in their country?"

George sighed. "There has long been trouble in Reede. The country was attacked by a vicious queen from the Mountains of Glacier and her cruel armies. The invaders were successful only because the people of Reede were paralyzed in their fight against them."

"Why?"

"Why?" George leaned back in his chair. "I don't know, Henry. Their king was frightened that such an army could not be defeated, and so he surrendered rather than risk the lives of his people. However, when he did that, he lost his country and its freedom."

"Where's the bad queen now?"

George shook his head. "She's long gone. She was defeated largely because our country went to battle for the people of Reede."

"Didn't they fight too?" Henry said incredulously.

George's face was very grave. "They couldn't. When people lose their freedom, they often forget what it was like to once have freedom. Forget what it means to be free. This was true for the people of Reede. But"—George's face cleared—"this was long, long ago. And it is not what you have come here to learn." He directed us back to the map. "Now look north again, and what do you see?"

"The Sunflower Forest," I said quickly, and George nodded.

"Queen Charlotte says it's enchanted," Henry added.

George looked thoughtful. "I wouldn't be surprised. It is reported that even on the coldest day of the year the sunflowers bloom there as if it were the middle of summer."

"And even with the trees above them blocking the sun, the sunflowers can grow as tall as fourteen feet," I interjected.

"A magical spot," George agreed. "Now what do we see west of the Sunflower Forest?"

"The Fairy Grove?" Henry looked carefully at the map.

"Correct," George smiled, "Fairy Grove is a beautiful part of the western region of our country. And an area where the plague has been particularly severe." George's face grew sad.

"Why is it called Fairy Grove?" Henry asked.

George smiled. "Because it's rumored that centuries ago, fairies lived in the low valleys there."

"Really?" I asked.

George smiled even more broadly. "That's the rumor, though no fairy spotting has been reported in two hundred years."

"Oh," I said, and sighed with disappointment.

"Now, let's look again at the map. Move south of the Fairy Grove and what do you see?"

"The Western Valleys, and the Mountains of Nylorac," I said confidently.

"Right," George said. "And what do you know about that area?"

"The Mountains of Nylorac have mines?" Henry guessed.

"Right again. The Mountains of Nylorac are filled with mines and old caves. A person could spend a lifetime exploring those caves and still have more to see. Now, what do you know of the Western Valleys?"

"There are a lot of orchards there," I volunteered.

"Yes." George nodded. "Most of our country's orchard groves are there. And what do you find in the central region?"

"Farms," Henry said, pointing to the map.

"And cities," I added.

George smiled, a quick satisfied smile. "Very good. Now I'm going to put you to work making your own maps."

"What kind of maps?" Henry pointed to one of the topographical maps. "Can we make one of those?"

"Such a map would take days and months to complete. However, it's a good idea for you both to make different maps." George frowned, thinking. "One map will be detailed and very specific, like our map with the careful painting"— he gestured to the old map—"and one shall be a larger map covering a greater expanse of land."

"What are we mapping?" I asked.

"Henry, do you think you could make a map of Tiege's wild gardens?" George asked, handing Henry a large white canvas and a bundle of paints.

Henry grinned. "I could try."

"Amelia." George turned to me. "Why don't you try to make a less detailed map than the garden map, and try to map out the entire palace grounds. Be sure to remember to include the creeks, the Lake of Swans, and all roads that lead up to the palace."

"Okay," I agreed, settling down next to Henry at the large table.

An hour later, Henry and I both had rather poorly drawn but still fairly accurate maps.

George sat down, looking pleased. "You have both been very diligent scholars this morning. I'm especially impressed with the focus and attention you've given this—you've been working a long time!"

As we prepared to go to lunch, George stopped us. "I have something for you both." He drew two small velvet bags from his pocket, one blue and one green. "Amelia." George placed the green velvet bag gently in the center of my palm. "And Henry." George handed him the blue bag.

I hesitated before opening my gift, wondering what secret was nestled inside, then slowly I drew open the silk strings and slid out a cold, round silver object. It looked like a large locket, and carved into the silver was an image of the Lake of Swans with the willow trees bending before her shores. I looked at the object curiously, trying to hide my disappointment, and decided that it was a kind of small paperweight. Henry held a nearly identical object in his hand, though on his was carved a small likeness of the Winter Palace and the Blue Mountains; two swans flew above the palace, their graceful necks extended.

George smiled at us. "Do you know what you're holding?"

Sheepishly, I shook my head and George smiled again. "Here," he said as he took the object from my hand and pressed an almost invisible latch. With a tiny click the top sprang open, revealing a compass. It was my turn to smile. I turned north and the needle swung north, and then I turned south and again the needle spun. I looked closely at the inside lid of the compass and read the curling script carefully. It read: *This is the property of the fourth princess of Gossling, Princess Amelia, so she will always find her way.*

Henry peered over my shoulder and read my inscription aloud, and then read his: *For Henry, so you will always know the direction your adventures lead you.*

I closed my lid gently, and it locked with a smart snapping sound. "Thank you, George, I love it!" I gave him a hug. "It's perfect—I can't wait to use it."

George winked at me. "I know you'll use it well. We could use you as an official map reader—we'll have to tell your mother that your sense of direction is impeccable."

I beamed at him. Next to me, Henry was standing very still, looking down at the compass and the message inside it. "Thank you," he said simply.

❧

In our second week without an official tutor, when Mother was just about to give up all hope and teach us herself, a telegram arrived from the University in the West. The telegram arrived at breakfast, and Mother opened it, reading aloud:

your highness: I have heard of your search
for a tutor for the youngest princess, and send
one of our best students. he is a librarian, well
versed in the arts, sciences, humanities, and
mathematics. he is of high character.

Mother read the rest of the telegram to herself, and then smiled. "This boy sounds promising; he'll arrive tomorrow, and if he seems a good match, you'll have afternoon classes in the library."

Henry and I grinned at each other across the table. Mother's interviews were notorious, and surely the reason we still were without a tutor. Mother refused to hire anyone less knowledgeable than herself. Whoever this young student was, it seemed unlikely he would be able to match her.

❧

The following day brought rain—a terrible storm from the east. Henry and I snuck into the sword room, trying on the heavy armor and lifting the large jeweled swords from their stands. With the storm outside, we happily decided that there wasn't a chance the new teacher would be able to reach the palace through the wind and driving rain. But we were wrong, and during the noon meal, Theo was announced.

One of the butlers—starched and prim—entered the dining room. Behind him stood a tall boy, dripping miserably on the marble floor. The butler bowed stiffly and said, with a hint of disapproval in his voice, "Your majesties, the librarian from the university has arrived."

Theo stepped forward looking wet and uncomfortable, his damp hair curling across his forehead, glasses slipping down his nose and fogging slightly in the warm dining room, his hands clutching a satchel. He was young. He seemed to be only a year or two older than Merrill, and he blushed as we stared at him.

Mother, ignoring the puddle forming around him, stood and smiled. "Welcome!" Then gesturing to each of us, she briskly introduced us. "Lily and Rose, the twins, our oldest daughter, Merrill, and our two youngest pupils, my daughter Amelia and our dear friend Henry. Now," she smiled pleasantly at all of us, "won't you please excuse me? I wish to dine privately with Theodore in the library."

Dripping and blushing, Theo followed my mother from the room. When they left, Henry and I smiled at each other, knowing there was no way the tutor would survive the interview. We were certain it was to be another day of holiday: Theodore from the west was a sheep meeting with a wolf.

But at the end of lunch, Mother returned in high spirits, as light and easy as she'd been in the weeks before the exodus of Madame Bellow. "Theo will start with you both in twenty minutes," she said to me and Henry, then smiling happily at my father, "He'll make a fine tutor."

My father smiled in return. Mother turned to us. "Go wash up," she ordered sharply, and—feet dragging—we walked slowly toward the study room. My mother's voice followed us, cheerful now, "Hurry up! You've missed enough school!"

In our large classroom, a cozy fire danced in the fireplace, and the rain drummed lightly against the windows. I sat down with a sigh and flopped back in my chair, rolling my eyes at Henry, who was rustling around inside his desk looking for the book he'd been reading before Madame

Bellow left. I looked at the clock: one o'clock. Four hours of the school day stretched before me, and I didn't imagine those hours to be much different than the hundreds of hours I had already spent in school. But I was wrong.

Theo, drier and more relaxed, entered the classroom and perched on the edge of the teacher's desk. "Before we begin, I think we should get to know each other." He smiled broadly at our blank faces. "I'll begin. I'm the oldest of eight children, four boys and four girls. I grew up near the Blue Mountains, by the twin lakes, Orion and Fox. So even though I can ice-skate; very well, I never learned how to swim because the water is too cold, even on the hottest day in August. Both my parents are professors, so I always assumed that I would be one too. And so, when I went to the university, I studied everything, but when I graduated, I was most interested in teaching."

He leaned forward a little on the desk. "Now," he said, "tell me about yourselves."

Henry and I stared at him, and Theo smiled encouragingly. "Why don't we start with you?" He gestured to Henry, and, haltingly at first, Henry told him about his mother's death, and how he came to be a part of two families when he was just a few hours old. He explained that his father was the palace's head gardener, organizing the more than seventy gardeners who worked to keep the expansive grounds of the palace beautiful.

When he was done, Theo said, "The gardens of the palace are visited by many of the world's most esteemed botanists and landscapers. Even through this rain, it is easy to see why. Do you share your father's love of flowers, or do your interests lie elsewhere?"

Henry's eyes shone and he looked pleased. "My father's the expert, but he's taught me a lot about flowers and plants. And I don't know what I want to do when I get older, but I think I'll probably have a really good garden."

Theo nodded. "I'm sure you will! Now, what do you like to read?"

Henry loved to read, and so the list was long. As he rattled off the names of the books he'd read over the past six months, Theo nodded and smiled, commenting on each one. "I loved that book too. And have you read the dragon books? What did you think of the pirate series?"

Henry's face was pink with pleasure; we had never had a tutor take a real interest in what we read or what we thought of what we were reading. Soon they were talking like old friends, and I felt a snake of jealousy tighten around my throat. Even though Henry was an excellent student, we had always shared a mutual hated of our tutors, and now Henry was looking at Theo as if he were a dragon slayer. Watching them, I vowed that I would hate Theo, and do everything I could to get him fired before the week's end.

Theo shifted his attention from Henry and smiled at me. "What about you, Princess Amelia? Tell me about yourself."

I shrugged and smiled a tight-lipped smile. "There's nothing to tell. I'm the fourth princess. I'm ineducable."

Henry looked troubled, but Theo's smile didn't change. "What do you like to read?"

I glared at him and folded my arms tightly across my chest. "Nothing. There's nothing I like to read."

Theo waited for me to say more, but when I didn't, he seemed unconcerned. He said mildly, "This afternoon, we're going to do some work so I can see where you are in your studies. I've a pile of report cards from Madame Bellow on you both, but before I read them, I'd rather assess you myself."

Although I was trying to hate him, I still felt a rush of gratitude, thankful that he was not reading what I knew were terrible reports. Theo handed us math sheets first, and as usual Henry flew through them, finishing in half the time it took me. As Theo waited for me to finish, he asked Henry to read aloud to him, and try as I could to focus on multiplication, I found myself distracted by Henry's reading. He was reading aloud quietly, but it was beautiful: a story about a lonely stag in the forest who is befriended by doves on the edge of an enchanted stream. Henry's voice lifted and changed with each character, and my pencil hovered above my math paper, listening. When he was done reading and had started working on an essay, I slowly finished the equations.

Shuffling up to Theo's desk, I put my math sheet facedown, knowing that half of my answers were wrong. It wasn't that I was bad at math, in fact, I was quite decent, but when I went to write down the answers, things got jumbled up, and so my sheet was covered with erasures and scratched-out numbers.

Theo didn't seem to notice; he studied the sheet briefly, then put it down. "Shall we do some reading?" he asked.

I shrugged.

"Here," he said, and handed me the book Henry had been reading, and I looked at it, horrified.

"Begin here," he pointed to the first paragraph of the second chapter.

Where Henry's reading was melodious, mine was choppy and broken, filled with misread words and skipped lines. I waited for Theo to stop me, but when he didn't, I pushed grimly on. When I was finished with the chapter, I slammed the book closed and stared defiantly at Theo, daring him to say anything. In the past when I'd read, Madame Bellow had nearly shaken in wrath. Her tirades about my ignorance spanned two languages, with Madame shouting at me in both English and French. But Theo didn't say a word, just looked thoughtful.

"Okay, Amelia, I'm going to ask you a little about what you just read. Can you tell me about the chapter?"

I couldn't, though, and I felt my stomach sink. I could have told him anything about what Henry had read, but I didn't understand a thing that I had read aloud. I shrugged and waited for Theo to yell but he didn't. Instead he did something unusual. He said, "Now, I'm going to read aloud, and I want you to listen."

So I listened, and when he was done, I easily answered all the questions he had about the reading.

When he was done asking questions, Theo's face was hard to read. "Good," he said briskly.

The next morning when we reached our classroom, Theo did the unthinkable: he sent us outside. Handing us each a book on botany, Theo ordered us to the garden with sketch-pads and an assignment to identify different leaves.

Later that afternoon, when lunch was finished and Henry and I were back in the classroom, Theo began his lesson to me with these words: "You're not stupid."

And I had rolled my eyes, because I had heard my father say the same thing a hundred times. Still, Theo laid out his case for me point by point: "You can't spell, but you're an excellent writer; you can't add on a sheet, but you can multiply large numbers in your head; you can't read well, but you can easily answer comprehension questions about what's been read to you. Someone who can do those things is not stupid." And he looked very pleased at the thought, as though my brain was extra special, and clever in its differentness.

"I believe," Theo continued slowly, "that because your brain learns in an unconventional way, that you need to be taught in a different way."

"Do you think I'll learn how to read?" I asked, and realized I was holding my breath.

Theo nodded. "Oh yes. Absolutely. It won't happen overnight, but it will happen."

And it did. Not overnight, but slowly, slowly, I began to read. As spring turned to summer, I was reading like an eight-year-old. True, I was twelve, but reading like an eight-year-old is much better than reading like a five-year-old—and I *was* reading.

As a result, my parents called Theo a miracle maker, and loved him. And it turned out they were not alone.

CHAPTER 5

Plague

SOON AFTER THEO ARRIVED, Merrill began spending more and more time in our classroom, helping us with our studies and helping Theo with his teaching. Merrill had always been the most patient of my sisters, and although I was curious about her sudden interest in our schoolwork, I was happy she was there. Theo had made my schooling a group effort, and the more help there was, the more I improved. Henry quizzed me on spelling words and math facts, Theo concentrated on teaching me to read, and Merrill helped me learn to write what I meant to write.

During classtime, both Merrill and Theo were focused completely on teaching, yet as soon as class was over, they would settle into long talks, discussing articles and books they had read, debating policies in our country, the spread of the plague, poetry, astronomy—everything, anything; their cups of tea cooling before them, forgotten. By early May they were spending so much time together that Henry and I joked that they were in love.

"Theo loves Merrill!" I sang out as Theo entered the library with Merrill one day after lunch, the two of them deep in conversation.

"Please, Amelia!" Theo blushed a deep purple.

And Merrill, usually controlled, looked briefly furious. "Honestly, Amelia!"

For a moment I felt shocked and then pleased—I hadn't really believed that they were in love, but this was proof.

On Thursday mornings Mother taught us history. She lectured to us about any and all subjects that were relevant to our knowledge of the kingdom: the history of sugarcane, the development of the school system, city planning, agricultural development, elimination of mines, social reforms, flooding . . . Mother's knowledge was endless—she told us funny stories about our grandfather and sad stories about the wars of neighboring countries; her lectures were long and filled with facts and large words and statistics. Although I didn't love history, I loved our Thursday-morning lessons, was drawn in despite myself.

One Thursday in May, while Theo and Henry were out examining trees with a group of scientists, Mother entered her drawing room late, looking rushed and distracted. We had been waiting for close to thirty minutes: Merrill draped like a cat on a chair, reading book reports that Henry and I had written, the twins playing an elaborate game of jacks, and me looking longingly out the window toward the river, where I knew that George, Henry, and Theo were spending the morning.

Mother was brisk. "Girls, come to the table please! We're

already getting a late start and we have much to cover. Perhaps I'll shift today's lesson to one of genealogy—that's the study of one's own family history," she added for my benefit. "This is a lesson I was saving for later in the month, but you all look like you could use a break from ocean life and plants." She smiled slightly when I vigorously nodded. "At any rate, I think it's time I tell you your family history—the history of the White Queens and the origins of your magic."

We sat up, instantly attentive.

Mother laughed at our sudden interest. "Well, well! Now I have your attention!" She paused before speaking, as if weighing her words carefully. "What you must first know is that you—all of you—are White Queens."

"But," Lily interrupted, confused, "I thought Merrill would be queen."

Mother nodded. "She will be queen of Gossling. She is also a White Queen. You're all princesses of Gossling right now, of course, but you are also White Queens. You have the power of your great-great-great-grandmothers alive in you, and it is a powerful blend of magic and something more."

"What are the powers, Mother? Are you going to teach us?" Rose's voice was high with excitement.

"In a moment we'll get to that. First, you should know that the White Queens are most powerful when they are united. My mother was the oldest of three sisters, and their power combined was greater than mine alone. I had no cousins or sisters, and my gift was weaker for it; I had to learn how best to use my powers alone. Your power, the power of four, will be great once you have learned your gifts, how to use them individually, and how to use them together."

"What if we had all been boys?" I asked.

Mother laughed. "Well, I would have loved you anyway. But I think you are asking if the son of a White Queen has her power, and he does not. Only daughters. The gift passes only through women."

"Queen Charlotte!" The door swung open with such force that Merrill's papers were blown to the floor. We all turned as George, red in the face from running, panted his message. "The king asked that you come quickly! The plague has moved into the eastern valleys."

Mother's face tightened with worry and her voice was heavy. "Thank you, I'll be in the library in a moment. Gather the advisors again, though what we shall accomplish, I wish I knew! Girls," she turned back to us as George closed the doors behind him, "we shall continue this lesson again in a week's time. We shall discuss powers, genealogy, and the history of our family." She stood up and her eyes were sad. "I wish we had more time." She sighed, and then straightened, as if to steel herself from what she was about to hear. She strode to the door and as she opened it, turned back to us. "Next week we will continue."

❧

But we never had the chance, for the next week the plague continued to spread through the low valleys, and Mother and Father traveled to the University in the East hoping that a scientist there might hold the answer. As the plague continued to spread and spread, and as one week faded into another, our meetings with Mother were put on hold, and the story of the White Queens' power and how it was used was never told. And then, of course, the plague crept closer and closer to the palace and we were sent to the Blue Mountains so the story remained untold, but not forgotten. The mystery of it was still there, like a mouse nibbling in the corner of my mind.

But that comes later. In the weeks that followed, Mother and Father spent almost every moment concentrating on the spread of the plague and how to stop it. All the while our life continued in a more or less ordinary way. Mother had insisted that, since we'd missed so much school after Madame Bellow left, Henry and I continue school for at least a part of the summer. So Theo moved our classroom outside and we began a butterfly study, learning science under the shade of the willow trees. To me, the days seemed long and lazy. Henry and I taught Theo to swim in the Lake of Swans, Dori invented a new cookie, and the twins performed well in a dance festival. Merrill and Theo continued to spend hours together, taking long walks, their heads bent close in conversation. Watching them, Mother and Father exchanged secret smiles, though their eyes were concerned, for it was not proper for a princess to love a commoner—even one as uncommon as Theo.

❧

With my reading improving, in midsummer Mother decided that every afternoon I should read for two hours.

Even though I protested, I didn't really mind because now that I *could* read I actually liked reading, and anyway most days Mother read next to me, on one of the benches by the Lake of Swans. Merrill had made a reading list, and the books she had chosen for me were perfect—books about pirates and explorers and acrobats and knights. All adventure tales, all detailing the exciting days of exciting heroes. As I read, I wished I could climb into the stories—wished I could follow them on their adventure rather than stay in the garden reading about it.

"I'm bored," I said one day, slamming my book closed. "I wish I was doing something exciting."

Mother looked up from the chart she was studying and smiled a small, grim smile. "And I wish this summer was a little bit less exciting."

"That's easy for you to say," I grumbled, "because you're always doing exciting things and I'm always doing ordinary things, like dancing and lessons."

Mother laughed suddenly. "Like everyone else, I live both an extraordinary and ordinary life. And here's a secret: the days that have been the most extraordinary ones to me would probably be considered the most ordinary ones by others. For example, the rainy day that we picnicked in the palace tower, or the time we spent hours building that enormous fort of blocks in the playroom, or the afternoons where I've just walked through the gardens with your father, or the early mornings I've spent laughing with Dori on the sunporch, or the lazy hours I've spent reading under trees." She winked at me. "Those are the memories of days I cherished the most.

My most wonderful days haven't been the days where I've worn beautiful long robes, or attended huge balls, or made grand speeches. No, my most wonderful days have been the ones that you might call dull or boring or ordinary. As unbelievable as this may seem, someday you'll realize that the best days are very, very ordinary ones. And they are the days I would relive a thousand times over. Be happy for the everyday days, Amelia."

I sighed and opened my book again, trying to get drawn back into the story about trained penguins. I didn't say it aloud, but I couldn't help but think that Mother was wrong—of course, no one wanted the kind of excitement that the plague brought, but an extraordinary day every now and then would certainly be a welcome change.

୧୨

Yet, from far in the east, reports continued about the spreading plague. It crept closer and closer, circling most of the country in a cloak of fear and disease. Every day messengers arrived with more bad news, and Father, Mother, George, and all the top advisors met frequently behind closed doors, their faces drawn and tired. Doctors and scientists came to the palace from faraway places, anxious to help find a cure. Under their recommendations, all the water was tested— each small stream, each strong river, the air was tested, and the blood of those who were sick was drawn and analyzed again and again—searching for some sign, some clue, as to the cause of the illness, as to how it was spread. As a precaution, Father decreed that all water be boiled before drinking or bathing. And then, as the sickness continued its rapid spread across the country, further restrictions were recommended—that no animal or fish be eaten, that all citizens stick to a strict regimen of exercise, that vitamins be consumed every day. And so the country subsisted on a diet of vegetables and fruit and grain; we took vitamins and exercised every day, we drank in the air that the scientists swore was clean and swam in the water that had been tested and retested and found pure. But the precautions were in vain, for still the sickness raged on. Raged on as if the country, once considered bountiful and blessed, was cursed.

CHAPTER 6

The Blue Mountains

AT THE END OF AUGUST, with Theo and George acting as teacher and advisor, we were sent to the palace in the Blue Mountains for safety: Merrill, Lily, Rose, Henry, and I. The other children in the palace village were encouraged to join us, and we were a caravan of thirty children, eight nurses, ten nannies, and fifteen handmaids. Together we left the warm green valley and headed two hundred miles away to the cold snow of the Blue Mountains.

Except for that summer, I had spent every July in the Blue Mountains with my entire family, and it was one of my favorite places on earth. But it felt odd to be there so close to fall. The tops of the Blue Mountains were already frosted with snow, and the air was crisp and almost cold after the warmth we had left behind.

The decision to leave had been made quickly. With the plague coming closer and closer to the capital, Father and Mother had grown more and more concerned, and that afternoon they had taken a long walk. Their figures were hunched and tired as they moved through the gardens, up and down the winding paths.

"What can they possibly be talking about?" Lily wondered, watching them from the window of the Children's Library.

Rose looked up from her painting. "Probably the plague."

I nodded in agreement, but Merrill stayed silent, her head bent over her book.

"What do you think, Merrill?" Lily asked.

Her eyes still on her book, Merrill said, "The plague, perhaps. But whatever it is, if we need to know, they'll tell us."

At dinner we were told. Father cleared his throat and took a quick swallow of water, then gravely announced that we would be leaving for the Blue Mountains in the morning. Without them.

Merrill paused, her ice-cream spoon in midair. Theo exchanged a look with her that made me believe that the topic of us leaving the palace had come up before, and that perhaps they had been a part of such a discussion.

Rose and Lily burst into tears, and Henry's pie lay untouched before him, two thick tears rolling down his cheeks.

I scowled into my custard, trying not to cry. Our family had never been separated before for more than a night or two, and that was only when Mother or Father went to another part of the kingdom on an official visit.

The dining room was quiet. Father cleared his throat, and then Mother began speaking—her voice crisp, even a bit teasing. "Now, now, this isn't a time for tears. All the village and palace children are to travel with you—it will be an adventure!"

"No, it won't," Rose muttered darkly into her water glass, and Lily shook her head, her blond hair lifting and sighing with the force.

Mother's voice grew serious. "There is no other choice. So, I suggest you all make the best of this and think of this journey as an adventure, rather than something to be dreaded."

"Besides," Father said with false heartiness, "with any luck, this plague will end and you'll be back before harvest, wishing it was still summer holiday. Now let's eat our dessert!"

But no one had an appetite for the ice cream, thick lemon custard, or chocolate soufflé. The pies went untouched, and the table was silent.

❧

On this last night, we all slept in my room—the old nursery. This was in part because of necessity—with so many suitcases to be packed, my sisters' rooms were bright with lights and filled with housekeepers. Even with the door firmly closed we could hear the maids hurrying up and down the halls. It seemed as if the whole household was to make the journey, with only a few members of the palace staff staying behind.

"Why is everyone going to the Blue Mountains, Mother?" Lily asked.

Mother was perched on the edge of Lily's bed, neatly folding the last of my fall dresses into a suitcase. Now she paused, choosing her words carefully. "Because, my Lily, if I believe this palace is unsafe for my own children, how could I allow the children of others to remain?"

"But if it's unsafe, then why don't you come to the Blue Mountains too?" Rose cried. "You can rule just as easily from there."

Mother shook her head, and her eyes flicked briefly to Merrill, and again I had the feeling that this had been discussed. "It's true we could rule from the Blue Mountains, but the country is panicked. Uprooting the king and queen feeds into that panic. Staying here allows us to monitor the spread of the plague more easily because this palace is located in the heart of the kingdom. It can take a full day for a message to reach the Blue Mountains, and by then the message may already be inaccurate. No," she sighed, "we must stay. And we will stay with as few staff as we can manage with—only the advisors will stay, one of the cooks, and Dori. After all," she smiled, "I know how to make my own bed and hang up my own gowns, and your father can cook an excellent omelet."

We didn't smile in return, and the room felt heavy and sad. Tucking a final sweater in, Mother zipped up my suitcase and placed it by the door, laying my winter coat on top of it.

"Tell us a story, Mother," I prompted her.

Mother smiled at me. "That's a wonderful idea! Especially since it's time for all good princesses to be sleeping." She patted my pillow, waiting as the twins settled under the covers, and Merrill kicked off her slippers and slid into bed.

75

The room was quiet, and in the soft light Mother smiled and then crossed the room and sat on Merrill's bed. "I will tell you my very favorite story, the best story I know. Once upon a time there was a king and queen who very much wanted a little girl. And the day they got her, they believed they had everything." Mother kissed Merrill's forehead and lightly touched the curve of her face. "My first baby," she said, and suddenly there were tears in her eyes.

I looked anxiously at the twins to see if they had noticed, but they hadn't, their eyes were already closed, both of them drifting toward sleep. Mother left Merrill's bed and went to their two beds, kneeling between them. Her voice was softer now. "Then the king and the queen hoped for another baby, and instead of getting one, they got two. Beautiful babies . . ." Mother paused again, and her voice became almost a whisper. "Twins who believed they were the same, but who would find one day they were different." She kissed them both gently, but they were asleep and already dreaming.

Mother came to my bed, where I was still sitting up. "Lie back, Amelia," Mother said. "Lie back, and I'll tell you the rest of the story."

I lay back on my pillow, and Mother pulled the quilt up around me. She smoothed my hair, pushing it from my forehead and curling one strand of it around her finger. "That's better, now you look ready for sleep. Well, just when the king and queen thought there would be no more babies, the queen remembered something so important that she felt ashamed to have forgotten it. Do you know what that was?"

I smiled at her. "That there was to be one more."

Mother nodded. "That's right, and when that princess came, she made her mother and father so proud, so happy! They wept with joy—they couldn't believe their luck, couldn't believe they had been blessed with such gifts. And the queen knew something about the fourth princess that no one else knew."

"What was it?" I asked, suddenly very awake.

Mother smiled at me and kissed the tip of my nose. "It can't be told, it must be found."

I rolled my eyes with impatience. "Is that the end of the story?"

Mother kissed me again. "It's the end of the story *tonight*, but the story isn't over. Far from it, Amelia."

❧

Dawn came, hot and thick. At six o'clock in the morning heat hung in the air, heavy as a blanket and hot as midday. The sky was gray though, and filled with dark, pregnant clouds. One of the coachmen looked at them hopefully. "Maybe there'll be rain later to break the heat."

A groomsman nodded, his hands holding the reins of a horse steady as the carriage was loaded. "We can only hope."

One by one, carriage after carriage disappeared down the drive. We were the last carriage to leave, and the four of us stood before Mother while Henry leaned miserably against my father, Father's arm wrapped hard around him.

"You'll be back before you know it." Mother tried to sound gay, though her eyes betrayed her.

Lily and Rose smiled weakly, their eyes puffy from crying,

and I glared at the ground, scuffing my foot back and forth along the stone. Only Merrill seemed calm, her eyes quiet. Mother and Father hugged us each in turn—long hugs to let us know that we were special, that we were the most precious. Mother held Merrill in her arms a moment longer, and she pressed her mouth to Merrill's ear, whispered something to her.

Then we were in the carriage, driving toward the Blue Mountains, waving and waving to our parents long after we stopped being able to see them.

※

Although we missed our parents, Mother had been right, there was a sort of holiday feeling at the enormous Winter Palace. It felt packed with people—they spilled out of bedrooms, they piled into the guest cottages, and they slept in the rooms above the stables. All day the cooks worked to feed everyone. In the night we could hear babies crying and the soft, soothing songs of the nursemaids and mothers trying to lull them back to sleep.

In addition to the sheer number of people, we had never been away from home with any children other than Henry and ourselves. Now suddenly there were children everywhere: our friends from the palace and village children we didn't know. Together, we spent hours climbing trees and playing elaborate games of capture the castle, and hide-and-seek, and tag. With colored chalk, Rosemary drew complicated hopscotch boards on the slate stones of the courtyard, and we drew thick mustaches on the statues in the statue garden.

Patrick showed off by doing a handstand on the back of a prancing horse, breaking his wrist in the process, and we all spent hours ice-skating on the large lake in front of the palace.

While we played, Merrill and Theo spent long portions of each day with the advisors behind the heavy doors of the library. As my parents had done at home, the talk of the plague continued, and the same worry that had etched lines into Mother's face now showed in Merrill's eyes, even when she smiled.

At night the four of us slept together in the nursery. This was done out of necessity—with so many children in the palace, Merrill had said it would be selfish for us to each claim our own rooms. She was right, though it was crowded in the nursery with toys, dolls, and books spilling out of the shelves and toy chests. Clothing and suitcases still covered the floors. They had been half-unpacked by the maids before Merrill had ordered them to focus on whatever was most crucial to the well-being of a palace half choked with people.

When Lily, annoyed with the mess, had tried to complete the unpacking process, she found it almost impossible because the closets and dressers were so packed with outgrown clothes from past summers. She and Rose had done their best to sort through the clothes and shoes, ordering them to be distributed to the children in the palace, correctly assuming that many of them had come with suitcases packed with enough clothes to last only for a week. When they had cleared as much as they could, they found that the closets were still too small for the belongings of four half-grown princesses and finally gave up in frustration. As a result, the room had a temporary feel to it too—as if to reinforce that we wouldn't be in the Winter Palace for long.

Still, even with the clutter and the chaos, and the anxiety of the plague, and the terrible ache for home and Mother and Father, there was still something about the weeks that were wonderful—with long stretches of time devoted to nothing more than game playing.

As Lily noted one night before bed, her voice wistful, "This must be the life of ordinary children."

Merrill laughed. "Don't be silly, Lil! Just like us, they spend most of the day in school, and unlike us, they don't have the privilege of special dance lessons or the responsibility of being princesses. Instead, they work to help their parents tend to younger children, or do their homework, or help with dinner, or chores. This isn't real life for them any more than it is for us!"

Rose didn't smile. "I'm glad this isn't real life. I wish everything was normal again." Lily nodded in agreement, pulling her blue blanket up over her.

I grinned from my bed. "I don't. Ordinary is dull! I wish Mother and Father were here, but other than that, I like it this way—no school, no rules, and best of all, no bedtime."

Merrill snapped the light off and hopped into bed. "Think again, Princess."

CHAPTER 7

Long Live the Queen

WE HAD BEEN THERE for three weeks when Lily asked Merrill the question that I had nearly forgotten to ask. It was hard to believe how cold the nights were in the Blue Mountains; it didn't feel like September, it felt like February, and my teeth chattered as I quickly stepped into warm flannel pajamas, shivering as I slipped between the cold sheets. A fire was roaring in the fireplace, and frost traced the window with cold hands. Lily sat on her bed in a thick pink robe, brushing out her blond hair so it gleamed like gold in the light of the fire. I stared at her hair enviously. "I wish I had blond hair."

Lily laughed. "Well, I wish I had red hair, so I guess we're even."

"Rose." I turned to Rose, who was busy closing the heavy drapes, hoping to keep out some of the cold, her slippers whispering on the floor as she walked from window to window. "Do you wish you had red hair? If you say you don't you're saying you don't want to be like Lily . . . ," I teased.

Rose rolled her eyes. "If Lily wants red hair, then I guess

I do too, but if she doesn't care, then I guess I'd say that I'd prefer to stay blond."

Merrill pulled a long nightgown over her head. "Well, I'd swap with any of the three of you—I'd happily be blond or red, as long as I didn't have to stay brown!" She laughed. "Dori and Mother would hate this conversation. They'd say we should be happy with the hair we have!"

Lily put her brush down on the nightstand and turned to look at Merrill. "Speaking of Mother, what did she say to you when we were getting into the carriage?"

Merrill's face looked troubled, and for a moment I thought she might not answer.

We all looked at her expectantly. "Merrill?" Rose asked after a moment.

"It was nothing," Merrill said, though her face was still troubled. "She said: 'You were born to be queen.' "

Rose laughed and picked up Lily's hairbrush, running it quickly through her hair. "Well, of course you were! And you will be—someday!"

Lily laughed too, as if relieved that the message was something so simple, but Merrill was not smiling, and neither was I.

Mother never stated the obvious, and so for some reason, what we had all known as fact—that Merrill was born to be queen—was no longer fact.

❧

Another week passed uneventfully. Then, on the day that changed everything, we were ice-skating, or, well, nearly everyone was; I was refusing. Meg, Lily, Rose, and Merrill slipped effortlessly by on the ice; the blades of their skates flashing and winking in the weak light. Most of the children were playing a game of tag on the ice, and even little Ralph, with Theo's help, skimmed along the edge of the large lake. I bent over my skates, pretending to tighten them and scowling. Henry sat next to me on a green bench.

"Come on," he begged for the tenth time.

"I'm not going. You go! I don't care." I glared across the ice at Meg, who was showing off with double spins and graceful leaps.

"Fine." He stood up, looking miserable. "I'm *really* going." He looked at me hopefully for a moment and then sat down again. "You know it's not fun out there without you. Who cares about Meg? She's just trying to make you mad. Ignore her! Come on—" Henry stopped midsentence and his mouth dropped open. "Look!"

I looked where he was pointing. Coming up the long iced driveway was a horseman in court colors galloping at full speed.

On the ice, all skating came to a halt, as everyone watched the horse race toward the palace steps where—half collapsing—the rider slid to the ground.

"Maybe the sickness has ended," Meg finally spoke.

Merrill shook her head. "I don't think so. He would have stopped and told us. Look at his horse—it's exhausted— he's been riding all day and night." Her voice was troubled, and I saw her glance at Theo, saw his face tighten.

We stared wordlessly as the silver horse was led to the

barn by a stable hand. The animal was clearly exhausted and it shivered with sweat and the cold of the mountains. I found myself suddenly chilled in the breath of silence that followed; only the horse's hooves clattered on the slick cobblestones.

Merrill sat on the bench then, and began unlacing her skates. "Continue skating," she ordered. "I'm going to greet our visitor."

When no one moved, she gestured toward one of the ladies-in-waiting, who clapped her hands. "Come children, let's play a game!" Reluctantly the group turned back to the ice, skating slowly over toward her. Theo sat next to Merrill as she slipped into her shoes and asked, "Do you want me to go with you?"

She smiled faintly at him. "No, better that I meet with him alone." She squared her shoulders and stood up.

When she was halfway across the lawn, I began to unlace my skates and Henry did the same. Theo, who had been watching Merrill, turned to us. "Why are you taking off your skates?"

"To get dry gloves," Henry said matter-of-factly, holding up his own wet pair.

If Theo hadn't been distracted, he would surely have seen through the lie and stopped us, but his face was worried as he watched Merrill climb the steps, and he only nodded. Stepping into our shoes, we walked quickly toward the palace steps, just as the large doors closed behind my sister.

❧

In the palace, Henry and I walked purposefully past the doorman and attentive butlers, down the hall, and in the direction of the library. "Do you think they'll be in there?" Henry whispered.

I shrugged and whispered back, "Probably."

We were right: they were in the library. And so it was that Henry and I walked into the library in time to see the messenger kneel on one knee before my sister.

"Princess, I come with the saddest of news," the messenger began and his voice broke. "King Bryant and Queen Charlotte are dead." Then his voice cleared, and again he bowed his head. "Long live Queen Merrill."

Merrill, steady, reasonable, unflappable Merrill, burst into tears and fell against George. And I—forgetting that I was supposed to be outside skating—cried out, "No! No!" and felt Henry's and then my sister's arms around me, their tears mixing with mine. I felt a storm of grief, and then welcome darkness.

❧

Someone had carried me to my bed, and when I awoke the room was dark and Henry slept in a deep chair next to the fireplace, where a fire was slowly burning out, our wet skating clothes drying stiffly before it. For a moment, I pretended that it had been a terrible nightmare, that I had only dreamed about the messenger and his awful message, that my parents were alive at home still worried about the sickness, but still certain it would end. Henry shifted in his chair and cried out in his sleep, and even in the darkness I could see he had been crying, realized there was no use pretending.

I slid out of bed and stood uncertain for a moment about where to go. Then, still unsure, I moved soundlessly out of the room and into the hall. In the hallway, I realized with a start that I had gone to bed without tea or dinner. With my throat dry as sand, I tiptoed down the hall to the dark kitchen, where I pulled cookies out of a jar and poured milk from a blue pitcher into a glass. A blue pitcher the color of my mother's eyes.

"My parents are dead," I said aloud, tasting the bitter words on my tongue and feeling the pricks of tears against my eyes.

I bit into a lemon cookie. They had been delicious at lunch, but now they tasted like dust to me: chalky and too dry. *This is what grief tastes like*, I thought to myself, and felt suddenly like I might throw up. I tried to picture life without my parents and couldn't. Felt my eyes fill again with tears, my throat choked with grief. I sat on the cold stone of the kitchen floor and wept until I could cry no more. Then I leaned against the cool counter, my body hot, my eyes stinging. I sipped the milk and took another small bite of cookie. Funny that life goes on, that I could be hungry, that my feet could feel cold against the stone.

Down the hall, a light burned and spilled into the darkness, and voices bounced out in a blur of sound. Unmistakably, I heard Merrill's voice and walked to it. Peeking around the library's door, I counted six advisors spread around the table, huge books open before them. Standing in front of the map wall stood a seventh advisor, his face drawn as he studied a map of Gossling, black pins denoting the spread of the plague. I squinted at the map and saw a sea of black across the gentle green of our country. In the far corner of the room huddled together in three deep chairs sat Merrill, Theo, and George. Merrill's hand was hugging a teacup, and her face was drawn with worry and almost gray with grief.

I walked over to them and leaned against Merrill, who hugged me tightly against her. "I'm so sorry," she said, and again I felt the bitter tears teasing my eyes, felt a lump rise in my throat.

"Me too," I whispered.

"We'll be okay, though," Merrill said. She cleared her throat, and drew her arm around me. "I promise."

"Why is everyone awake?" I wondered.

Merrill passed a quick hand over her eyes. "No reason, really. Shock, maybe. Also, I'm eight weeks away from my eighteenth birthday," she paused, and in that pause I remembered the party my parents had been planning before we had left for the Winter Palace: fireworks, cakes, a dance, gardens of flowers filling vase after vase. I wondered if Merrill was remembering it too, though she didn't seem to be. "Until I'm eighteen, there is to be an interim ruler."

"What is that?"

"A temporary ruler. Someone to rule for those eight weeks before Merrill's birthday," Theo explained.

"What about George?" I crawled onto George's lap and he wrapped his arms securely around me.

Merrill laughed. "Smart princesses think alike. That was

my idea too, but George says there's a problem with me selecting a ruler. You see, it seems we have an uncle. A great-uncle, really, and according to ancient law, when there is a relative, the relative has the right to rule until a princess or prince comes of age. And if there is both a male and female relative, then by ancient law the male relative has the right to rule."

Thinking, I frowned and said, "That's dumb. They're both dumb rules. Why shouldn't the most qualified person rule? And why a boy before a girl? And anyway, I don't remember Mother or Father ever saying anything about an uncle."

Merrill sighed. "Nor do I, but he exists." She lifted a book off her lap, and pointed to the family tree inside it. "See, Mother's mother, our grandmother, had a stepbrother, our great-uncle Raven. I am told that he lives up near the lakes of black ice. He must be a bit odd, because no other creature lives there . . ." Merrill's face clouded and she tugged on her lip, worried. "Still, a messenger has been dispatched with a message for Count Raven to meet us all at Gossling Palace in a week's time. He shall begin his seven-week reign then."

It was only luck that I was not at Gossling Palace to greet the count with my sisters, though it did not seem at all lucky at the time.

CHAPTER 8

Metamorphosis

"THEY ARE NOT CHICKEN POX!" Meg shrieked, staring in horror at her face in the mirror. Her reflection scowled back. She looked like an aggravated leopard—her milky skin covered in angry red spots. Henry, his skin indistinguishable from Meg's and mine, met my eyes across the room. Meg had been shrieking for hours.

"They *are* chicken pox!" Perched on their suitcases, Lily and Rose pushed hands up to their mouths, covering their smiles in an identical gesture. It was true that we looked ridiculous—the doctor had dabbed us with pink lotion, and a nurse had tied socks to our hands with bright ribbon to keep us from scratching and scarring ourselves.

"Hey, I'm a sock puppet," I said, and held my hands up, pretending to make one socked hand talk to Meg. "Face it," I said in my best puppet voice, "they're chicken pox!"

"Shut up! Shut up!" Meg screamed at me, turning from the mirror, her face a furious mask of pink lotion and spots. "Shut up! Shut up! Shut up!" Then she burst into tears.

Across the nursery, Henry, his face stiff with pink lotion, rolled his eyes. All of us—Meg, Henry, and I—were in complete agreement about the chicken pox situation. For one thing, we found it very unfair that we'd been placed in the children's nursery together. The doctor had decided that it would be easier to care for us if we were all together in one room. That, and he'd decided we should be quarantined to prevent a chicken pox outbreak in the palace. "Besides," he said heartily, surveying our sulky faces glaring out at him from plumped pillows, "think of the fun the three of you will have bunking in together!"

"Oh yeah," Henry said with mock seriousness, "lots of fun."

Meg's whimpering and whining was enough to make me truly ill, and although I didn't want to admit it I didn't want to be separated from my sisters, who were to return to Gossling Palace. The thought that they could become ill with the plague as my parents had, that they too could die and I would be left alone, was too frightening to imagine, though there was a rumor that the sickness had ended as quickly as it had begun.

Merrill rushed into the nursery wearing her coat and sat on the edge of my bed. She squeezed my hand and smiled across the room at Henry. "I'm sorry to leave you," she said, looking genuinely sorry. "The doctor says you can leave here in three days if your fever breaks. In the meantime, Cook is making cake and meringues downstairs, and—"

She was interrupted by a long howl from Meg, and

Merrill suddenly looked both annoyed and concerned. "Maybe we *should* stay here. I'll send word to the palace that Uncle Raven should wait for us. Or perhaps meet us here . . ." She began to shake herself free of her coat.

"Oh, please! We're not babies." I glared across the room at Meg. "You don't have to babysit us. Besides, Theo is here. Go see Uncle Raven."

Merrill looked relieved and kissed my head. "Okay, Miss Sensible!" she teased. "We'll miss you. Feel better!" She pulled her coat around her, ruffled Henry's hair, and strode out the door followed by the twins.

"Feel better!" the twins called over their shoulders, turning to wave and blow kisses as they ran down the stairs after Merrill, their long blond curls bouncing behind them.

Without my sisters, the nursery was suddenly silent. Henry flopped back on his bed and groaned, "Boring!"

Meg swallowed a sob.

Downstairs I heard the great doors close, and I ran to the window that looked out over the long driveway. I saw the twins and George vanish into the waiting carriage, and then saw Merrill lean into Theo and kiss him for a very long minute on the lips. Then Merrill climbed into the carriage too, and with a quick slap of his whip, the driver urged the horses on. Theo stood alone on the front step, and I stood at the window, both of us waving to the carriage long after it had disappeared.

Merrill

When I was five years old, my father took me for a walk toward the edge of the palace grounds, to the large Lake of Swans. There was a bench under one of the willow trees and we sat on it together, watching the swans dip and rise over the water and high reeds. We had walked without speaking; we didn't always need to speak to know how the other felt. Besides that, my father was a quiet man, and I was a quiet child, and I had not thought the walk was anything more than a walk.

But sitting on the bench, my father took one of my hands in his own. "Look at the willow tree, Merrill. Many find this a sad tree because of how her branches seem to touch the ground. People say she is weeping. What do you think?"

I studied the tree, and said I thought maybe it was weeping. My father very gently pulled a branch toward us. "See this, the velvet softness?" and he touched the pad of the willow lightly. "This tree is not afraid to be soft. See the green of her branch? She is an old tree, but she is covered with these green branches. She is not afraid to be new or young. Change does not frighten her. See the roots of this tree? See her thick trunk? She is strong. And yes, I see that this tree weeps with her branches, that she is not afraid of tears. But now see her in the wind."

We watched the branches bounce lightly in the breeze. "She is not afraid to dance," my father observed.

And then my father told me that someday I would be

queen. And I knew why he had described the tree and her qualities, for they were the characteristics of a good leader. I'm afraid it's silly to say so now, but I had always imagined us ruling together—Mother, Father, and me. I did not imagine that I would be queen by my eighteenth birthday, did not imagine my sisters and myself orphaned by plague, our kingdom devastated by disease and death.

And I know this will sound strange, but I knew, *I knew*, that when my parents sent us to the Blue Mountains, that I would never see them again. The messenger and his message did not surprise me.

My mother was known as the White Queen by very few. Growing up, I didn't know how she came by this title, or why. I did know, in the fuzziest of ways, that my mother held a power that extended beyond human understanding. My mother was not a sorceress, nor was she a witch. She was herself: a White Queen. She held a power that I pray she passed to us, some magic, but more important, some strength of character—some virtue of self. And I pray—beg—that Amelia is safe, that she is protected by the generations of White Queens before her—for now he goes after her.

Lily and Rose

We were named for our grandmother, and for the sweetness of our newborn faces. Father called us his flowers. Mother called us the two elements. She meant wind and water.

Wind because of our hair, which is so fine and thick that it seems to be always moving, as if lightly blown by an unseen wind. Water because of our blue gray eyes. Theo, soon after he first met us, said we were two of the four elements, that Merrill must be earth, and Amelia, with her red hair and temper, fire.

Flowers. Wind. Water. Mother said that when we were babies we couldn't bear to be separated from each other—would cry and cry, and could not be consoled until we were joined again. Dori says that when we were toddlers we invented a language that only we spoke and understood. It wasn't long before people began to say our names as one: *LilyandRose. LilyandRose.* Finally our names joined together and became one: *Lillianrose.* Tiege says we are part of a quartet of sisters, two middle children of four, but we are from one egg. We have each other, we tell her again and again.

Even now, like this, we have each other.

CHAPTER 9

Cries the Raven

THE MAN ARRIVED IN A STORM. It had been nearly one hundred years since the palace valley had seen this kind of storm. Powerful and gray, it swept against the houses, tearing at the shutters, whining and screaming at the doors as if it wished to come in. Rain slashed knifelike into the dark soil, and crops not yet harvested were lost under the blows of the wind.

In the palace stables, the wind rocked the heavy doors and shook the windows, hail pounding the glass like pebbles, the lights dancing on and off. The storm made the horses nervous and they pawed and kicked at the doors of their stalls, anxious. The groomsmen played cards on a table in one of the back rooms, while the guardsmen drowsily watched the stable boys sweep the broad boards, betting when the storm would end.

Perhaps it was because of the noise of the storm that the men didn't hear the horse approaching the barn, didn't hear the shattering rush of clacking hooves on the wet cobble-stones. It was only when a young stable boy gasped as he looked up from his broom at the exact moment that light-ning lit the courtyard that anyone noticed the huge horse and its rider.

"There's a man out there!" the boy shouted.

The heavy doors were opened by two guardsmen, who struggled and fought to control them in the strong wind. As the doors swung open, rain pushed its way in and an avalanche of water spit across the clean floors. The groomsmen—their game forgotten—straightened their uniforms and steeled their bodies against the sudden cold of the rain. The men were flustered and apologetic as they grabbed the lead of the huge horse. They were embarrassed to have missed the man's arrival, embarrassed not to have heard him, the great-uncle of the princesses, Count Raven, embarrassed to leave an old man in the rain.

They ushered the count into the warm barn, and when the wind followed him—a swelling wave of wind that swal-lowed the lights and blew in the doors—they apologized for the storm. The man's own horse was huge and dark, and the rain had made his wet black coat darker and he smelled of wood rot. As the groomsmen led him to an empty stall, the other horses screamed, rolled their eyes back, and bared their teeth, oddly frightened, as if they sensed something evil in this stranger and his horse. Again, the head grooms-man apologized.

"Animals get odd in bad weather," the stranger said, and

he smiled at the groomsman, his face half covered by his cloak. The groomsman felt a tickle of unease; felt himself spooked, like the horses. Even after the man began his long walk to the palace, despite the groomsman's offer to drive him there by carriage, the sense of dread lingered in the barn. To lighten the mood, one of the stable boys began to whistle the tune of the Gossling anthem and one after another, the groomsmen joined in, trying to drown out the thunder and the high-pitched screams of the frightened animals.

❧

After his fast, fierce ride, the old man journeyed toward the palace slowly; he was in no rush now. The man at the gate-house had confirmed it: three princesses awaited him. On the edge of the lake, the swans gathered under the willow trees, seeking shelter from the cold rain, and the man stopped to watch them. Then he did a remarkable thing, seen only by the shivering swans; he threw back his cloak to reveal his black hair and sharp beaked nose, and he lifted his long arms into the driving rain. There was a shock of lightning then, and the man's shadow showed the sharp outline of a raven, of that dark bird. There was darkness again, and then the man lifted his hands to the storm and as he did, lightning charged down into his fingers—he held the fury of the sky—a pulse of electricity between his palms. Then he dropped his hands, and began to walk up toward the palace, replacing the dark hood to hide his face.

Under the shelter of the willow trees, the swans shuddered

with fear and cried out a warning that was swallowed by the mouth of the storm.

❧

Merrill, Lily, and Rose both expected and didn't expect the arrival of their great-uncle that night. After all, the storm was severe and roads were blocked by flooding and fallen trees. Still, they kept dinner waiting, just in case. When the hour grew still later, they finally moved into the living room. Lily sat at the piano playing the same few notes over and over, until Rose glared at her. "For heaven's sake, stop playing! You'll make us all insane!"

Lily glared back and then closed the piano with a bang, and flopped onto the pink sofa with her twin. Outside the wind clawed at the windows, and the rain was thrown against the glass like stones. Merrill sighed when the clock in the corner of the room chimed ten. "In thirty minutes, I think we should all go to bed. It's likely he can't make it through the storm. The weather is dreadful!"

George nodded, his face was a knot of concern and his gray hair seemed slightly disheveled, though his suit was still as crisp and neat as it had been at eight that morning. The older man paced the living room, up and down, up and down. The sound of his clicking shoes on the polished floor was the only noise in the room.

"Please sit down," Lily urged.

"Yes, do." Rose smiled. "You're making me nervous! Won't you have more tea?"

George smiled apologetically. "My apologies. Thank you,

yes to the tea. Sorry to make you nervous. The storm puts us all on edge, I'm afraid."

Rose poured him a cup of tea and neatly dropped two sugars into it. As she passed it to him, Merrill, who had been slouched in a chair pretending to read, sat up. "That was the door!"

Lily and Rose listened. "It wasn't," Rose said after a moment. "It was just the wind battering against something."

George sipped his tea and listened for a moment too. "Nothing," he agreed.

Then suddenly there was the sound of heavy footsteps hurrying down the hall followed by a lighter pair, almost running to keep up. Moments later the door frame was filled by a large, stooped man, his face hidden in the shadows of his dark cape. Behind him a rushing maid breathlessly apologized, "So sorry—"

"No, no," the old man cut in smoothly, interrupting her with a gentle hand on her shoulder and stepping slightly into the room. "It's true, I've charged in unannounced, yet who can blame my excitement at seeing the three beautiful daughters of my dear niece, rest her soul." The man slid the hood from his head. "Allow me to introduce myself. I am your old uncle, Count Raven. I do not know if your dear mother ever spoke of me. I never met her, though her mother, your grandmother, was my stepsister Elizabeth."

As he spoke, they studied him: even stooped over he was a tall man, and his face was pale and heavily lined. Merrill guessed he was close to ninety years old, although George said he wasn't older than seventy-five. The twins later said they thought he was ageless, maybe one hundred years old, maybe two hundred. The man's nose was long, and his hair jet-black, like his suit. He looked like a raven; as if he had taken on his own name.

The rush of words stopped and the room was suddenly very still, the fire spitting behind the grate was the only sound. The count was still standing on the edge of the door frame, rainwater dripping from his dark cloak. "Won't you come in and get dry before the fire?" Rose said faintly, and then they all remembered their manners.

"Yes, please do." Merrill nodded toward the maid. "Nancy, please bring Count Raven some dinner. Can I pour you some tea, Uncle Raven?"

The man warmed himself before the fireplace and smiled. "Such lovely manners," he murmured. Then he sighed and turned, the light of the fire casting strange light and shadows on his face. "Tea would be perfect. Now tell me your names, my dears."

Merrill introduced herself, and he looked at her gravely, and then nodded as if deciding something. "You have been raised to rule. A serious princess, but lovely. You remind me of your grandmother Elizabeth in character, and you resemble her—your gray eyes are the same. Sad that you never knew her. And who are you two beauties?" he asked, his eyes sliding toward the twins.

"Lillianrose," Lily volunteered, sliding their names together unconsciously.

"Everyone says—said—we look—like mother," Rose added, a lump suddenly in her throat.

The count nodded sympathetically and murmured, "A terrible thing to be orphaned so young." He sighed sadly, his pale forehead wrinkled.

He turned gracefully from the girls. "I don't believe we've met," he trained his sharp eyes on George, who had remained sitting on the couch, watching.

George stood now, and held out his hand. "I'm Lord George Glascow; I was King Bryant's top aide and oldest friend."

"Then you'll be of great assistance to me. Such a shame about all of this." Count Raven gestured around him, and then as a maid rolled dinner in on a cart he smiled. "Ah, dinner . . ."

He ate swiftly, almost methodically, and without pleasure. When he was finished, he stood up. "It's late, and I can see you're all exhausted. Grief will do that. And worry. Certainly is it past the bedtime of young princesses and old counts. Though before we retire to sleep, I'm sure you are anxious to formalize the security of your country by naming me its ruler."

"Interim ruler," George said sharply.

"Of course," the count looked offended for a moment, his dark eyes opened wide in a gesture of innocence and quiet outrage at the implied accusation. "Like you, I am anxious to be of help, and then in seven weeks' time, I'm sure I'll be anxious to return to my quiet lake. Modestly, I never fancied myself king, even an interim king." His voice was smooth, sincere, but George felt a bristle of fear rising along his neck, a suspicion of this velvet-voiced count.

Merrill too felt unsettled, nodding briskly. "You're right, Uncle Raven, we are exhausted, so let us make it official." She stood and opened the door to the library, gesturing to a butler who waited there at attention. "Please call for the swearing-in officials."

The butler nodded and disappeared. When he left, the room was silent again and even with the heat of the fire there was a chill. Unconsciously, Merrill shivered.

Minutes later the officials were gathered around the great table, a sleepy group of concerned lords and advisors. Papers had been drawn up earlier in the week in preparation for the transfer of power. The papers stipulated that because, according to ancient law, the Princess Merrill was too young to rule, that Count Raven, as the next male relative, would be king for seven weeks until her eighteenth birthday. On the dawn of her eighteenth birthday, Princess Merrill was to assume the role of queen of Gossling, and Count Raven would step down from his temporary post as king.

The room was very quiet as a pen was produced. There was silence, a certain stillness, as Merrill's hand hesitated above the paper. It was a strange pause, as if the very room itself were holding its breath. Then Merrill signed the paper, and the room exhaled. After she signed it, so did Lily and Rose, and then George, his pen also hesitating above the paper reluctantly. Then five other advisors signed, and finally Count Raven. It was surprisingly simple, this official transfer of power, witnessed by ten men and three princesses, as the clock chimed midnight.

"Thank you for rousing yourself from your warm beds on this stormy night." Count Raven smiled nicely at the officers. "I shall try to rule well for this fine country."

The men nodded gravely and murmured, "We wish you well. Please let us know how we can help you in the coming weeks. We are here to serve and aid you."

Count Raven nodded his thanks. "Much gratitude. Could you give me a private moment with my nieces?" It was more a command than a request. "Thank you, and good night."

Before leaving, the officers bowed stiff, short bows before him. "King Raven." George stood slowly and did not bow to his country's new king, his tone curt, "Good night, *Count*." Then his voice became gentle and his kind face softened as he turned to the princesses. "Sleep well, my dears, I shall see you at breakfast."

Count Raven closed the doors slowly behind the man, and turned to the three girls. "Now it's just us, just family. It's funny, looking at you, I see my stepsisters, the White Queens. Other sisters of another time . . . Ah, there will be plenty of time later for remembering. It is time for bed now, dear children. But there is one thing that would make me feel more secure in stepping into this difficult role." The old man smiled serenely. "It would mean so much if you would give me your blessing as king."

"Of course I do," Merrill said after a pause, her voice stiff.

"Yes, but it would mean so much to me, if you would say the words," he implored, his voice sweet as syrup.

"You have my blessing as king," Merrill's voice was ice now.

The count smiled. "And you, my dear," he asked, turning to Lily. "Do I have your blessing?"

"Yes, Uncle, you have my blessing as king," Lily said prettily, and Rose echoed her sister, "You have my blessing as king."

The man nodded his head, his smile growing and growing, and then suddenly the lights flickered and the man himself seemed to grow, his shadow curving for a moment into that of a bird. In the dimmed lights, his black eyes glowed with triumph. "I've waited for this moment for fifty years. Waited for the White Queens to give me permission, to bless me with the throne, waited for the spell to be complete, and now I have done it. Nothing stops me now, first Gossling will be mine, and then her neighboring countries, and their neighboring countries . . ." He smiled at the three princesses, at their confusion, at their muteness, at their horror. "Yes, dear children, it was a spell. A spell made by my mother, a promise that if a set of sisters—a set of White Queens— were to give me their blessing to rule, that I could rule forever. And rule forever I shall!"

His voice rose crazily and the princesses stepped backward, mute with horror. Staring at them, the count's face twisted into something like a smile. "Oh, I shall seek my revenge on your country. I shall pay back the wrongs your grandmother and her sisters cast on me and my mother— pay them back tenfold! I promise you, sweet sisters, you shall see the people of Gossling starve, the crops fail, the animals killed in the forest, the streams and brooks polluted and dried, the children of your country hungry for food, uneducated, half-human, half-animal in their starvation and poverty, the old men and women shall die lonely and frightened. This country shall be torn with violence and fear!" He smiled, the wild smile of a madman.

Lily and Rose stood frozen, their faces blank and pale. Merrill made a low cry and seized her chest, as if to hold her heart, which grew heavier as the man spoke. "Impossible!" she whispered her protest.

He shook his head, smiling. "No, princess, not impossible! The blessings of the White Queens cannot be undone now: I have all I need: one, two, three girls," and he held up three fingers and laughed, a brittle, harsh sound. "All the children of the White Queen—the only descendants of my stepsisters. *All* the children, a *set* of sisters, have given their blessing to me, and so easily too, and it cannot be undone . . . a set of sisters." He smiled apologetically, spreading his hands out before him.

"But there are four of us!" Lily blurted out angrily, and then realizing what she had done, grew silent too late.

"Four?" The count's face grew white, then red, then dark with rage. "Four sisters? Impossible! I was told there were only three!"

"There are only three, she's lying!" Rose's voice was high and edged with desperation.

"No, no." The man smiled smoothly, his emotions under control again. "There's a fourth sister. Where is she? She must be here."

"You won't find her." Merrill's voice was low.

"No, I suppose I won't find her here, then," the man agreed

in a pleasant tone. "But I will find her, and when I do, I'll have the final blessing." He turned toward the windows where the rain slashed hard against the glass. "But wherever she may be, you mustn't be allowed to warn the fourth princess, nor can I have you here still worshiped and adored by the people of Gossling. No, I shall find the princess and get her blessing, and when I do, my power—already strengthened by the blessings of three—shall be unconquerable with the blessing of four. The missing fourth princess is a setback, but a small one. Oh"—the man turned back to the girls—"we aren't through, no!"

His eyes narrowed into hard slits. "Such pretty princesses, such a pity that they shall be seen no more . . ." And then he stretched out his hands:

You who are light become white with feather, light of wind,
And you, who are dark, grow roots like the trees;
Cry into the water your tears.
Forty days and your fate forever seals!

There was lightning and darkness and a shattering of glass as the doors leading to the balcony gave way. In the confusion that followed, it would have been impossible to see that two identical swans circled the palace beating their wings and crying, or to notice that another willow tree wept into the night lake. In fact, in the coming minutes as maids and a butler hurried into the room, hammering wood over the open windows, sweeping away glass and mopping water from the rugs, no one even asked where the princesses were. That would come later, but not yet.

Unnoticed, the man picked up his black cloak and slipped down a back corridor like a dark shadow. At the end of the hallway, he saw a young maid. Feigning the confusion of an old man he asked sheepishly, "Please, I'm ashamed to admit it, but I have forgotten the name of my youngest niece, the fourth princess."

"You're meaning Amelia," the girl smiled, "the most energetic of the princesses."

"Of course, Amelia," the man purred. "Named for my own dear stepsister, bless her soul. And where is the child?"

"Don't you know? I thought everyone had heard. She's in the Blue Mountains getting over the chicken pox." She grinned good-naturedly. "Probably driving them all batty there."

The man smiled back ruefully. "Old age." He tapped his head with one finger. "Bless you for helping an old man."

"Of course," the girl said, bobbing into a deep curtsey. When she stood up with a smile, the man was gone. The girl looked up and down the hall, but there was no sign of him, just a burst of wind from an opened door somewhere. In the sudden draft, she shivered.

❧

The doors of the barn were open and rain slashed through them, making the soft, warm wood of the floor black with water. In the courtyard, the stones were wet and slick with the pounding rain, and the groomsmen struggled to control the new king's horse, who had kicked down the door of his stall—splintered it with the force of his giant hooves.

The head groomsman, sweating and exhausted, was surprised when the old man appeared at his elbow and said, "Allow me. I heard him screaming down here. I'm afraid the strange barn and the storm upset him." The count gestured apologetically at the ruined stall. "I'm going to take him for a ride to calm him."

"But sir, the storm—," one of the stable boys protested.

"Count Raven, I must insist you stay; it's too dangerous," the head stableman began, as lightning again lit the sky. But the man was already on his horse, his cloak drawn tightly over his face. The dark animal reared up again, its silver shoes glinting, and the men stepped back in fear as its huge hooves shattered the courtyard stones. Man and horse raced from the courtyard, the storm thundering above them.

❧

But the count had not been cautious, for one had watched him unseen—watched him change the twins into swans and their sister into a willow tree, heard his promise to find the fourth princess—and a power that had lain quiet for nearly fifty years was awakened by anger. For Count Raven had miscalculated twice, and both were dangerous errors. His first mistake was in believing that there were three princesses when there were four. It was a logical mistake, for his stepsisters had been three. His second mistake was assuming that his stepsisters, all those White Queens, had died. For they had not.

❧

The old woman drew upon her powers and called the wind to her, whispered its ancient name; a secret name, and one that it rarely heard. She waited only a moment before the wind came and knelt by her; laughed with the woman, flattered that someone remembered its true name. And the wind, which sees everything, remembered the old woman as a young girl, a young princess, knew that she was one of the White Queens—grown older, but not weaker—and promised her whatever she wished. "Snow," the woman cried. "Snow!" And instantly the noise of the dark rain was silenced and the sky was filled with a white blanketing snow.

"Faster," the old woman urged the wind, "it must storm!" And as one storm ended, another began.

The woman nodded, satisfied, but she had another favor for her old friend, and she whispered a name into the ear of the wind. A name and a message: "Lia! Come! The Raven flies for the fourth child!"

And far away, the message was received and answered, a return message sent on the strong back of the wind: "I leave now!"

CHAPTER 10

The Story of the White Queens

MY SISTERS HAD ONLY TRAVELED HOME to Gossling Palace the week before, but already Henry and I were bored. In the course of the afternoon we exhausted Theo—learned every card game he knew, insisted he teach us how to play chess (which we did, badly), played jacks and gambled pennies, listened to Theo read aloud, ate rice pudding and ice cream, and did our best to ignore Meg's whining. The next morning when the doctor examined us, he looked satisfied. "In a day or two, I'd say you three can head back to Gossling Palace—you're not contagious anymore, and you don't have fevers."

Theo looked relieved. "Good. You'll all rest this morning, and then maybe in the afternoon we'll begin packing."

But we didn't because something very odd happened: a snowstorm came, a blanket of white and ice so heavy that the palace seemed all but sealed. Theo was chagrined, peeking through the heavy drapes, his forehead wrinkled in confusion about the sudden change in weather, mumbling, "A snowstorm in *September?*"

But he soon recovered, and now Theo was excited, ready to teach. "Meg, sit up, please. Henry, up. Now, let's take a look at the weather charts . . ."

It was a lesson that was not to be, for at that moment the large windows of the nursery burst open, the curtains blowing back under the force of the storm. Snow swirled into the room and the fire flickered in the fireplace, stroked by the wind.

Meg screamed, and Henry and I stared—frozen—as two large swans flew through those open windows, circling the room, their heavy feathered wings beating fast.

Confusion followed. Theo rushed to close the windows as if he feared other birds would follow, Meg buried her head under the covers, screaming, and one of the long, muscled wings of a swan brushed against a vase of flowers, knocking it to the floor, where it shattered, flowers and water spilling everywhere, and then the nursery door opened.

Henry leaped out of bed. "Dori!"

I turned, and there she was. Dori stood in the doorway, plump as a dove in her white coat. Her face was creased in a frown, and she surveyed the room with some displeasure. She pulled off her gloves in one neat gesture and said crisply, "Meg, stop shrieking. Henry, back in bed, you're still sick, you know. Theo, latch those windows tightly. Girls, stop circling. And Amelia, close your mouth, you look like you're catching flies."

111

I closed my mouth, and Dori stepped into the room, pulling the door shut behind her. She smiled at Theo, who had successfully locked the windows and drawn the curtains. "Find us another chair, love, we're to be one more."

Theo, nodding wordlessly and looking dazed, lifted the chair that perched before the dressing table and carried it carefully over in front of the fireplace. Dori sighed then, as if satisfied, and dropped into the deep pink armchair, kicking off her shoes. "Now, that's better!" The two swans settled next to her on the rug and puffed their feathers in front of the fire, warming themselves.

In the sudden calm, Meg began to cry; huge hiccupping sobs, done more for attention than out of any real fear. "Meg!" Dori said sharply, pressing one hand to her forehead as if to stop a headache. "That's quite enough!"

Before Meg could reply, the door flew open for the second time and a small old woman with a wrinkled face and red hair as bright as mine entered the room.

"Dori!" the strange woman cried.

"Lia!" Dori leaped from her chair as if she were no more than a girl, and nearly ran to the old woman. The two women embraced and then separated, studying each other's faces, smiling and half-crying.

"Who is that?" Henry whispered to me.

I shrugged, eyeing the swans.

"This is my sister," Dori said, leading the woman into the room. "And Henry, you shouldn't whisper."

"You have a sister?" My eyes were wide with surprise.

Dori laughed. "Does that seem so impossible?"

The other woman laughed too, then winked at me.

A maid appeared in the doorway with a tea cart and Dori smiled at her. "Hello, my dear, we're going to be two more for tea today, and my swans will need water with just a dash of sugar in it." She said it like swans came to tea every day.

Eyes wide, The maid dropped a curtsey and disappeared.

Dori pulled the deserted tea cart close to the fireplace and began deftly transferring sandwiches onto delicate pink china plates.

"Theo"—Dori's face sharpened as if remembering something important, and a look passed across her face, one that I had seen before but could not read—"why don't you ring for a maid to bring Meg down to the main hall for tea. There is to be a huge *proper* tea set up there for all the children of the court. I would send Amelia and Henry down as well, but I'm afraid they still look like spotted owls. Meg"—Dori nodded at her approvingly—"looks as lovely as she always does."

I looked with some astonishment at Henry—Dori had always deplored Meg's vanity, and told us never to compliment anyone who agreed too completely with your compliment. From his bed, Henry raised his eyebrows just slightly in response, as if to say he didn't understand either.

Looking pleased, Meg was out of bed in an instant, pulling on a lacy pink robe, her fingers flying as she buttoned the small pearl buttons. As Theo called for a maid, Meg smoothed down her gold hair and smiled smugly at me. "I'll be sure to tell the other children that you send your regards. No doubt you'll be missed."

"Thanks," I said shortly.

A maid appeared, crisp and efficient in her uniform, and Dori said rather grandly, "Won't you please escort Lady Meg to the main hall for tea? Stay with her the entire time in case she feels dizzy or tired. Then, when she is ready to return, *you* must bring her back. She's still delicate, and I worry she could feel faint."

Meg smiled a brave smile at the maid. "I'm sure I'll be all right," she said prettily.

Dori shook her head and her voice was firm. "No, I insist that you be escorted. How could I explain to your poor mother that you'd collapsed on the stairs?" She turned again to the maid. "Please stay close to Lady Meg."

Meg held her head up importantly, pleased to be called Lady Meg. Looking back at us with a brief triumphant smile, Meg sailed grandly from the room. I stuck my tongue out and crossed my eyes, but it was wasted because Meg was already heading down the long hallway. The maid dropped a quick curtsey to Dori and hurried out of the room after her. There was a brief silence, then Lia stood up and looked down the hallway before closing the door with a quiet click.

"Well," Dori sighed, leaning back again in the soft chair, "I hate to ruin the other children's special tea and that poor maid's afternoon, but what I'm about to share must *not* be shared with Meg. And the reason for the escort, of course, is to stop her from listening at the door frame—a habit of hers that I despise."

Dori set the bowls of sugared water down onto the floor by the large swans. "Lily and Rose, let me know if you wish for more sugar."

I stared at the birds, then cleared my throat. "Lily and Rose? The swans have the same names as my sisters."

Before Dori could reply, one of the swans said in a very cranky voice, which sounded just like Lily's, "We have the same names because we *are* your sisters!"

The room was very quiet for a moment, and I felt my heart thumping hard in my chest, then Henry spoke in a reasonable, even tone. "But you can't be. You're swans, not princesses! Right?" He looked at Dori.

I felt fear tighten around my throat, suddenly certain of the answer, and Theo sat down heavily on the edge of Henry's bed, as if his legs could no longer support him.

Dori ignored Lily's announcement and Henry's question, and began to pass out plates of tea sandwiches. "We haven't much time, and there is a lot to tell. Amelia,"—she looked at me sharply—"there is no easy way to say this: you're in danger. You are in danger, and so is the kingdom. The twins, of course, have been transformed into swans." She gestured to the two birds. "And Merrill into a tree."

"A tree?" Theo said faintly.

Dori nodded. "Oh, and this is such a long story. And really it starts long ago when I was a young girl, not much older than the twins." She sighed heavily. I closed my eyes for a moment, trying to picture Dori young, and couldn't.

Dori leaned forward slightly on her chair. "Perhaps the place to start is to tell you that I am your great-aunt. Lia and I both are. Your grandmother Elizabeth was our oldest sister, your mother was our niece."

"You're my great-aunt," I echoed dumbly.

Dori smiled slightly. "Yes, meaning that, like you, I am a princess of Gossling, and, like you, I am a White Queen."

Lily lifted her head, her voice hopeful, "You're White Queens too? Do you know what the powers are?"

Dori held up her hands as if to stop her. "Let's begin this story in order, I think it will answer any questions you have. Theo, please pass me that sketch pad and a pencil."

Theo passed them to her, and Dori made a quick drawing and held it up. "This is your family tree; it might help you during this story."

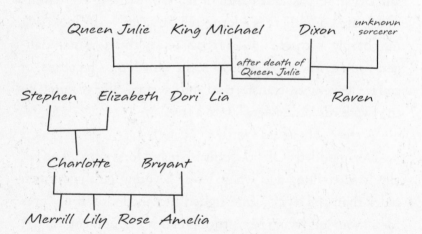

Family Tree of the White Queens

Lia nodded at the drawing and leaned back in her chair, as if to get comfortable, then began. "This story begins long ago with your great-grandparents, our mother and father." She gestured to the drawing. "King Michael and Queen

Julie. Our mother and father had been very much in love, and my sisters, Dori and Elizabeth, and I grew up living a charmed life. This changed one terrible October morning when our mother grew ill. By nightfall she was dead. Our father was devastated; shocked and sickened with grief. We could do nothing to console him."

When Lia grew suddenly quiet, Dori continued the story. "Five years passed, and still our father was consumed with his grief. Grief blurred his mind and made him a tentative ruler, where before he had always been decisive and strong. When Father set off on a journey of neighboring countries, it was almost a relief, for we were certain that such a tour would shake him awake, turn him back into himself."

"It was to be a six-month holiday," Lia added. "Elizabeth had just married, and she agreed to rule in the interim of his absence."

"Did the trip fix him?" Henry wondered.

Dori grimaced. "It did, and it didn't. Father traveled from country to country, trying to escape his terrible sorrow. Winter turned to spring, and spring to summer, and Father found himself far from home in the hill country, Laomongole."

"Where is that?" I interrupted; trying to picture the maps that George had showed us in the map room.

As if she could read my thoughts, Dori shook her head. "No, Amelia, you've never seen its map. The country is so far from here that I don't think we have any accurate maps, only what those who had once visited could piece together."

Lia continued. "Maps or not, the country of Laomongole is beautiful, and yet it is home to many secrets. Some of its vast forests are peaceful as cathedrals; their soaring trees arched and light dappled, but other woods are thought to be inhabited by something evil and unseen—dark and shadowed. No human dares step into those woods, for it is where the ancient witches are said to reside—shape-shifters, holders of an evil old as the world itself."

"Do you think the stories are true?" Theo asked, and in spite of myself I grinned, hearing the academic tone creep into his voice, as if he meant to take notes on the country's folklore, ready to challenge them.

Dori smiled a tired smile. "It doesn't matter what I believe—it matters that the people of Laomongole believed it. Don't be so quick to dismiss their superstitions, Theo. Isn't there darkness and light to be found everywhere? Our country is not so young that our people don't have their own superstitions, fears, and irrational beliefs. And in this particular case, the people were not wrong to fear those woods."

Theo blushed, but before he could say anything Lia continued the story. "It is there on the edge of the Black Forest that in a storm Father sought shelter inside a small jewel of a palace. For more than four hours, Father's horses had fought their way through driving rain, the trees shuddering above them, and the wind howling through the empty branches, a frightening, ghostly sound. The rain had washed out the roads, and in the darkness of the forest and night, Father and the drivers knew they were hopelessly lost. Although he did not wish to alarm the men he was traveling with, Father had watched a muscular black panther following them for close to an hour—jumping from tree to tree—casual and graceful and feral, its green eyes flashing. A dangerous escort. When the lights of the palace beckoned, Father was washed with a sense of relief. It seemed to him that when he saw those lights the storm slowed, and the panther that had seemed to stalk the carriage for so many miles also disappeared.

"Inside the gilded door of the palace, Father met his hostess, a woman in an emerald dress that made her green eyes greener. She wore a slim gold crown on her head, which let Father know that she, too, was of royal birth. Father held her slight hand in his own, and asked her name. *Dixon,* the woman replied, and Father thought her voice was lovely. In a month's time our father was back in Gossling with his new wife, our stepmother, Dixon."

Dori sighed deeply and stirred the fire.

"Was she nice?" I wondered, though I thought I knew the answer.

Lia shook her head slowly as if to shake it all away. "She seemed nice, but she was not. She was very beautiful, though, and sometimes people confuse the two, think that those who are beautiful on the outside are also beautiful on the inside. Dixon was lovely to look at. She had skin the color of the softest, pale fawn, her hair was midnight black—so smooth and glossy it was almost a mirror—and her eyes were the green of the sea. And she was graceful—her fingers as skilled as a spider's, weaving the smallest stitches into her tapestries. Elizabeth always suspected that she had bewitched Father, but I disagreed—I think he loved her because he was lonely, and because he believed that she had given him back his life." Lia looked sad for a moment.

Dori seemed to share the memory. "We recognized immediately that our stepmother Dixon was one of the ancient Dark Ones. An almost extinct form of witches who hundreds of years before had brutalized countries with their cruelty. A strong power of evil—they were shape-shifters who could change into almost any form."

"Like a panther?" I asked.

Dori nodded. "Yes. But that was not her only power. She knew spells and potions that had been dead to the world for centuries, and she had the power to call them forth."

Lia looked grim. "We recognized who she was, and she recognized who we were."

Dori lifted her hands to her temples, as if the memory hurt her. "She was rightly threatened by us, yet she was also a threat to us. And so our home no longer felt like home. We were living with an enemy. And the enemy was unrecognized by Father; he looked at Dixon, and only saw his life reborn. He did not see the danger. And Dixon did not move into our castle alone. She brought her son, our stepbrother, Raven."

"Count Raven?" Lily asked.

Dori nodded. "He was an odd, sullen teenager, only a year older than Lia. Yet he seemed both younger and older than she. Most often he was nothing more than a petulant child, determined to punish those around him for imagined crimes and small slights, but sometimes he seemed older— as if he carried a secret that no one else could know. We knew his secret, though: Raven was the son of a witch and a sorcerer, and powers were stirring within him—powers he was not old enough to understand or control, but powers nonetheless.

"With his dark hair and ghost white skin, he seemed to be everywhere in the castle, listening at closed doors, standing in the shadows of the hallway, hidden by the tapestry and darkness, and always, always listening. Elizabeth used to laugh that we never spoke of anything serious, interesting, or important enough to be worth all his eavesdropping. But still, it was unsettling to be under his ever-watchful eyes, to hesitate before speaking, to first make certain he was not around." Dori looked thoughtful for a moment, as if remembering. "He tormented Lia with small spells and pranks, and was cruel to the animals he managed to trap in crude cages. He tortured them, and often killed them—it was awful. His mother had groomed him to be king, but not the kind of king our father was. She had not raised a gentle or kind son; she had not raised him to be a measured or thoughtful man. She had raised him to be suspicious and angry, greedy and cruel. He had none of the characteristics a king should possess."

"There was a part of me that always felt a little sorry for Raven," Lia said softly.

Dori shook her head. "Your sympathy is misplaced. You can feel sad for an unhappy child, but he was not a child when we knew him, and at a certain point people are responsible for the lives they live. Raven grew from an angry and manipulative teenager to an angry and manipulative adult. A man capable of doing tremendous damage and harm. And thus far, he has been successful."

"What happened to Dixon?" I felt fear stirring inside me.

Lia stood and poked at the fire. "Your grandmother Elizabeth was pregnant with your mother when our stepmother Dixon decided that she wanted to rule Gossling. She had decided that it was time to awaken the legion of witches who still slumbered in the world. With them she planned to destroy all that was light, and she meant to start with Gossling. We knew that we had to bring together the power of three White Queens to drive her from Gossling forever."

Dori's eyes flashed, and her chin went up in sudden defiance. "We met in secret, and practiced until our powers were stronger, a circle of sisters. We had anticipated the strength of Dixon, but we had not counted on the strength of her son, our stepbrother Raven."

"Raven," Lia practically spat his name, her lip curling up in disgust. "A witch's child is not necessarily a witch— he might be a sorcerer, a warlock, a wizard, or nothing at all. But Raven was different because his birth was drawn from two evils, and these two evils meant a cruel inheritance. Raven's powers were erratic, like his temper, and so he was not always in control of what he would one day master. Still, although he was young, there were two powers that he had learned well. From his mother he had inherited the ability to transform himself into something half-bird and half-man, and the power to transform others into animal, tree, or bush." Lia looked ruefully at the swans before continuing.

"And from his father, a man unknown to us, and perhaps unknown to him, he inherited a gift for grand spells."

Lia lifted another tea cake from the stand and licked the melting pink icing from her fingers. "The story of the exile of Dixon and Raven is long, but ultimately Dixon was trapped in a slice of amber—trapped in stone. Raven's power was not strong without his mother to guide him, and enraged, he banished himself to the Black Lakes, swearing revenge on the White Queens and all of Gossling. Before he left, he cast his mother's last spell, one she had created when she knew that her own fate would be sealed forever. She believed that if she could not rule Gossling, then her son would. That would be his inheritance. The spell stated that one day he would have the blessings of the White Queens and with those blessings, thus rule."

Dori rubbed at her temples. "We were naïve, though, and we paid little attention to his threat. We had our father to comfort on the loss of another wife, and then months later, our own grief as our sister Elizabeth died giving birth to your mother."

"You raised Mother!" I said to Dori.

She nodded and gestured to her sister. "I did. With Lia, for whom you are named, Amelia. Still, when your mother became queen, we thought it best to hide who we were; allow the country to forget us. Your mother was a strong ruler; the threat of Dixon was gone, and we believed Raven had gone mad because he had disappeared. We thought it better for the country to have one ruler, and we thought it safer for Raven to *forget us*. After all, his grudge was against his three stepsisters, not one of their daughters.

"Then, shortly before the birth of the twins, Lia went north to the country of Reede. There she joined her powers with a small but strong group of fairy witches, for Raven had succeeded in freeing his mother, and she'd laid ruin on that country."

Henry interrupted, turning to me, "Remember when George told us about the bad queen who invaded Reede?"

Lia's face was sad. "A bad queen indeed. We were successful in driving Dixon into stone again, but the damage was done. The country of Reede lay half in slumber, dazed by her rule. Their king was near crippled with his loss of power. I stayed, but there was little I could do—the king had lost faith in himself, and his people had lost faith in their country."

"Then six months ago, in the border forests of Gossling, animals began to die. The fairy witches and I studied them, we tried magic and medicine, and yet nothing helped—the animals continued to die. We noticed that the trees were filled with ravens; every day more and more black birds filled the trees. Later I heard of the sickness that spread down through the mountains, this time killing people, and I wondered if ravens hid in those trees too."

"Tell how he turned us into swans, and Merrill into a tree," Rose interrupted.

Lia sighed. "It's a spell using the elements—in his case lightning. Using a spell and the strength of the lightning, he transformed the girls."

"Can't you reverse it?" Theo spoke for the first time in nearly an hour.

"No." Dori shook her head. "But it can be reversed. However, for it to break, the four sisters must be united and they must draw on their own elements to create their own spell. If the spell is not broken before daylight on the fortieth day, it shall be permanent. No power can reverse it. We have thirty-eight days to determine what that spell is."

"Thirty-eight days," Theo echoed weakly.

"Thirty-eight days and I'm happy for it!" Dori said adamantly. "Raven's power is not strong enough to contain White Queens in a single night—his spell takes forty days to seal. Good thing too, or the girls would be trapped forever. Anyway," she finished briskly, "the spell cannot be broken now, because Amelia will not return to Gossling Palace right away."

"What? Why?" I asked indignantly.

"Amelia, haven't you noticed that we've been turned into swans? Do you want to become a swan too?" Lily said meanly.

"I wouldn't be dumb enough to let that happen," I shot back.

The swans hissed at me.

"Girls, enough." Dori held up her hand. "The snow will hold the Raven back for now, but not forever, and we need a plan. A good plan for how we are going to solve this. Now let us eat quietly for a bit."

When she had finished her tea cake and a second cup of tea, Dori stood up and stirred the fire. "Amelia, you will travel with Lia and me to the Western Valley. There is an old fairy hollow where we are welcome. There in the safety of the hollow we shall be well hidden until we create a plan. Theo, you will travel with Meg and Henry to the Golden City. Like us, you will move quickly because it is likely that Raven will mistake Meg for Amelia. He has no idea what Amelia looks like, and since Meg's long blond hair looks like the twins', a mistake could be made if she remains here, and there have been enough changes in girls already." She paused and looked meaningfully at the swans. "Lily and Rose, you will return to your sister and the Lake of Swans. Wait for us there, we shall arrive with Amelia as soon as we are able. We shall leave tomorrow at first light."

"Can you teach us some magic?" Rose asked suddenly.

Dori shook her head. "You're not ready, and now certainly is not the time to start learning."

Lia frowned. "What better time, sister?" Without waiting for an answer, Lia turned to us. "Here is a transforming spell— a spell of motion. It can bring you from one place to another, but only in times of grave danger. If it is used when there is no danger, then the spell is useless."

I sat forward eagerly and Lia smiled at me. "So then, here is the spell of motion:

Wind of east
Wind of west
Wind of sea and shoreline's breast
Lean in close, lean in near,
Make this White Queen disappear!

Theo looked skeptical. "You're still here."

Lia gave an exasperated snort. "Aren't you supposed to be the children's tutor?"

Theo nodded.

"Then," Lia continued, "weren't you listening when I said that the spell is *useless* unless used in moments of great danger?"

Theo flushed and looked down at the floor, embarrassed.

"It rhymes," I observed.

Lia turned to me and laughed. "I make them *all* rhyme so I can remember them. In school, I was always dreadful at memorizing unless it was a song or a poem, and with so many spells to learn, well, I thought this might make it easier."

"Teach us another!" Rose prodded.

"Which to teach, though?" Lia mused.

Resigned to the spell conversation, Dori broke in, "How about the garden spell?"

Together the two sisters recited:

Blue coriander, rabbit-foot grass
Bittersweet September: flowers mass
Winter frozen, spring's rebirth
Guard with silence, guard with earth.

Summer brings her sun-tipped wand
Spreads her light to field and pond
Here let me hide, here let me stay
Protect and shield me for this day.

"But what does it do?" Henry wondered.

Dori looked at him and winked. "Good question. It keeps you safe from harm when you are in a friendly garden."

"A friendly garden?" Lily sounded doubtful. "How can you tell if a garden is friendly or not?"

Dori smiled at her. "I bet Henry knows how to tell."

"What else could we teach them?" Lia mused. "Something of use."

But before she got the chance there was a knock on the door, and the maid entered, followed by Meg.

"Another time," Dori murmured, as the maid left quietly.

"Another time for what?" Meg looked at us suspiciously.

"Another time for me to teach you all about flight patterns in birds," Theo said briskly. "In fact, that may be tomorrow's lesson plan."

"Good lesson," Lily said, and laughed, feathers shaking. Then she realized that she had spoken in front of Meg.

Meg's mouth dropped open, and for the second time that afternoon she began to cry.

Dori and Lia exchanged anxious looks, for a moment at a loss for words. Theo was not, however; he strode over to Meg and bent down in front of her.

"Listen," he said calmly, "Lily and Rose have been changed into swans because of an evil spell that no one understands. That's why Dori—their *nanny*," he stressed the word, "brought them here to be with Amelia, you, and Henry."

"What spell?" Meg gulped, her face red and blurred with tears.

"A spell that their Uncle Raven may be responsible for," Theo said delicately.

Meg sniffed, her face frightened. "Why would he do that?"

Dori shook her head, and her voice was gentle. "Nobody knows why, sweetheart. But it is important that you tell no one about it."

❧

Before bed that night, the nursery was busy. A maid brushed Meg's hair one hundred times as Meg droned on and on about the tea party we had missed, explaining loudly to the maid that she—Lady Meg—was the most important guest at the party. Theo kept looking distractedly out the window into the heavy storm, and I wondered if he was thinking about Merrill, alone in the snow. Henry was explaining to Lia the plot of the book he was reading, a complicated story of dragons and talking dogs, while a maid stripped the beds of old linens, placing new blankets on our beds and piling the old next to the door, while another maid worked to build up the fire, and the twins, forced to stay mute as swans while the maids were in the room, sulked by the post of my bed.

Dori bustled about, pulling sweaters and heavy socks out of dressers and bundling them neatly into small packs.

Meg interrupted her story to focus on Dori. "Why are you packing?"

Dori frowned. "Didn't you hear the doctor, my dear? You're to be going home tomorrow."

Meg looked confused. "What about the snowstorm?"

Dori smiled. "We'll play that by ear—if the snow stops, then we're ready to head home to the palace, if it doesn't, then we'll stay right here, cozy in front of the fireplace."

Meg made a face, as if the idea of spending time with Henry and me was more than she could bear, then she turned back to the maid and continued her story.

Dori resumed packing, once passing my bed as if only to drop off a fresh nightgown, she bent down next to me.

"Remember," she breathed the message into my ear, "we leave at first light."

CHAPTER 11

Gone!

THAT NIGHT I DREAMED my mother sat on my bed and stroked my hair. "Chicken pox girl." She smiled, but then her face became tight with worry. "Amelia, the count is coming tonight." Suddenly I saw him, a man moving like the wind on a dark horse, pushing through the snow, a flock of ravens casting a dark cloud above him. My mother's voice was soft, but clear. "You must leave now. Go to the Sunflower Forest, you'll be safe there. Go now! Wake up, Amelia! My darling, wake up!"

And I awoke.

Here is the funny thing about dreams. Sometimes it is best to ignore them, best to roll over and say *That dragon wasn't real*, or *I'm not going to fail my math test*, best to curl back into the covers and sleep. At other times, though, it is best to listen to your dreaming self and act. So, shivering, I dressed in the dark, pulling an old pair of Henry's pants over my pajamas, then a sweater, and then heavy boots of fur.

"Where are you going?" Henry hissed from his bed across the room.

In the darkness it was hard to see him, and I crept across the room on tiptoe until I stood right above him. Henry was blinking awake, the very faintest shine of pink calamine lotion on his face. "Where are you going?" he repeated.

"Shhh! Go back to sleep," I whispered, buttoning my sweater.

Henry sat up, annoyed and suddenly very awake. "Where are you *going*? Amelia, what are you doing, and where are you going?"

"I'm leaving. I have to leave right now. I'm going to the Sunflower Forest."

"What about Lia and Dori?" his voice rose.

"Shhh!" I glanced over toward where Meg was sleeping. "There isn't time to tell Dori and Lia. Anyway, they have to stay here and protect the others. The Raven is coming for *me*!"

"Well, you're not going alone." Henry stood up.

"Yes, I am! Now get back in bed!" I ordered.

"Either I come or I'll go next door right now and wake up Dori, and she'll stop you! I'll do it, Amelia!" Henry's voice held the threat.

I paused for a moment, trying to decide if he was serious. Decided, I sighed, "Fine, come, but hurry!"

Then from the corner, a second voice piped up, not whispering and clearly irritated. "Where are you two going? Do you know what time it is?"

I groaned, and Henry said soothingly, "Sorry, Meg, we're really sorry. Go back to sleep now."

But she was awake, her long gold hair tangled, and her blue eyes blinking out sleep and sand. She did look like the twins, I thought. Even in the dark, she looked like my sisters far more than I did. It would be easy to believe she was the fourth princess; it was smart for Theo to take her away from Count Raven's magic. Then I realized with a sickening thud that leaving Meg here with Raven on his way meant she would be turned into a bird, or a tree, or a rock, or perhaps even worse. Especially once he realized she was not the fourth princess.

"Okay, fine, let's go. Get dressed," I sighed.

"What?" Henry half-whispered, half-yelled.

"I'm not going anywhere just because you say so." Meg glared at me. "You're the fourth princess, not the first!"

"Suit yourself." I shrugged. "I just figured you'd rather not be killed by my uncle—he would hate to find an imposter when he is looking only for me."

"I truly hate you." Meg's face looked confused and angry. "Why would your uncle kill anybody?"

I shrugged. "I don't know, but I wouldn't stay here if I were you. You might be turned into a swan if he thinks you're me."

"This better not be some stupid trick," Meg said.

"It's your choice," Henry said generously. "Come or stay."

Meg climbed out of bed, shivering. Within minutes we were all dressed, hot in our coats and hats and mittens. Henry stuffed the tea cakes from the deserted tea table into his pockets, as I pushed as many blankets as I could into the packs that sat waiting by the door.

"What about our swords?" Henry whispered.

Meg gave a short laugh. "As if you know how to use one!"

Ignoring her, I opened the door of the closet and took out both our swords. "Just in case," I said to Henry.

❦

Lily and Rose were curled together before the large hall fireplace, and although we were quiet when we slipped from the room, they awoke, and both spoke at once.

"Where are you going?"

"You can't go anywhere without Lia or Dori!"

I took a deep breath. "Listen, I just had a dream with Mother in it—she said I have to leave. We're going to the Sunflower Forest. Mother warned me! I have to go!" I heard my voice rise, felt suddenly hysterical, certain they would stop me.

The swans, my sisters, looked at each other for a long moment and seemed to make a decision. "You can't go alone," they said at the same time.

Then one swan spoke, "I'll go with you, and Lily will stay here and wake the others. When you've reached the forest, I'll fly back."

The two swans stared at each other. "You will go, and I will stay," Lily repeated, and they nodded, decided. My twin sisters who would not separate.

❦

Outside, the night was very dark and the half moon hung heavy, shadowed, and low in the sky. Around us, the ice and snow glistened in the white light and snowflakes fell from the sky, steady as rain.

"Do you even know where this forest is?" Meg asked meanly, shivering.

I nodded and whispered, "George showed us on a map during one of our geography lessons. And anyway we've been there a dozen times in the summer."

Henry added, "The forest is slightly to the north of the Blue Mountains." He faced east and took two steps.

"North, Henry." I grabbed his arm and turned him around. "And they called me ineducable . . ." I shook my head.

"Shhh, we must be as silent as possible. Now follow me," Rose whispered, and in one graceful gesture her body rose into the cold, still air. On the ground, Meg, Henry, and I began to walk, the fast-falling snow covering our tracks, while Rose flew above us, like a lone sentinel, white against the dark night sky; leading us.

❧

The Sunflower Forest is beyond the Blue Mountains. To reach the forest, you must cut through the mountains and across the Otter River. In the late spring and early summer it was a two-hour hike to the Otter River. And it was worth the hike. It was a beautiful river—come spring the grassy banks were thick with daffodils and bright tulips, and the fast-racing river chuckled and gurgled as it bounced over smooth white rocks. It was the perfect spot to picnic, just the place to play tag or read on the soft green grass. Not tonight, though; in the icy dark reaching the river was difficult. We reached it after four hours, stiff with cold and slow with exhaustion, all of us quiet as we crawled down the steep embankment.

The cold made us clumsy. I could feel my feet sliding under the slick rocks, and my fingers were stiff and awkward as they grabbed on to roots and branches on the way down the half-frozen bank toward the river. Meg slipped on an icy rock, banging her knee and falling solidly down on the hard snow by the river's edge.

Henry reached her quickly. "Are you okay? Come on, get up!" He offered her a hand.

Meg glared up at him and didn't move. "I'm tired!" she whimpered.

Rose swooped down and landed in the stiff snow next to us.

Meg looked defiantly at Rose. "I'm too tired to keep walking." Her voice curled into a whine, "I want to go back! I'm tired!"

Rose tilted her head to one side, as if considering something. "It's okay, Meg," she said after a moment. "You should all rest for a while. I'm going to fly ahead a little, but I'll be back soon."

Henry and I exchanged worried glances as she lifted into the air again. Although Rose was a swan, she was still Rose, still older, even if she was powerless to protect us. The river raced by, chunks of ice floating in its cold water. Meg shivered in her coat and began to cry. Henry put an arm around her. "Rose'll be back," he said reassuringly, meeting my eyes over her head, his forehead crinkled with worry and doubt.

Meg shrugged his arm off her and glared at him meanly. "Don't talk to me, gardener's boy."

I could feel my hands curl into tight fists inside my red mittens, ready to fight, but Henry shook his head at me, and stood up. "She's not worth it," he murmured.

I nodded, but still felt something hot and angry boil inside of me—livid that Meg would be mean when Henry only offered her kindness.

Henry and I moved away from Meg and stood watching the river pass, the ice chunks banging against each other in their fight downstream. The moon was veiled with clouds and it seemed darker somehow, the trees stark and lonely in the snow. I shivered.

Minutes later Rose was back. "Half a mile upstream the river is narrow and shallow, and the tip of the Sunflower Forest lies just beyond it on the far bank. The ice seems thick enough to walk across in some places, but even if it breaks, it's still shallow enough to wade through. It will be cold, though," she added grimly.

Henry and I stood up, but Meg stayed sitting, her face stubborn. "Come on, Meg, get up!" Henry said.

She tilted her huge blue eyes up at him. "I'm not going," she sniffled. "I'm too tired. I can't keep going."

Rose landed on the ground gracefully. "Meg," she said sweetly, "this is a princess adventure. See, you're just like a real princess, going on this special trip, and just like a real princess you're in danger." She paused and said meaningfully, "Maybe even more danger than Amelia."

Meg shot me a self-important look and sniffed again.

Rose took a deep breath. "But, Meg, we can't go on without you, and we can't leave you here. If you don't come now, you'll be in danger, Amelia's in danger—the whole country is in danger!" Her voice took on a coaxing tone, "You would be doing everyone a huge service! You'd be helping the whole country."

I held my breath, wondering if she would believe this. And she did; Meg stood up and squared her shoulders. "Okay," she said, "I'm ready!"

Henry sighed. "Let's hurry!"

❧

The drifts were deep and cold, and that last half-mile seemed to take a lifetime. We walked in single file—Henry first, pushing through the nearly waist-deep snow, Meg and I following him, walking in the path he created. The storm had started again, and the night was colder now, the moon all but hidden in clouds. With snow swirling down around us, Rose flew lower, sometimes in front of us as a guide, and sometimes right above us, like an umbrella, shielding us from the worst of the storm.

Finally we reached the narrow throat of the river, and Rose landed beside us, fluffing her feathers against the cold. Rose was right: here, the ice had clogged so that it had created a bridge to cross from one bank to another. We stared at that frozen bridge with trepidation.

"It's the easiest way," Rose said in a low voice.

Henry stepped forward. "I'll go first."

I shook my head. "No, let me. I'm lighter, and remember— even if it breaks, it's shallow water." I moved tentatively onto the ice, testing it, wondering if it would hold my weight. Below me, the ice creaked and groaned, and I stopped, frozen and afraid of plunging through the dark ice into the wintry water.

Behind me, Henry urged, "Keep going—it's holding!" I took another step forward, and another, until somehow I was across the bridge of ice, and my foot was stepping onto the hard ground of the other bank.

A moment later Meg joined me, and then Henry. Rose landed lightly next to us, her voice thick with relief. "This is the Sunflower Forest."

In the excitement of crossing the bridge I had forgotten the forest, and now I turned and saw it huge and looming ahead of us. The Sunflower Forest had always been one of our favorite places to picnic in the summer. Unlike most forests, it was not dark—sun filtered through the delicate leaves of the high birch trees, making snowflake patterns that danced on every surface. The forest floor was thick with tall sunflowers and plush moss, perfect to spread a picnic blanket. In this long night, though, the forest looked menacing, frightening. Through the trees I could see the large heads of the sunflowers bobbing crazily in the wind, shaking like the weak heads of rag dolls.

"It looks strange at night." I almost said *scary*, but caught myself in time.

Rose looked anxious. "You're sure this is where Mother told you to go?"

"Positively sure," I nodded, shivering a little.

She looked skeptical.

"Some people believe the wood is enchanted," Henry said stoutly. "Anyway, Queen Charlotte wouldn't send us someplace dangerous."

"It's warmer here, at least," Rose said, watching as Henry and Meg made their way to the edge of the flowering trees with their packs. In fact, it was oddly warm, as if in crossing the icy river, we had stepped from winter back to fall. A light wind ruffled the tops of the trees and the leaves whispered together, an odd sound after the clicking noise of the bare branches along the Otter River.

"Amelia." Rose hesitated for a moment. "Be safe. I would be sick if anything happened to you. Please, be so, so careful."

"I will be," I promised, and hugged her.

"I'll see you soon!" she whispered, and then she lifted into the air, circled twice, and was gone.

Six steps into the dark woods, Henry had found a tree that was built like a bunk bed, three flat limbs growing almost perfectly one on top of another. He had already pulled blankets from the pack and was spreading them carefully across the long, level limbs of the tree. Meg sat away from him, leaning against another tree, her eyes drowsing shut. I set down my pack and looked around—the waxy leaves of the forest made a canopy above us, and with no moon now, the forest was almost black. Henry finished crafting makeshift pillows out of sweaters and looked at me. "Sleep?"

Meg sighed dramatically and stood up. "Finally."

Henry was still looking at me, questioning. "Should we sleep, or do we need to keep going?"

Meg stamped her foot. "It's time for sleep."

And because I couldn't think of anything else to do, and because it was the middle of the night, I agreed, crawling to the top branch and falling into a deep and dreamless sleep.

Rose

Amelia is brave. She is brave as I could never be. It would never occur to me to leave at night, to leave alone. Lily did not want to fly alone with them. I believe she was afraid to go. But I am not afraid: there are no hunters in Gossling, the only things to fear are Raven and the sickness. And I cannot fear them when children younger than I are brave enough to travel on.

There is something that I love about flying, a part of me that has always waited to fly, has always waited to lift off the ground and become weightless. Lily does not feel this way, I know. Which is so odd, because to me, this love is as easy as my love of books and chocolate, as natural as breathing. Yet our loves and hates are usually so similar, it is rare when they differ.

The night is clear. Cold but clear. There are stars everywhere, a pattern of stars, a map to guide me home.

Lily

Without Rose, the fireplace is cold. I watch the clock at the end of the hall, and when the clock strikes one thirty I look for Rose, search the sky, but do not see her. I call for her—a honking sound, but one I believe she will recognize. I wait for an answer, listen for one, but there is nothing.

I have not seen Raven, or heard him, but there is something in the air, a vibration, the shivery sound that is left in a room after a harp is played. And the sound is familiar: wings. There is a sense of wings.

I wait one minute, two, five, ten, and then I can wait no more. I push open the doors to the bedrooms; cry out, "They're gone! They're gone! The ravens are coming!"

"Who is gone?" Theo asks, sitting up in confusion and blinking with sleep. But in their bedroom next door, Dori and Lia seem to know.

"Where is Rose?" Dori asks sharply, stepping from her bed and reaching for a robe, and I have no answer, but then suddenly see her in my mind, a snapshot, a flash of white following a ladder of starlight, and far behind her, not yet visible, a cloud of dark wings.

Once they were dressed and awake, they were angry we had not woken them earlier.

"The Sunflower Forest!" Theo pressed a hand to his head as if he had a headache.

But Dori—her face creased with worry—looked thoughtful, her voice no longer angry: "Tell me Amelia's dream again."

And after we had told them a second time, Dori nodded briskly. "Well, done is done. We must change our plan, and we must move quickly."

CHAPTER 12

Three Prophecies

HE ARRIVED IN THE BLUE MOUNTAINS before dawn, pushing his way against the wind and driving snow, his dark, huge horse tireless even in the cold, thickening drifts. Then, once the animal was securely in the stable, the count turned toward the castle, and as he had done before, when the butler opened the palace doors, he played the part of the old uncle, concerned about his young niece.

His dark cloak all but covering his face, the count was escorted into a large dining room. "The storm made me worry. A child in delicate health, secluded in such a place, it seemed wrong she should be here without relative or friend," the count said, warming himself before the fire and gladly drinking the hot tea a cook had been roused from her bed to make. The butler nodded, and stifled a yawn. "Now"— the count set down the teacup delicately—"shall we go up to the nursery?"

The butler frowned. "As you wish, sir. However, she should not be woken, as she has been ill."

"Of course," the count agreed, "I'll simply peek in on her—merely to reassure myself that she's all right, and then in the morning we'll get to know each other."

The butler nodded, and wordlessly strode down the darkened corridor, up a long flight of stairs, and down another dark hall, before finally stopping at a closed door. "The nursery, sir." The butler bowed stiffly in front of the door, and walked briskly down the hall, happy to be returning to the warmth of his bed. The count waited until the man was gone, and then slowly opened the door.

The room was dark, but the slow burning remains of a fire offered some light. In the glow of this small light, the count took in the darkened pink room: a fireplace with stuffed chairs before it, the dollhouse in one corner, a rocking horse, easels; he saw four beds, three of them tightly made. In the farthest bed, he saw a small lump and a swatch of blond hair peeking out from under the covers.

The count stood before the fireplace and spoke to the sleeping child in a soft, sweet voice. "Here I am, your old Uncle Raven. I have come for my blessing, little one." He smiled, showing his small, sharp teeth. "Do you wish to join your sisters in flight or earth?" he mused in a softer voice, his tone still gentle and light.

Then in two sudden steps he reached the bed, and his voice changed—became cold and hard. "Let's find out, come and wake up!" He reached out a bony hand to shake the child awake, and then when she did not stir, he threw back the blankets, revealing an old doll, her blank glass eyes staring and her red frozen lips smiling benignly up at him. That is when he noticed the soft white feather on the sheet, a signature of Lily, who had tenderly tucked her old doll into bed—a decoy.

A cruel, shrill shriek filled the palace and pierced the dreams of all who slept. A scream like an icicle falling. And the scream did not sound human—it sounded more like the wail of an angered bird.

The count searched and searched, but the castle was empty of the fourth princess. In the courtyard, he called for his horse and the huge dark animal was brought to him at once, its feet stamping with impatience. With the morning brightening around him, the count cursed the sky. Above him in the trees, ravens rustled their restless black wings, waiting for their orders. "Find the fourth princess," the count commanded, and the birds scattered north, south, east, and west; their gleeful cries shattering the quiet of the pale morning.

The count mounted his horse and faced him toward Gossling Palace, where he knew that in the night his armies had arrived, spread through the palace, city, and all across the kingdom. He was angry but he was also confident, for he had no doubt: the fourth princess *would* be found. And when she was, he would be king forever and ever.

Merrill

It is difficult to be still when others are helping, difficult to be trapped by roots, trapped in the soil of the country I love.

Powerless to help. Yet perhaps as a tree I played some small role because I was the first to hear of the prophecies, the first to hear the announcement of our "deaths." But now I am losing the order. Far away in the Blue Mountains, the snow had stopped and our uncle Raven, filled with rage, turned his horse back toward the castle—determined to find Amelia and sure that his ravens would.

The ravens arrived before the man did. They flew— crying and diving—around the palace, making the sky black. Later, men in dark armor arrived on dark horses and soon af- ter, Raven arrived. *What a gray morning it was!* The sky was heavy with clouds and thunder, and rain whipped through the air; so I was surprised when the tower's bell rang, calling the townspeople and court to meet. An hour later, hundreds had gathered. They met—an anxious somber group—at the lake's gazebo, once my father's favorite meeting place, though now the gazebo was draped in black for mourning, the crepe paper hanging in heavy strips, dripping in the rain. With dark umbrellas raised, the townspeople exchanged anxious glances and whispered slips of sentences to each other, their eyes asking questions they were too frightened to voice. Waiting.

Count Raven crossed the lawn heavily; his head low, steps slow and measured. Behind him followed two men I had never seen before and whom I rightly assumed were his advisors. Like their leader, the advisors wore black and their dark hair was long against their pale faces, their eyes follow- ing the count with hungry, searching looks. The crowd was scared; apprehensive, as if they sensed bad news and feared it. The count himself paused on the lawn, and slowly drew a handkerchief from his breast pocket, blowing his nose delicately, his face a mask of carefully arranged grief. I felt a flicker of fear, sensing a trick. A large raven circled above him and then flew to me, landing soundlessly, its sharp talons gripping my branches cruelly.

Uncle Raven stood before the messengers, writers, advisors, and townspeople, and shook his head sadly. "I have terrible news," and his voice broke as if with grief, "the four princesses, my nieces, are dead of the sickness."

There was a shocked silence, and then a man called out, "It's not true! The littlest one, the Princess Amelia, is in the Blue Mountains!"

The count nodded in reluctant agreement. "It is true," he said sadly. And I felt the lie. Felt his lie with every inch of my heart, knew somehow that my sister was alive. "It is true that the Princess Amelia *was* in the Blue Mountains," the count's voice was heavy. "The sickness found her there. I watched her draw her last breath." Here he paused again, as if struggling to compose himself. He was a wonderful actor, his face a mix of sadness, anger, and regret.

Some in the crowd began to wail, a terrible weeping, and the count nodded his head, as if he too wished to do nothing more than join them in their grief and disbelief.

"This sadness shall cover our kingdom, even the heavens weep on us!" He raised his hands to the rain, proof of the sky's tears. "However, we were a close family, united in our vision for the country of Gossling," the count continued, drawing himself up. "And before they died, the girls gave me their blessing as king."

This, I thought grimly, *was at least partially true. Stupid, but true.*

"And," he went on, though no one challenged his right to the kingdom, "the eldest three penned their approval in their own hand," and he held up the document that we had all foolishly signed. "It pains me now, that during this time of acute grief that I must begin to govern. Yet this is the burden of kings." He paused. "And it troubles me greatly that I must begin my reign with first this bad news, and now another."

The crowd murmured uneasily, and the question went unasked: *How could there possibly be more bad news?*

The count glanced at one of his advisors and the two men exchanged a brief, sly look, and the count almost smiled, though his face was grave as he faced the people again. "As greatly as this act wounds me, one of my first acts as king is to close the schools."

There was a sharp intake of breath and a sudden silence—the crowd mute. We are an educated people: our schools are strong and filled, and anyone who desires to study may learn for free in any of our universities. To close the schools was a shocking act.

"Why?" A woman demanded from the crowd, her face a blur of confusion and still streaked with tears over the false news of our deaths.

"The cost," the count said apologetically. "It takes a tremendous amount of money to run, and I'm afraid that the royal family's accounting skills were poor!" He laughed gently, regretfully.

Another lie. Each year, my father and mother planned the country's budget with care and prudence. And their first priority, the first planning, was of the country's schools. For the schools, they believed, were the most important. "A country with an educated people can do anything," my father said a thousand times. If there was one thing I knew for certain, it was that there was money in the schools. So much money—money to run the schools for years and years even with a cropped budget. I knew this, and knew that the count lied.

But no one else knew that. The crowd, already distressed, became angry, frightened.

"Impossible!" a man shouted.

"I don't believe it!" another man cried out, and other voices joined them.

"The schools must stay open!"

"How will the children learn?"

"Silence!" one of the count's advisors roared, and the crowd quieted for a moment.

And then another voice rose from the people, "You can't close the schools!"

The count's face grew dark. "I can, and I have. Good day, that is all," and with that he was abruptly done.

The dark birds stirred in the trees above him, and as he walked back toward the palace the two advisors rushed to keep up with his long stride. A pale sun slid out from behind the dark clouds showing the count's shadow: a raven.

The count was gone, but the crowd remained. A stunned and quiet group now.

"Amelia lives," I whispered, though I did not know this for absolute certain.

A woman near me looked around nervously, and then suddenly, as if struck, she began speaking, her voice high and desperate. The voice of hysteria. "Princess Amelia lives! The fourth princess, our young queen lives, but she has gone into hiding! There will be three signs—one for each of her lost sisters—to let us know she is among us: the rivers of Gossling will be crossed without bridge or boat or ice, haloes of light will crown the mountains, and a night sky will turn white."

I groaned, but the people began to nod. "A prophecy!" one man whispered with reverence. And a woman cried out, "Three signs!" A cheer went up from the crowd, and then another: "The fourth princess lives! Three signs and the queen shall return to Gossling!" The raven in my branches gave an enraged cry, and beating his dark wings, flew toward the palace.

❧

In the time that followed, there were many changes in the palace. George, along with all of my parents' advisors, was placed in the palace prison. There they were close enough to mourn the terrible changes that the count would continue to make, and close enough to ensure they would not be set free to lead an uprising. Meanwhile, the count staffed the palace with his own advisors, his own strange men in black cloaks, all with the same small, cruel eyes and sharp, grabbing hands. As if they were ravens who had taken on human form. These men were soon sent out into the country and cities to loot and rob for Count Raven—collecting taxes, taking the most precious art from the museums for the count's own collection, and seizing people's treasures at their own whim. Sparkling wedding bands, silver cups, anything they fancied they stole at gunpoint. And all week the meetings at the gazebo continued, each day worse than the day before, as Count Raven decreed that all public places were to close; all libraries, all theaters, all parks, all museums, all town halls.

And then, when it seemed there was nothing left to take, all arts funding was halted, all musical performances and plays were stopped. And with each cut the count apologized, and when people questioned him, he had them imprisoned, or threatened them with death for treason, for rising up and challenging a king. Soon and the jails began to fill and swell, and the people of the country who once might have stood up against oppression, were near blind with fear and hysteria. Soon people stopped questioning him, and the cuts went on: no street cleaning, no garbage collection, and no water purification. And then the count began to tax in earnest, he taxed the water, he taxed the roads, he taxed the farmers so much they could no longer farm, he taxed and taxed and taxed. And the money of the kingdom, the money of the people—the money people had sacrificed to save—it all went to him. He filled the rooms of the palace with his stolen gold.

But still there was hope. I heard it, the faintest of whispers in the quiet crowds that gathered in the square outside the castle gates. "The princess lives. There will be three signs!" It was a false prophecy and one made by a desperate woman, and yet the people of the kingdom believed it, and I began to wonder how we could make those prophecies come true. Wondered in those long days when Dori, Theo, Rose, and Lily would return. Wondered where Amelia was. Whether she was safe.

CHAPTER 13

The Sunflower Forest

Amelia

I awoke to the sound of humming. Not one sound of humming, but the sound of many things humming many different songs. I kept my eyes closed, but then something fell on my chest, and I opened my eyes to see a sunflower seed. I looked up, and the most extraordinary creature I had ever seen looked down on me curiously.

The creature was lovely. A bit smaller than a house cat, it had long lavender scales and large beautiful gold wings tucked behind it like a fan. It looked to be half-lizard, half-dragon. According to our ancient books, our kingdom was once filled with gentle mystical creatures, magical animals and dragons; sweet oddities, all described with the glittery sugar of fairy tales. As children we had read about them with Dori, marveling over the descriptions and delighting at the idea of talking animals and gallant dragons.

In our old nursery, years and years ago, Merrill had asked Dori if the stories were true. Dori had looked thoughtful, tapped her finger lightly against an illustration and smiled slightly. "I'm not arrogant enough to believe that only humans speak and think in our kingdom. Surely our animals communicate in ways they do not in the other kingdoms I've visited, and surely there are other unexplainable things in our lives that do not fit into what we know and what we can prove. Look at the universe and the millions of stars, who can explain such wonders without using just the slightest bit of imagination? We live in a varied and wondrous world!"

Months earlier, when Henry had asked Theo if such creatures still existed, Theo had laughed and said, "Only in our imaginations."

But now here was proof of the impossible, proof that those ancient careful artists, who had so painstakingly reproduced the world they saw around them, had been accurate, not simply whimsical. Such creatures had indeed existed, and existed still.

"Henry," I whispered down to him. "Wake up!"

Henry blinked awake as suddenly as if I had shaken him. "What?"

"Look." I pointed to the creature just as it lifted into the air and flew away.

"Wow!" Henry sat up and grinned. "Wait until I tell Theo—" He broke off suddenly, as if remembering where we were and why we were here. "Is it morning already?" He yawned.

I looked around, puzzled—the forest was lighter than it had been when we had arrived, but it didn't seem to be light enough to be morning. "I think so," I said slowly, "maybe. Anyway, climb up here," I ordered Henry, "if we keep talking like this we're bound to wake up Meg."

Henry swung up on the branch next to me, but it was too late: Meg was awake. Awake and furious.

"I can't believe I let you drag me to this stupid forest!" She stamped out of bed, her hair tangled and her eyes puffy with exhaustion. She looked up to where we sat looking down on her. "Ugh, there you are! How am I supposed to bathe in this forest?" she demanded indignantly.

I looked around helplessly. "I don't know."

"Good morning to you too," Henry said sweetly.

Meg ignored him, though her eyes narrowed meanly. A bird landed next to us on the branch, and two of the small winged creatures swooped by playing some kind of game with each other. Seeing them, Meg's lip curled in contempt. "What are those *things*?"

"I'm not sure," I said, and shrugged.

"Of course you wouldn't know! Oh, I hate this forest, and I hate these dirty flying things." She stamped her foot hard, then she looked back at us. "And most of all I *hate* both of you."

I glared down at Meg. "Well, the feeling is mutual!"

❧

Henry grabbed a handful of sunflower seeds from a nearby flower and began to eat. Through a mouthful of seeds, he said to Meg mildly, "There's a stream for bathing through the trees

156

over there. No more than a two-minute walk." He pointed straight ahead of us where I could see a running stream.

Meg snatched up her pack, and without a word stormed off in the direction of the stream.

I sighed. "Do you think she's going to act like this all the way back to Gossling Palace?" I asked Henry.

He smiled. "If she is, then it's just one more reason to get back there really, really fast!" He wiped off his hands and began to climb down from the tree.

"Where are you going?"

"You mean where are *we* going?" Henry grinned up at me.

I sighed and started to climb down after him. "Fine, where are *we* going?"

"*We* are going to pack up our beds and then we are going to the stream for water," Henry said matter-of-factly. "And then we're going to make a plan to get out of this forest and back to Gossling Palace."

❧

When we came to the stream, Meg had already bathed and was dressed in a clean gown. Her long, wet golden hair—the color of dark honey—hung down her back. She was staring at her reflection in the stream, and I couldn't help but think she would have looked beautiful, except that her face was twisted into a sulky pout.

Henry knelt down and dunked his head into the stream. He came out sopping wet. And he shook his head like a dog, splattering everything with water. "Cold!" he said.

I shivered just looking at him. "I have a feeling we're going to be dirtier before the morning is over, so I think I'll save my bathing for later."

"Dirtier?" Meg wrinkled her nose at me. "Is that even possible for you?"

Henry nodded cheerfully. "It is. I've seen it!"

Gingerly I washed my hands and face in the cold water, wiping them dry on the edge of a blanket. Then I dipped one of the cups into the clear water, and drank.

Henry looked at us. "Anyone hungry? I've got the leftover tea cakes in my sack." Before we could answer he pulled a blue linen tea towel from his pack, unrolled it, and took out tea cakes. "Here." He handed one to me, and then walked over to where Meg sat against a tree and handed her one.

Meg took a delicate bite and made a face. "It's stale."

I shrugged. "It's this or sunflower seeds."

"I'll eat it," Henry volunteered through a mouthful of cake.

Meg narrowed her eyes. "I didn't say I wasn't going to eat it, I said it was stale."

"Better to eat them now," Henry said, "before they get more stale. Anyway, we need to keep our strength up. We have a long way to travel in the next few days, and we have to be careful of ravens."

Meg's lower lip pushed out into a full pout. "I'm so tired of hearing about the ravens. I just want to go home." For a moment, her lip quivered and I thought she might cry. "First we left home and went to the Winter Palace, and then we had to leave there and come here"—she gestured to the forest around her—"and I hate it here!" Her voice had become hard and whiny again, and I sighed. For a moment—just a moment—I had been feeling sorry for Meg.

❧

We explored the border of the Sunflower Forest, walking along what we imagined was the edge farthest from the Winter Palace. There the Sunflower Forest faded into an ordinary wood—a sort of tangle of trees and sparse bushes. Henry led us into it, checking his compass every few feet, before finally coming to a stop.

"Doesn't this take us farther away from Gossling Palace?" Meg asked.

I looked at my compass too. "It does, but we might have to find a roundabout way to get home. After all, Count Raven's armies will expect us to take one of the main roads."

Meg sighed. "I'm bored with this."

It was then that we saw the dark birds. There were just a handful of them, no more than five, but they shrieked and cawed when they saw us. Meg waved her arms at them in irritation. "Go away!"

The birds' cries became louder, more piercing, and Meg wrinkled her nose. "Shut up!"

Henry looked concerned. "I think we should go back to the Sunflower Forest." Turning, we began to quickly retrace our steps. Yet as we walked one bird followed us at a distance, hopping from tree to tree, crying angrily. Then, suddenly, when we were just steps from the safety of the Sunflower Forest, it swooped sharply down and bit Meg, before gliding swiftly back up into the tree—wings flapping hard.

"Ouch!" Meg looked angry. "That bird just bit me!" She flipped over her arm and we saw a thick line of blood stretching across the pale flesh. Meg frowned, picked up a stone, and threw it at a dark bird, which now sat in a tree just outside the border of the Sunflower Forest. The stone missed, and the bird gave a mocking cry before rising again into the sky and flying west.

"That was a raven," Henry said in a low voice.

"I don't care what it was—it bit me and now I have a mark," Meg complained, turning her arm over again to examine where the bird had bitten her. Yet, oddly, now there was no mark, and the blood was gone, as if her skin had absorbed all signs of the attack.

Henry looked mystified, but Meg smiled, content that there would be no scar, no bruise to remember the bite of the bird by.

"That's strange," Henry said, frowning. He slid his eyes over to me, and his face was worried.

❧

Back in the Sunflower Forest, Meg insisted on resting, so Henry and I discussed a plan: we would return to Gossling Palace and hope that the others were there too. It was a risky plan—returning to the home of the enemy—but we didn't know where Lia's house was and we didn't know where else to go. The route we had created to return to the palace was a winding, twisting one, using shortcuts that favored forests and wooded areas rather than towns and cities, because Henry and I had agreed that this was one way to hide from the ravens that we now suspected flew over the entire country searching for us.

As we packed in the dim light of the next morning, Meg sulked, pacing back and forth in front of the tree that we had slept in for two nights. "I don't understand why we're leaving." She kicked Henry's pack as she passed it. "If we're safe here, then why should we leave?"

"We can't hide here forever. Except for Amelia, there's no Gossling princess that can stop Count Raven," Henry replied curtly, shoving the last of the blankets into his pack.

Meg's lips curled into a sneer and she folded her arms hard across her chest. "What makes you think Amelia can stop him? She can't, and she puts *us* in danger by making us return to the palace with her."

"Stay here then," Henry shot back.

But of course she wouldn't. Scared of being by herself and eager to return to a palace—even one ruled by a mad count—Meg would not stay in the enchanted wood alone. "Fine, I'll go with you," she grudgingly conceded, as if she were doing us a favor by agreeing.

❧

Standing on the edge of the forest as we readied to leave, Henry turned to say something, but stopped, his mouth half open.

"What?" I asked.

"Look at Meg," Henry said in a low voice. I turned and

saw that there was a stripe of black running through her long blond hair.

"Why are you staring at me?" Meg asked meanly.

"Your hair—," I started to say.

"Is gold," Meg finished smugly. "Gold the way a *proper* princess's hair should be."

"Merrill's hair is brown," Henry pointed out reasonably.

"Well, maybe that's my point—if she were a proper princess, her hair would be like spun gold. Like mine. Now shut up!" Meg's voice was icy.

"Fine," Henry shrugged, "but your golden princess hair has a black stripe in it."

Meg's face turned red with rage, and she stalked to the stream. On the mirrored stream's grassy shore, Meg kneeled and bent so close to the water that her long blond hair nearly touched the surface. She smiled at her reflection, and then her smile froze as she saw the thick black stripe running through her hair. She lifted her hand slowly and fingered the stripe lightly with her hand. Then she smiled, a strange, strange smile.

"I'm more beautiful now," she whispered in a soft voice. "Even more now."

"Weird." Henry looked at me, and I nodded. It was strange, as if the bite of the dark bird had somehow left its mark on Meg. Given her its poison. I felt a shiver of dread, and shook my head as if to shake away the feeling, but it remained.

Merrill

Twelve days after they had left the palace, Theo, the twins, and Dori returned. As when they had left, there was a terrible snowstorm on the night they arrived. It was a blinding snow—whiting out the landscape so I could barely see to the edge of the pond. It was an unnatural storm, and it gave me hope, a cautious hope that Dori was returning. And I was not disappointed; they came under the cover of the storm, arriving in the darkest hour of the night.

I heard them before I saw them, whispered voices on a curl of wind. And then they were there; the twins huddled under the shelter of my branches, and Theo shivering in the cold and snow. Only Dori looked calm and unruffled in the terrible wind.

"Merrill?" Theo's voice was uncertain and strained.

"Yes," I sighed, "you are looking at the first princess of Gossling, a willow tree."

Theo fell to his knees, his face a mask of sadness and something else, something unreadable.

"Do not kneel before me, Theo!"

"I bow before the one I love."

"You love a tree!" I cried out in irritation.

"I love a queen," Theo said solidly, as if that ended all conversation.

Before I could reply, Dori broke in, her voice soft but firm, "Stand up, Theo. There is no *time* tonight to speak of love. Tonight we plan, and plan quickly. The longer we remain together, the greater the risk that we are discovered, and if we are discovered, the Raven will believe, rightly, that we gather for the sake of Amelia."

"Where *is* Amelia?" I asked, my voice strained. "The count has announced her death to the kingdom."

"We heard," Theo said grimly. "When we traveled here, we moved through the small towns bordering the northeast, where it was least likely we would be discovered. Even so far from home, people spoke of the death of the fourth princess."

"Did you hear of the prophecies?"

Dori looked startled, her wrinkled face sharp and quizzical. "What prophecies?"

I sighed. "The people of Gossling believe there will be three signs, and that after those signs, the queen shall reveal herself."

"That's ridiculous!" Dori looked annoyed as I told them of the prophecies.

"I don't understand," Rose said, shifting slightly. "Do the people think Amelia's dead, or do they think she's in hiding?"

Dori rubbed at her temples. "When people are frightened they believe anything—true or false, as long as it offers hope. The prophecies offer hope, so the people believe them."

"But they also believe Amelia is dead! We heard that in every town we flew through—that the fourth princess was dead. So their beliefs contradict themselves!" Lily exclaimed.

"It doesn't matter," Dori said mildly. "What matters is that some of the people are holding on to hope. After all, Amelia is not dead, nor are any of the other princesses, so having hope is not such a foolish thing, no matter how it may seem."

"Where is Amelia?" I asked again.

Dori looked worried. "Twelve nights ago, Amelia, Henry, and Meg disappeared into the Sunflower Forest, reaching the safety of that enchanted wood just hours before the Raven arrived at the Winter Palace. And we left the Winter Palace with haste too, became as invisible as we could be. For safety, we split up. Lia went to Central Gossling to see if the plague has progressed, and to see if Raven has sent his armies there. The twins joined a flock of swans as they flew south, and through the sheer number of birds, disguised themselves. Theo and I traveled through the small border towns, pretending to be gypsies—an old grandmother and her grandson."

"Are they still in the Sunflower Forest?" I wondered.

"I believe they are journeying here," Dori said gravely.

"Why?" Rose exclaimed.

"How do you know?" Lily interrupted.

"I don't know for certain." Dori looked thoughtful. "But I feel that they are. Amelia is far from here, but I believe she will come home because she will not know where else to go. And, if we are detected here, then our very presence is a threat to her."

"Where will you go?" I asked.

"I will join Lia, and Theo shall again accompany me. Lily and Rose will leave the Lake of Swans."

"Why can't we stay with Merrill?" Lily protested.

Dori sighed and looked sorry. "Although it would be an easy disguise for you to be here among so many swans, it is possible that Raven would somehow detect you and that is a risk we cannot take. For now, you should go to one of the great central lakes. So, finally, we come to Amelia and Henry and Meg." Dori sighed again. "Amelia will come to you, Merrill. And when she does, you must send her far from here." Dori looked worried. "Amelia's job is a big one for such little shoulders. She must help break the spell placed on her sisters, and she must help the people believe in themselves. Both almost impossible tasks. *Almost.*"

"What should I tell her?" I asked.

"We will stick with the original plan. Tell her that she and Henry should travel to the fairy hollow on the edge of the Western Valleys. Enough magic resides there to keep us safe from the prying eyes of the ravens. We will meet there, and shall try to create a plan to fulfill the prophecies. Fulfill them and the people will join us in war against Raven. Win, and the princesses will be transformed, and the country shall again be free."

"I hope so," Lily said doubtfully, and the ravens in the trees around us shrieked with mocking laughter.

CHAPTER 14

Back to Gossling Palace

Amelia

The trip home to the palace was long. We wound through a labyrinth of woods, using the shallow streams as a guide and the sun to mark the passing hours. In a few days' time, we grew used to camping. I could build a fire far more easily than I could embroider, and Henry—with his father's knowledge of plants and leaves—was skilled at identifying sweet berries to eat. He knew where squirrels stored their winter nuts, and which herbs, roots, and leaves could be boiled into a sort of soup. All of us were bad at catching fish, and disliked eating it, though with so little food it was necessary. Days passed and with each passing day, Meg grew odder and odder—and her blond hair slowly became striped with more strips of black.

We traveled in the woods that edged the farms, knowing that the woods, at least, provided us with some cover from the ravens that seemed to always fill the skies above us. Still, as Henry joked, the ravens weren't likely to have identified us anyway. He was right: in this short time we'd come to look raggedy and worn. Of the three of us, Meg had somehow managed to stay clean, her dress with its threads of gold running through delicate foam-green cloth hadn't torn, and her hands were still soft and smooth, though her blond hair with its dark stripes gave her a strange look.

"We're a messy group. I don't think there's a raven in the land that would mistake either of you for princesses," Henry remarked cheerfully one night as we sat around the small fire I had built, fish roasting slowly before us on crude spits. We had spent most of day walking through brambles and thick trees, and much of the late afternoon building a little camp to sleep in. Catching fish had made us wet, and all of us were covered in with soot and ash.

However, at his comment Meg's head snapped up, and her pale eyes were furious, glowing red in the light of the fire. "Amelia has *never* looked like a princess and I always have! And I do now!"

I wasn't offended to be told I'd never looked like a princess, and I shrugged, leaning forward to carefully turn the spits. "True enough," I said mildly to Meg.

But Meg was still angry. She turned to Henry. "Apologize to me!"

Henry's mouth curled obstinately. "No."

Meg stood up and stamped her foot hard on the forest floor. "Apologize to me now, or you *will* be sorry."

Henry's face tightened, and his voice grew low. "No. What I said was not meant to offend, it was meant only as truth, and I will not apologize for truth."

Meg stormed away, out of the light of the fire and into the dark woods just beyond the camp. Henry and I looked at each other in silence.

This is how Meg had become. A joke was twisted to mean an insult, a kind word was worthy only of suspicion, her demands irrational. Meg had always been mean, but she had become far worse. Some shift was occurring—hard to pinpoint, but there still. Henry and I ignored her comments and complaints as best as we could. Tried to shrug them off with excuses—blaming her behavior on exhaustion or homesickness or her generally unpleasant nature made worse by worsening circumstances. Still, it made us uneasy.

Then, when we were only about a two days' walk from the palace, Henry heard Meg talking to herself as she gathered water for our lunch, and realized that we were in danger—that Meg herself had become a part of the danger we were fleeing.

Henry rushed back to where I was trying to build a fire without too much success. "Listen, I think Meg's gone mad!"

"You're just thinking that now?" I grinned at him, bent over the firewood I was arranging. "Pass me those branches." I pointed toward the scrappy branches I'd managed to gather while he was gone.

"No, listen!" Henry took a step toward me. "There's something really wrong with her! I mean, she seems crazy. When I was looking for berries, I overheard her at the stream. She was admiring herself . . ."

"So?" I interrupted. "What else is new?"

"She said she'd kill you to become queen," Henry said flatly.

"What?" I heard a note of fear creep into my voice.

"She said she'd *kill* you," he repeated. "I think when she was pinched by that raven, he infected her. Maybe that's why we keep seeing ravens everywhere. Maybe they're following Meg, because it's easy for them to find her. I don't know, but whatever is wrong with her, she's dangerous and we have to leave her."

"We can't leave her! Especially if she's sick." Even if I hated Meg, leaving her, no matter how miserable she made us, didn't seem right.

"We have to! We're close to a town—we passed its edges this morning. She won't starve if we leave her here. Come on!"

I dropped the kindling on the forest floor, listening. I could hear Meg singing by the river. Her voice was sweet and pure, though hearing it now, I shivered.

"You're right, I suppose. Let's go," I said to Henry, and lifting our swords and packs we left quietly, crept from the safety of the forest toward an open field dotted with loose haystacks. "We should hide. It's too dangerous to walk in the open during the day, especially with ravens everywhere."

"And Meg," Henry added. "She'll be looking for us, and we would be easy to spot walking across an open field."

"Where should we hide, though?" I looked miserably at the shorn field.

Henry paused, looking at the fields beyond it, all of them identical and empty. "There's no place to go except into the hay. Come on!"

We ran across the field and tunneled quickly into a high prickly haystack. Moments after, we heard Meg's voice—faint and far away, calling for us. She called and called for close to an hour, and then her voice faded as she moved deeper into the forest.

With the sun warming the hay, we slept. Hours later we woke up itchy and too warm. Still, we stayed hidden in the fresh hay until it was night, and then we crawled out and stood up stiffly in the dark field, brushing thistle from our clothes and packs before traveling along the worn cow paths toward the palace. The night seemed to hum around us: tree frogs hiccupped and crickets tuned their wings, chirping; animals rustled in the bushes and a deer ran before us, his high white tail stiff. The cow paths were twisted and knotted with rocks and yet they were well outside the border of the woods, and that night it seemed freeing to be beyond the canopy of dark trees. Freeing to look up into the velvet sky and see the soft curve of the moon, the gentle, blue glow of her light.

I followed Henry as he made his way down the steep slope of the path, thinking about how in just days we would see Merrill, and maybe Tiege.

"Wait." Henry stopped so suddenly that I fell against him, nearly knocking us both over.

"What?" I said, annoyed.

"We can't go back to Gossling Palace this way. The ravens were following us because of Meg, and Meg knows that we were going to the palace. Even with us gone she'll assume that's where we're headed, and so will the ravens. We can't go," he finished miserably.

I looked up at the stars and fought back a sudden urge to cry. We were so close to home, so close to Merrill. Still, Henry was right: we couldn't go home. At least not by this route. Not with the ravens following us. I pulled George's compass from my pocket and turned to the east, suddenly decisive. "Okay, so we can't go home for help or answers." I looked at Henry. "Let's go to the Night Forest, maybe we'll find some answers there."

"The Night Forest?" Henry shifted uneasily under the weight of his pack. "You want us to see the witch of the Night Forest?"

"Yes," I said, sounding more confident than I felt. "She may know some magic to help us."

"Have you ever been there before? Ever met her?"

"No," I said obstinately, "but I think she'll welcome us."

Henry shook his head doubtfully. "Welcome us, or kill us."

Still, he picked up his pack and followed me as we retraced our way up the cow path and into the dark fields.

CHAPTER 15

The Night Forest

WE WALKED EAST, moving more quickly than we had before, knowing that daylight was just hours away, and knowing that we needed to be as far as possible from where the ravens might think us to be. The night seemed less friendly now; the open sky with its too-bright moon and twinkling stars seemed dangerous.

We walked east through barren fields, crossing dusty country roads, weaving through the high grass of pastures, and around cow ponds, until finally the sky became dusty with light. And with day creeping onto the horizon, on the edge of a creek bed, we curled under the thick hanging roots of a linden tree and slept.

When I woke up it was nearly night again, and for a moment I struggled to remember where I was; blinked at the roots that hung like witch's fingers around me. Then I heard Henry's quiet breathing behind me and remembered. I listened for a moment, my ears straining to hear the cries of the ravens, but I only heard the running creek rushing by. Then I turned and shook Henry awake.

❧

"It's spooky to eat breakfast at night," Henry whispered to me as we sat eating berries on the bank of the creek.

I nodded in agreement. I swallowed, and then whispered, "I feel like we should be sleeping."

"Well, we should be," Henry pointed out reasonably, making me giggle.

When the berries were gone and we had drunk long cool drinks from the creek, we started east again. For two nights we did this, waking up when the moon rose, and going to sleep when the first hint of dawn appeared.

On the last night of our journey, as dawn was just beginning to tinge the sky a dusty blue, Henry and I reached the narrow, overgrown road that I knew would lead us into the Night Forest. We fought our way down the road, Henry ahead of me, carefully holding back branches. Still, nettles and bushes soon scratched us both. As we came closer and closer to the forest, the trees seemed to hang lower, and the shadows grew longer.

On the edge of the Night Forest, hollyhock and black ivy seemed to quiver and murmur a warning: *Visitors beware, visitors beware*. An enchanted forest. We stepped gingerly into the darkness of the woods, blinking our eyes to adjust to the sudden blackness.

"Are you sure we should be here?" Henry sounded doubtful and scared.

"Uh-huh." I tried to make my voice confident and firm, but the moment was ruined because a great bat swooped above us and I screamed.

Henry gave a small forced laugh. "It's just a bat. Come on, let's go find the Great Witch."

"As if it's easy to find her," I muttered, still embarrassed by being frightened by a bat.

Henry shifted his pack over his shoulder. "A long time ago, Tiege told me that the Night Witch can be found within the Three Circles of Stone in the heart of the forest. That must mean the middle."

"How does she know?"

Henry laughed. "How does Tiege know anything? She just knows!"

We began to walk deeper into the dark, dark forest. Long, wet Spanish moss hung from the trees, and it seemed to caress and grab at our ankles, trailing its wet fingers across our legs and making me shiver. "How much farther do you think?" I asked Henry, holding tightly to his hand.

"I don't know. Soon, maybe," he whispered.

We walked a bit farther, and suddenly I noticed that the forest had begun to thin, and then suddenly we stepped into a clearing, and before us were the largest, whitest stones I had ever seen, stones as white as cream and arranged in a giant circle. I gasped. Henry gulped, looking up at the huge stones.

"Do you think we just walk in?" he asked.

I looked tentatively through a narrow gap between two stones. "We can try." I slithered between the gap, and Henry followed me. We blinked, looking around. For we now stood inside the first circle.

"That was easy," I said slowly.

"I don't think it's going to be as easy this time," Henry said, eyeing the smooth wall of stone before us. We circled the wall twice, but there was no entry, no small space to squeeze between. Henry and I peered up, but the stones were so tall that it was difficult to judge where they ended.

Henry pushed gently against a stone, but it did not move. He pushed harder, and then harder still, his face becoming red with the effort.

"Help me push, Amelia," Henry ordered, and together we pushed with all our might, straining against the weight of the stone. It did not budge.

"Wait." Henry stopped suddenly. "Tiege also said that to visit the Great Witch, you had to believe that you could reach her."

"What does that mean? *Believe* you can?" I stopped pushing too and sat, exhausted, against the wall.

"I have an idea." Henry jumped up and reached down a hand to help me stand. "Amelia, close your eyes! We're going to walk through this wall!"

"That's dumb," I sighed, pushing away his hand and staying slumped on the ground. "The stone is real, not imaginary. We can't move it with both of us pushing as hard as we can. It's solid rock. Why do you think we can walk through it?"

"I don't know. Do you have any other ideas?"

"No."

"Then let's just try this. It could work."

I stood up. "Fine."

Henry clasped my hand in his. "Now, close your eyes," he ordered.

I closed my eyes. "Okay," Henry said, "now we're going to walk through the wall."

Right, I thought, *we'll just walk through stone.*

"Amelia," Henry said sharply, "*believe* we can walk through it, just for a minute." His voice softened. "Please."

I closed my eyes again and imagined us walking through the stone, and as I did something cold shivered through my body. Scared, I opened my eyes. We were standing in the second circle, the stone behind us and another wall before us.

Henry took a shaky breath. "Ready?"

I nodded. We gripped hands and again I pictured myself walking through the marble wall in front of me. And again I felt my body pass through something cold, and I opened my eyes.

In the center of the circle, on a yet another white stone, sat a woman. She was taller than anyone I had ever seen, and beautiful. Her skin was the warm brown of chestnuts and her eyes the milky brown of hot cocoa. She smiled at us and when she spoke her voice was low and kind. "I knew you would both make it through the circles. Only the true of heart can pass through this forest and into the heart of the stone." She paused and looked from Henry to me, studying me with curiosity. "So, you are the youngest princess, the fourth. I knew your grandmother well, though you do not favor her. You look like my old friend, your great-aunt Lia. A stubborn, stubborn woman." The witch smiled as if remembering a joke, and then her face grew serious. "I hope you have inherited more than her red hair. And you," she turned her piercing eyes back to Henry, "the milk-twin of the princess. Queen Charlotte spoke of you often to me. She imagined greatness for you."

Henry blushed.

"You knew Mother?" I said, flashing a quizzical look to Henry.

The witch said nothing, stared at us thoughtfully as if considering us. "You've traveled so far," she said finally, "and at such great risk." She frowned. "And you've traveled to me for answers—answers about your powers, answers on how to lead, and answers on how to save your sisters from the spell that traps them. You've traveled so far for these answers, but I cannot help you, for I don't have the answers you seek."

. I felt my body sag with disappointment, and yet it suddenly struck me as strange that she would know what had happened to my sisters, especially when all of Gossling imagined them dead. "You know about my sisters?"

The witch's face broke into a smile, which transformed her face. "Yes," she nodded, "I know much about Gossling. And I am not alone; there are many who follow the journey of the fourth princess. It is important that you succeed; much rests on your victory." She paused and her voice became soft. "You are very afraid, I know. But only your own power will do here."

"But I have no power or magic!" My voice rose up in frustration.

"Oh, but you do." The witch was no longer smiling and her face was serious. "You have your own magic. You don't yet know what it is, or how to use it." Her voice grew grave. "And Amelia, I cannot tell you, for I do not know. The power of the White Queens is known only to them, and each queen must find it in herself."

"Then we came here for nothing," I said bitterly.

The witch shook her head. "Wrong. I shall give you four things, one for each of your sisters, and one for the milk-twin." She nodded briefly at Henry. She held out her dark hand and upon it lay three white round stones. Against the dark ebony of her palm, the stones seemed to glow like pearls. "These are three stones from the Circle of Light. When you are in great need, wish on a stone and you shall have aid. But wish wisely, Amelia, as there are only three. My fourth gift to you is this: when the moment is right, when all four princesses are united, my magic shall join the power of the White Queens and shall aid you in casting the spell that shall free your sisters from root and feather. The moment must be right, however, or my magic shall do nothing."

"What will the spell be?" I asked eagerly.

But before she could speak there was a whisper around us, a sort of breath of air, and the Great Witch stood very still, listening. "You must go now. The time is right for you to move toward the palace again; the bats tell me that the ravens search for you in the south." Her brow wrinkled slightly. "A child moves with them. A strange child—this child is a danger to you."

"What about the spell?" I asked again.

The witch smiled at me. "Amelia, I don't know what the

spell will be, only you will know that. What I do know is what I've told you: when the moment is right and you cast that spell, my magic shall join yours."

"I don't have any magic," I muttered darkly.

The witch stared down at me, her eyes mild. "With time you will find your magic. Now, though, you must go. This forest protects you, but outside of its trees, you are alone, so travel with great caution. Go now, there is no time to lose. Merrill waits for you!"

We stepped toward the wall of stone, and again Henry reached for my hand. "Ready?" he asked.

I took a deep breath. "Rea—"

"Wait!" the witch commanded.

We turned back to the Great Witch and she plucked a gold envelope from the air. "Here is a message for the boy," she said, as she handed Henry the heavy envelope. He looked at it with awe.

"Open it," she ordered, and with shaking hands, Henry did.

He read aloud, "There shall be a moment when the fate of the kingdom shall be held by you. Have faith in yourself and in those around you. You too shall save the kingdom. The power of friendship and love is greater than any other. There is greatness in your future, and truth in your eyes."

The witch gave Henry a long look. "Your fate is also in the stars, milk-twin."

Henry nodded and looked down again at the letter in his hand, and in that instant I realized something. I looked at the witch in surprise. "You sent the envelopes to Mother and made the frog speak!"

The witch laughed. "I did—long ago! At times I see the future, my dear, and when I saw your young mother in the garden, I saw you! Go to the White Queens, children. It's time now, so do not delay! Go with courage."

Henry took my hand and we stepped through the stone.

CHAPTER 16

Homeward Bound

STANDING ON THE EDGE of the Night Forest, we looked forward. In the very far distance, the highest spire of Gossling Palace could be seen, its golden tip shimmering in the early light of the morning. Henry grinned at me. "Home still seems pretty far away, huh?"

I nodded. "Well, at least we can see it."

Henry laughed. "That's true; we won't need to use our compasses from George. We should be home in a few days' time." He took a deep breath. "Ready?"

"I guess," I answered doubtfully.

Henry picked up my pack and handed it to me, and then reached down and pulled his own pack off the soft green moss of the dark forest floor.

"Go with safety, White Queen and friend," the trees whispered at our backs, and with this blessing we stepped onto the old merchant road and began the long walk home.

We traveled for two days and two nights. The travel was not difficult—we moved easily under the cover of the trees, through the high, late corn, and along country roads empty of people or animals. Maybe because the travel was so easy, it was easy to forget that we were in danger. Or maybe it was that we could see home so far in the distance. For a day our travel was uninterrupted, and then on the morning of the second day it began to rain. The rain was the first small sign that autumn had begun in earnest, for the rain was cold and biting.

As the day wore on, the rain fell harder and the country roads flooded and the fields were turned to mud. By late afternoon our clothes were soaked, and our packs were heavy. Henry and I began to look for a place to spend the night. We had spent our nights sleeping under the stars, but now, with the rain beating down on us, we had to find shelter.

Finally, on the edge of a field, we saw a barn that seemed to be abandoned. The barn was tall as a cathedral; its weathered wood graceful, even in age. The rain whipping around us, we ran across the barren field and entered the barn cautiously. Although we hadn't seen many people, we were still careful not to be seen. Even a seemingly abandoned barn could be home to something.

Henry and I slid through the barn door and pulled it closed behind us. The barn was drafty; rain fell through the roof and the wind whipped through the cracked wood of the walls with a whistling sound. The walls and floors were covered in spiderwebs and dust, but still, it was mostly dry and it was warmer than outside. Best of all, it seemed empty: traces of old hay littered the floor and a rusty shovel leaned against one wall, beside it, a rickety ladder led to a hayloft. The thick dust that lay on the floor was undisturbed by footprints.

"It looks empty to me," Henry whispered, looking around warily.

I nodded. "Definitely empty, but very, very dusty."

Henry sneezed in agreement, the sound bouncing and echoing in the empty barn.

I giggled. "Let's go to the hayloft. At least the hay will be softer than the ground's been."

I picked up my wet pack again and slung it over my back, then slowly climbed the rickety ladder to the hayloft. The old hay was musty, and a cloud of ragweed and dust flew up when I dropped my pack on it. Henry quickly scaled the ladder and stood in the hay next to me.

"Well, it's dry, anyway," he said grimly.

A clap of thunder split the sky, and then lightning lit the barn with light. "Cheer up, at least we're not outside," I shuddered.

"True." Henry unsnapped his pack and took out two of the small green apples that we had picked earlier in the day. "Dinner?" he offered, tossing me one.

I bit into the apple and made a face. "Sour!"

"Yeah," Henry agreed. "I think they're not quite ready for eating, but it's something."

My mouth full of apple, I nodded and flopped backward onto my pack. Outside there was a rustling sound—a noise different than the wind, a sound like an animal. "Did you hear that?" I sat up.

Henry sat up too and listened for a moment. "Probably a deer. No animal likes cold rain, especially in October. They're not prepared for it—it feels like February!" He shivered.

Then, with nothing to do and the night growing darker, we arranged the old hay into mattresses and covered them with blankets.

"We'll start again early," Henry said, and yawned from his makeshift bed.

I yawned too and turned over. "If you wake up first, wake me up."

"Okay," Henry sighed sleepily.

The barn was very dark, and the rain fell in a sharp staccato on the roof. Except for the storm, the night was quiet. The steady tapping of rain made me tired and soon I was asleep.

It was the sound of crackling that woke me up . . . that, and the smell of smoke.

CHAPTER 17

Fire!

I WOKE UP SUDDENLY. The barn, which should have been dark with night, glowed as orange as the inside of a pumpkin. For a moment I was confused, my brain still half-asleep, and then, with smoke snaking around me, I jumped up and shook Henry awake. "Fire!" I screamed.

I peered over the edge of the hayloft and saw flames licking the wooden walls of the barn, heard the old wood bend in response to the fire, heard it split and moan as it surrendered to the heat and climbing flames. Behind me, Henry stuffed blankets into our packs while smoke billowed around us like soft clouds in the dust of the hay. I stood mesmerized and frozen, watching the flames. Then Henry's fingers were digging into the soft flesh of my arm. "We have to get out of here *now!*"

Wordless, I pointed down at the ladder, which was now engulfed in flames.

"There's another way out, there must be," Henry said more to himself than to me. "I've been in the palace stables with Patrick, and I know that haylofts have hay drops—somewhere there's a trapdoor that should lead outside! Help me look, Amelia!"

We waded into the old hay, climbing over disintegrating bales, until we reached the wall, then we began digging. Behind us the smoke grew thicker, and I knew with terrible clarity that when the fire reached the hayloft there would be no escape—that the hay would burn too fast. I began to dig, the hay scratching my hands as I clawed at the floors and walls, desperate to find an escape.

"Here!" I cried, my fingers brushing against a ring of metal on the side of the wall. Pushing the hay away I saw the edges of a trapdoor.

Henry knelt down next to me, and together we dug through the musty hay, until the outline of the hay drop was clear. Henry tugged on the large rusty ring, but the door didn't budge. He tried again, but the door stayed sealed.

Henry coughed, and when he did, I realized that the barn was now filled with smoke. Even my hands were hazy in front of me, blurred by the gray smog of the fire. The fire had climbed the ladder to the hayloft, hungry and eager to devour it, too. When licking flames touched the hay, it sparked like fireworks. The insatiable appetite of fire.

Henry and I pulled again, straining to open the door. There was a creaking sound, and then the trapdoor opened slowly. Cool, fresh air blew through the small door toward us, and we gasped, breathing it in.

We peered through the hole—the drop was a long one that led only to darkness. Behind us a section of the roof collapsed, the burning timbers crashing to the barn floor in an explosion of ash and flames. The fire breathed in like a dragon, spitting and sizzling. And with the fire behind us, there was no choice but to jump into the inky darkness. Henry pushed our packs through the trapdoor, and then looked at me. "Jump," he said fiercely.

I hesitated and then Henry's hands pushed me and I was falling—the air around me cold and clear. I landed hard on the muddy earth beyond the barn. Gasping, I looked up to where I had just fallen from and could barely see the open trapdoor. In the dark night the barn glowed and burned like a terrible furnace—red flames lighting the sky. The rain still fell lightly, but it did nothing to slow the fire. I waited to hear Henry's fall but it didn't happen.

"Henry," I cried out, my voice swallowed in the terrible sounds of crashing timbers. The windows of the barn exploded outward, a bomb of glass and fire, the falling shards like shattering ice around me.

"Henry! Henry!" I screamed. *Please*, I thought, *please let him answer.*

There was still no answer.

"Henry," I screamed again, my voice thick with tears. "Henry! Please! Please!" I fumbled in my pack, frantic to find one of the witch's stones. Grabbing one, I wished: *Please let him get out!*

There was a thud on the ground somewhere in front of me, and I ran toward the sound.

CHAPTER 18

Ravens

I RAN TO THE DARK, still figure on the ground and knelt down. Even in the darkness I could see how pale he was, his face bleached of color.

"Henry?" I whispered his name.

Henry didn't move.

I shook his arm gently. "Are you okay?"

In answer, Henry coughed—a faint, fragile sound that filled me with relief. The wood of the barn hissed and snapped, and there was a crunching noise as another section of the ceiling slowly collapsed. The barn tilted toward us, loomed over us like a terrible breathing serpent, threatening to fall. My heart beat crazily in my chest, but I tried to make my voice sound calm. "We have to go before the rest of the barn falls. Do you think you can walk?"

Still unable to speak, Henry nodded, wheezing; his breathing shallow and weak.

I helped him up and lifted both of our packs onto my back. Then, moving slowly, we backed away from the barn.

Henry's steps were slow and his breathing labored; still, his face wasn't quite as pale. I silently thanked the witch for her wishing stones.

We walked for what seemed like miles, stopping to rest only when the smoke of the burning barn was a whisper of white in the night sky, as if it were only a swirl of chalk on a blackboard, a faint cloud over the moon.

We stopped next to a clear creek; its water tripping and giggling downstream. The night was quiet, only the sounds of the sleepy forest sighed around us. Still, I could hear it: the shivery breath of the fire, the quivering of the hungry flames straining to lick and destroy whatever it could.

Henry and I knelt on the soft moss by the creek bed and dipped our hands into the cold water, cleaning the soot from our arms and faces. Then we drank and drank the creek's cool water. The water soothed our dry throats and washed the taste of fire from our mouths, removing the bitter taste of smoke and ash.

When we had drunk our fill, we sat back on the moss and leaned against our packs, exhausted. I looked at Henry—his eyes were closed and his face was a fragile white in the moon-light. "When you didn't come out, I thought something had happened to you," I whispered.

"Something happened," Henry said, his eyes were still closed, but his body no longer seemed relaxed, the muscles in his body suddenly tense.

"What?"

"When I was about to jump, another part of the roof

collapsed, and I looked back. When I did, I saw a raven." Henry's voice was flat.

I sat up and looked at him: his pale face, and his closed eyes, his clenched fists. "You couldn't have," I said evenly. "A bird could never have been inside the barn. No animal could survive there!"

"I know," Henry said soberly and his large eyes blinked open, "but it did. And when I saw it, for a moment I felt as if something were holding me there. Something wouldn't let me jump. Then I heard you calling me, and it was as if I woke up."

My stomach knotted. "You could have died."

Henry was silent, staring out into the dark forest beyond the creek. With the soft black night all around us, it was hard to believe that just hours ago we had escaped the fire. But I could see the memory of the flames reflected in Henry's eyes.

"We should try to get at least *some* sleep tonight," I said, looking at his drawn face, tight with exhaustion.

Henry nodded but looked uneasy, as if sleep was a new danger to face.

"We'll sleep in shifts," I said quickly. "You sleep first. Then I'll wake you up and you can stand guard while I sleep."

Henry hesitated for a moment.

"It's the only way." I pressed him, "We can't keep going without sleep."

He nodded reluctantly. "You're right. Promise to wake me, though."

I nodded, knowing as I did that I wouldn't wake him.

He fell asleep immediately, though he slept fitfully and

cried out in his sleep all the while, tossing and turning. It is frightening to be alone and awake in darkness—every sound seems dangerous, magnified, every noise could be the step of the enemy, the sharp snap of a breaking twig could be the hard, cold click of a readied weapon, the sliding fall of leaves the sound of a sword drawn from a narrow sheaf. The creek was cheerful though, bouncing and gurgling beside me, as if for company. Still, I lay awake, watchful and wary, my sword at my side, my hand wrapped hard around its handle. Waiting. When daylight began to touch the tips of the trees, Henry woke up, coughing hard. He sat up slowly, his body stiff from the fall from the barn. At first he seemed confused, and then as the memory of the night returned, his face darkened and grew grave. "I hoped it was a nightmare."

I shook my head. "It wasn't."

"You should have woken me up," he said accusingly.

I shrugged. "I wasn't tired," I lied. "Anyway, we're only a day from the palace. I was too excited to sleep."

Henry looked incredulous, but said nothing.

We bathed in the stream, washing away the lingering smell of soot and smoke. Then we ate a silent berry breakfast, collected our packs, and moved instinctively toward the dark trees of the forest, moving deeper into the woods where we would be covered. The raven—if Henry had truly seen one—hadn't found us here along the creek bed, but it was only a matter of time before they realized we weren't in the south, then they would change direction and the skies would again be filled with their small black bodies and sharp cries.

We traveled cautiously, the image of the burning barn

seared in our memory. We moved almost soundlessly, cutting between the whispering wheat of neighboring fields and down the gentle slopes of the path. At daybreak we reached the very back wall of the palace, where huge wooden gates could be opened to allow farmers' wagons onto the palace grounds. The dawn was a dusty blue, almost pale gray, the sky just beginning to be touched with light. In this half-light, we crouched under a lilac bush, its branches a veil around us, watching as one of Count Raven's guardsmen stopped a farmer and his wagon of pumpkins and squash, looking with disinterest at the produce before waving him through the gates.

"How will we get past him?" I whispered.

Henry ran one hand quickly through his curling hair so it stood up in stiff spikes. His face was troubled, then he grinned. "The door in the wall!"

"The what?"

Henry's words tripped over themselves in his excitement. "I found it with Patrick one time when we were playing hide-and-seek. It's along the far wall, about ten feet from the back of Tiege's garden. It's buried under morning glory vines—it would be impossible to spot unless you knew it was there."

I caught his excitement. "Do you think it's still covered?"

"Probably," Henry nodded. "The back wall is miles long, and I know that once when my father sent gardeners to clear it, the vines were so tenacious and the job so difficult that after a month they gave up." Henry smiled. "It's unlikely that Raven's men are so interested in the appearance of the back wall that they would have the persistence to cut those plants down. And anyway, my father decided that the morning glories didn't look so bad after all."

I smiled. "Let's go right now!"

We crept along the back wall of the palace grounds. It was easy to do unseen because the ground was thick with bushes and low plants, and the wall was overgrown with creeping vines. We had walked for close to an hour when suddenly, next to a huge bush, we stopped.

"Is it here?" I asked eagerly, searching the stone wall for signs of a door.

Henry shook his head. "No, not for another quarter mile, I think, but we'll bury our swords here," he drove first his sword and then mine into the soft soil below the bush so only part of their handles stood above the earth, then he quickly covered them with fallen leaves. Our swords hidden, Henry looked down the wall. Without the inside markers of the palace to show Henry how far we'd gone, it was difficult to judge where the door could be hidden, and I began to think that maybe the door was lost forever.

"It shouldn't be far now," Henry said, as if reading my mind. We walked close to the wall, peering at each poking branch as if it might be a doorknob. Finally, Henry pulled on a small, knotted branch, and then turned and smiled at me with relief. "It's here!"

Turning the doorknob, he leaned very slowly on the door, and grinned when it creaked open. It didn't open far, just enough to allow a child to slip through. Henry turned to me. "Let me go in first. That way, if they catch one of us, it's me. But," he added hastily before I could object, "I don't think we're going to be caught. When I'm through, I'll give a dove's call. Tiege's garden is full of those, so it won't be suspicious."

I grinned because Henry's imitation of a cooing dove sounded more like a honking duck. Ignoring my smile, he continued, "Once you're through, run to Tiege's cottage; I don't know why, but I don't think the ravens will be able to follow us there."

"The messenger doves would drive them away."

Henry stifled a laugh. "Or they'd get lost in all the flowers."

"Shhh," I pressed a finger against my lips and smiled too, imagining the ravens lost in Tiege's gardens, which resembled a wild jungle garden more than the formal gardens of the palace.

"And anyway, just in case, you know the garden spell," Henry whispered.

Henry slid through the door and ran. I held my breath, waiting to hear the cries of angry guards or the harsh shrieks of ravens. Instead, moments later, the call of a honking duck filled the air, and smiling, I slipped through the door.

CHAPTER 19

The Book of Spells

TIEGE'S STONE COTTAGE was on the edge of the palace wall, half-buried under climbing ivy, honeysuckle, and lilac. Even in early October, her gardens were arguably the most beautiful on the palace grounds, though unlike the other flowerbeds, they had no order: daisies grew among irises, and sunflowers smiled over the panther-faced pansies. To find Tiege among the blooms meant digging through a maze of flowers and searching carefully for the stone paths, which, like everything else, were half-buried by blossoms and high grass. The challenge was that even if you found a path, it was no guarantee that it would lead you to Tiege.

I slid through the open door of her green garden gate, where Henry waited for me, closing it behind me with a satisfying click. In the sudden safety of her garden we moved cautiously, trying not to trample anything precious, and still half wary of the ravens that we heard screaming and fussing in the trees near the palace.

"Ugh, I hate those birds," I shivered.

Henry nodded, then said in a low voice, "I think you should say the spell now."

"Okay," I closed my eyes trying to remember. I heard Lia laughing: *The rhymes help me remember* . . . In a rush, the words of the spell filled my head:

Blue coriander, rabbit-foot grass,
Bittersweet September: flowers mass.
Winter frozen, spring's rebirth,
Guard with silence, guard with earth.
Summer brings her sun-tipped wand,
Spreads her light to field and pond,
Here let me hide, here let me stay,
Protect and shield me for this day.

I opened my eyes cautiously. Everything seemed the same, but Henry nodded admiringly. "That was good."

"Do you think it will work?"

Henry shrugged and started down the path again. "It can't hurt, and I believe that Tiege has some sort of magic of her own."

"Like what?" I asked, curious.

But before he could answer, Snowy, Tiege's small white dog, appeared, wiggling with excitement and barking a greeting.

I bent down, petting and praising him the way I always did, but Henry clapped his hands sharply.

"Snowy, take us to Tiege," he ordered.

Snowy cocked his head and then, with a worried look, led us through the high grass toward a tangle of late wild roses. Lazy bees buzzed happily above the blooms, carrying away pollen on velvet feet. Nearby, hummingbirds sucked the long stems of lilies as if drinking lemonade through pale green straws. It seemed that Tiege was nowhere to be found, when below the high-waving stems of lavender, we spotted the tip of a straw hat.

"Tiege!" Henry shouted with relief and delight.

The tiny woman turned and smiled, her dark face smudged with streaks of pollen. Snowy jumped and barked with excitement as she hugged us.

I knelt down and gently petted Snowy's soft fur and long ears while Tiege fussed over Henry. "What a good day for a visit!" Tiege twinkled at us, finally letting Henry out of a hug. "Come this way, I've been hoping you two would arrive. Waiting for you, actually."

"Didn't you think we were dead?" Henry asked.

"Not for a minute!" Tiege looked shocked at the idea.

Henry seemed a little disappointed. "Well, I almost did die in a fire," he said importantly.

"*Almost* is not the same as *did*," Tiege scolded. "Now come!"

We followed her deeper into the garden until we reached the shade of an old elm tree where tea for three was set out on a round table. "You knew we were coming!" Henry exclaimed.

"I had a feeling . . . and so as soon as I woke up I began making gingersnaps for Henry and sugar cookies for Amelia."

I eyed the cookies, realizing suddenly that I was ravenous.

Tiege carefully poured out pink lemonade and Henry and I quickly chose cookies, sneaking bites to Snowy who wagged his tail in fierce appreciation. Settling happily into her deep chair, Tiege picked up a tangle of blue wool and began knitting, her needles clicking briskly together as we ate. All of us were quiet, and Henry and I devoured cookie after cookie.

When we slowed our eating, Tiege smiled at us. "Now, one of the reasons you're here is because you're looking for answers, but if I were to guess, you're not sure yet of all the questions. Is that right?" Tiege asked in her cozy voice.

Henry and I looked at each other and nodded.

"Well, eat, and think for a bit."

As we sat munching on cookies, my head swarmed with questions that I wanted—needed—answers to. Before I could ask, Tiege looked at me, her hands paused above her knitting and her black eyes sharp. "You're looking to know what the powers of a White Queen are. For you, that's the most important question, isn't it?"

I nodded.

Tiege sighed. "I thought so. And I wish I could give you an answer, but I can't because I don't know." She looked at us both gravely. "I think, Amelia, that this is an answer that you will need to find on your own."

"That's what the witch of the Night Forest told her," Henry said.

"Hmmm," Tiege murmured, and her face registered no surprise that we had been to see the witch of the Night Forest. Tiege's yarn tumbled from her lap to the soft grass

199

and she smiled at Henry. "Here, love, hand me that. Okay, now," she winked as Henry dropped the yarn deftly back into her lap. "How about I choose a story to tell you?"

We both nodded, our mouths full of cookies.

"All right then, here is the story of the forests."

❦

When Amelia's father, King Bryant, was a young prince, he loved animals—all animals: he would rescue baby birds that he found fallen from their nests and nurse them to health in small boxes by his bed, he would carry ladybugs out of the palace to the safety of the garden so they wouldn't be killed, he spent hours with his pet fox, whom he'd trained as if a little dog. He might have been a veterinarian if he hadn't been meant to be a king.

On the prince's thirteenth birthday his father gave him the same gift he had given the young prince's older brothers: he promised him anything he wanted. "It is an open wish. Name what you want—anything—and you shall have it!" The king said grandly.

The prince was very excited by his father's gift, for there were a great many things he wanted: cake for every meal, flying machines, another pony, a driving sleigh—he could think of dozens of things he wanted!

However, although he was still young, he was a wise prince, and he decided to save his wish. A wish this large needed thought, and the prince knew it was not a gift to take lightly.

That year the prince's birthday happened to fall on the day of the Great Hunt. The Great Hunt was the first day of hunting season, and all the men in the country celebrated this day with much excitement. At the palace, the royal family and most of the village celebrated the day with their own hunt followed by a huge meal in the palace's great hall.

Because the prince was now thirteen, his father decided that he could join the men on the hunt, and the young prince was very eager to prove that this was a privilege he deserved. At breakfast his mother had presented him with a new green bow and eight gold-tipped arrows. At thirteen, the prince was an excellent marksman, and many believed that the young prince would soon be a better hunter than his father and brothers, for his eyes were so sharp, his arm so steady, and his aim so precise that he rarely missed his target.

Outside, the stablemen held horses for the palace hunters to mount, and the hunting dogs barked with excitement. It was a crisp fall day—a light breeze blew and the leaves above them were a chattering canopy of gold and red and green. A perfect day, the men agreed, for a hunt. The men on horseback spread out, and the king announced that the hunting party would meet back at the great hall at noon. And with that announcement a trumpet sounded, signaling that the hunt had begun. The young prince began the hunt with his father and the royal advisors, but soon he found himself alone in the wood. In the distance, he could hear the cries of baying dogs in pursuit of game, and the laughter and shouts of men, and it made him smile to hear the hunt was on. Standing there, the prince imagined himself entering the great hall with his kill, and the look of admiration on his father's proud face.

On the edge of the embankment he had his chance. There stood the largest stag he had ever seen. It was a beautiful animal, and regal, his coat the color of thick chocolate and his antlers the color of the new snow. Such an animal would certainly be a prize. But as the prince lifted his bow, the stag turned and stared at him unflinchingly with his clear eyes, and the prince suddenly felt flushed with shame. *What right did he have to kill such an animal for sport? To kill just for the pleasure of boasting?* The prince lowered his bow and snapped his arrows across his knees, and the stag, undisturbed, turned away from the boy and moved deeper into the forest.

When the prince returned to the great hall, it was half past noon and the hall was filled with the merry voices of men excited by the hunt, and the clanking sound of plates and silverware being passed. On a platform above the villagers sat the king, the older princes, and the royal advisors; like the rest of the men, they too were laughing and joking about the morning's excitement.

The young prince did not stop to say hello to his friends as he passed through the hall, nor did he respond when someone called out asking how his new bow was. Instead the boy went straight to his father, the king; walked quickly through the great hall until he stood before him. Although he shook, his voice was steady. "I have come for my birthday wish, Father."

A hush fell over the hall. *What would the prince wish for? Gold? Silver? Palaces? Islands?*

His father nodded. "So long as it is within my power, your wish shall be granted."

"I wish . . . I wish that there will never again be a great hunt, and that animals in the country of Sarao be killed only for necessity, and never for sport."

Now a murmur went up in the hall, and the murmur soon became a roar of outrage. The king was a great sportsman, and he had killed some of the country's largest boars and bears. He had hunted the country's greatest pheasants, fiercest cats, most beautiful peacocks. "Surely," the men in the hall said to each other, "the king will not end hunting, he would not grant such a foolish request to a child."

It is true that the king was an excellent marksman, but he was also just and honest. He studied his son. "I have given my word, and you shall have your wish. So be it: there is to be no further hunting for sport in the country of Sarao, by order of the prince."

Years later, when this young prince was a young man, he fell in love with Princess Charlotte, who would one day rule her country of Gossling as queen. Because he was the fifth and youngest prince, he would never be king of Sarao, but with his marriage he became king of Gossling and ruled the kingdom with his wife. There were many laws of Sarao that the young king thought silly, or thought made sense for his old kingdom, but not his new one, but with Queen Charlotte's agreement, his first order as king of Gossling was the same as his first order as prince of Sarao.

And this is why the woods and streams of Gossling are some of the world's most beautiful, for no animal is endangered, no bird is shot at, none is hunted for sport, none is ever threatened.

"I chose this story for a reason: the animals of this country are your allies," Tiege said gravely. "Your friends are all around you," she gestured around the garden and suddenly it seemed to hum with life: there were rabbits nibbling on lettuce, swallows carrying straw and strands of colored yarn toward a nest, a small hedgehog running along a border of yellow marigolds. Two larks splashed in a birdbath. Snowy wagged his tail, his eyes hopeful as he watched Henry munch a cookie.

"Remember that—in a time like this, it is important to know who your friends are. Now," Tiege said, turning to me and smiling slightly, "you have not come here only to see me. Go to Merrill. I have told her you are coming, and she waits by the water for you. Go quickly and return quickly, for it is dangerous." Tiege stood up and handed me a small garden trowel and a large floppy hat.

I looked at her blankly.

"It's a disguise," Tiege said, and grinned. "Pretend you're gardening at the lake. That will attract far less attention than a child simply talking to a tree. And should you see me crossing the lawn with my gardening basket, it is a sign for you to return to the cottage at once."

I approached the lake from Tiege's side gate. From there it was a quick run to where Merrill stood, trapped. As I closed the gate solidly behind me, I could see the cluster of willow trees near the water's edge, and knew—even from far away—which one was Merrill. For even as a tree, my sister was regal.

I ran to her, and fought the urge to wrap my arms around the dark, rough trunk. When Merrill spoke my name I wasn't surprised, as I had been when Lily and Rose had first spoken as swans; instead, hearing Merrill's voice, I thought I might cry with relief. It's selfish, I know, but I couldn't help feeling that Merrill would somehow fix everything.

"Amelia." Merrill's voice was also thick with tears. "You're safe!"

I knelt down on the ground next to her roots as Tiege had instructed, pretending that I was there simply to garden. "Merrill—," I began, but I couldn't find the words I wanted. I didn't want to tell her how scared I was, or how frightened I was that I wouldn't be able to save her, the twins, and the kingdom. Didn't want to tell her how uncertain everything felt.

Before I could say anything Merrill spoke, her voice fast and almost breathless as if there was much she needed to say and little time to say it. "Tiege will tell you about Lily and Rose and Theo and Dori, but I should explain about the prophecies."

"Prophecies?" I echoed stupidly.

Merrill's voice was edged with impatience. "Uncle Raven has announced our deaths to the kingdom, but many believe you are still alive and that you will reveal yourself only after three prophecies have been fulfilled: that the rivers and lakes will be crossed without bridge or boat or ice, that haloes of light will crown the mountains, and that a night sky will turn white."

"What?" Confused, I looked up from where I was digging.

Merrill groaned. "I know, it's ridiculous, but there it is. Amelia, you'll have to find a way to lead the people, otherwise the kingdom will be destroyed. Count Raven is a terribly dangerous man, and he is intent on devastating our country and murdering our people. Others will help you stop him, but only you can lead and only you can break the spell that traps us."

"But there are only two spells I know, and I don't think either of them would help us."

"There's a book in the palace," Merrill hesitated. "It's in Mother's library. It is red and nondescript and looks like a dictionary, but it's not—it's some kind of history book. In it is the history of the White Queens, but also histories of all sorts of other things. And Amelia, I think it's important. I think it has spells in it."

"Spells?"

Merrill's voice grew softer, as if she feared the very grass leaned in to listen, to share her secret. "There is some magic in that book. I know it."

"How do you know?" I found myself whispering as well.

"When I was nine or ten, I was reading with Mother in the garden, when she asked me to go to her library and get her a dictionary. So I ran inside to the library and there on the center of Mother's desk a huge book was split open. Assuming it was the dictionary, I went over to it. But it wasn't a dictionary—the book was filled with strange illustrations.

"I had read only part of a page when Mother entered the room. She was across the room in an instant, and she snapped the book closed and said it wasn't for small eyes. But Amelia, here's the funny part: I have always believed Mother left the book open for me to find."

"What did it say?" I put down the trowel.

"Nothing that I could understand."

"What about the pictures?"

"The pictures were strange because they seemed real, almost alive, quivering on the page as if waiting to be spoken to, or waiting to speak."

"Did you think they were really alive?" I could feel my breath quicken with excitement.

Merrill laughed. "No, I don't think this was a book that one could jump into, or one where paintings might jump out. But I do think that this book was alive in a different way."

"What do you mean?"

Merrill said slowly, "I think it was alive in the sense that it had so much to tell. The pictures were of three women standing in a circle, and there was a light that seemed to come from them, or maybe it was just painted that way."

"A light like they were glowing?" I felt impatience wiggle inside me, trying to understand.

"I can't explain it—it just seemed as though there was a light that they had created, or they were a part of."

"They must have been White Queens," I said reasonably.

"That's what I assume now. That's why I think the book is important."

"I'm going to go get the book," I said, and stood up.

"No." Merrill's voice was sharp. "It's far too dangerous. There must be another way to get the book—a safer way. And if there is not, then the secrets of the book will remain just that. Secrets."

From the corner of my eye, I saw Tiege crossing the lawn carrying a gardening basket and pruning shears. She nodded at me, and I remembered our signal.

"I have to go," I whispered to Merrill. I picked up the gardening basket that was lying carelessly beside me, and quickly stuffed the small rake and trowel into them before standing. "I'll think of a way to get the book."

"Amelia," Merrill called after me as I ran to the white gate of Tiege's garden, but if she said anything else, I couldn't hear her. Breathless, I lifted one hand to wave to her, then stepped through the gate and was swallowed by the flowers.

❧

Over dinner that night I told the story of the three prophecies and explained what Merrill had told me about the book she had seen in the library. Henry's eyes were wide, listening, and then his face clouded over.

He put down his fork with a bang, his face dark with irritation. "Of all the books I read from that library, why didn't I read that one?"

Tiege chuckled, and then looked serious. "I imagine that book wasn't meant to be read by either of you. It was meant to one day be read and studied by Merrill. After all, it is Merrill who is meant to be Gossling's queen."

I remembered what Mother had told Merrill on the last day we had seen her: *You were born to be queen.* I looked down at the plate before me, and suddenly I couldn't eat any more. I sat remembering how life had been just weeks, months, years before: Mother and Father teaching Merrill, helping her, shaping her, so that she could one day be queen of Gossling. And now—now—it seemed like Gossling would not have the queen they had been promised, nor any queen at all.

"It is clear that we must get the book," Tiege said suddenly. "The book could be necessary, somehow, and we must find a way to get it."

"How?" Henry asked.

Tiege shook her head mysteriously. "Let us finish our dinner, and think. I don't yet know how, but someone must get into the library and find it."

Henry

Morning slid into the room, the sun stretching her arms wide to hug the walls and floor, making the room bright. I blinked awake. Down the hall, I heard the sound of a door shutting softly. I climbed out of bed and walked quietly from my room to the kitchen. Tiege stood at the table, a cloth bag before her. She smiled at me. "Did my sweetest godson sleep well?"

I nodded. "Very well."

Tiege lifted the bag from the table. "This is for you."

I wrapped my arms around the soft parcel, and sat on the edge of one of the blue-painted chairs, yawning.

Tiege's eyes twinkled. "A favor, please, sleepyhead."

I stifled another yawn. "Of course."

"In my kitchen garden, guarded by a den of bunnies, you'll find weeping lantana, toad flax, and hawk's beard. I need a bit of each."

I rubbed my eyes in confusion. "The flowers?"

Tiege bobbed her head. "The pink ones, all next to each other."

"Why those?"

Tiege smiled mysteriously. "Never mind. Just take the scissors, please, and cut me some."

The kitchen garden was defined by a low stone wall. Unlike Tiege's other gardens, this one had some order. Vegetables grew in tidy rows, and neat poles and green yarn held the tomato plants tall and straight. Herbs marched in perfect precision along one wall of the garden, and the back wall was bordered with the flowers, from which Tiege was able to coax mysterious cures. These flowers, with their whimsical names, when mixed with herbs could be transformed into sleeping potions, or aids to soothe poison ivy, or scents that kept skunks from spraying. As a child I had been warned again and again never to eat such a flower. "A flower is not food!" Tiege had told me a million times, and although they never passed my lips, I knew their power.

This early in the morning the garden was dusted wet with dew. The sun was still new to the sky and her warmth had not yet reached the garden; all around me the air was crisp, reminding me that autumn had arrived. On the garden's edge a shy fawn and her mother stood still as statues, and then, startled perhaps by my watching eyes, bounded away, their long white tails waving like flags behind them. Birds scolded from the birdbaths, chattering to each other as they dipped noisily into the water. It might have been any ordinary morning. I made my way over to the flowers and snipped quickly, all the while aware of the small den of sleeping bunnies tucked under the roots of the lemon tree, their pale pink noses just visible. I moved softly, careful not to wake them.

Back inside, I placed the flowers by the sink and kissed Tiege, who was stirring a chocolate batter. "Is this going to be for breakfast?" I asked hopefully, reaching in a finger to swipe some batter.

"This is for later, and *not* for eating," Tiege said, batting my hand away. "Breakfast will be ready soon enough, now take that off the table and into your room." With her mixing spoon she pointed to the bag.

I saluted her, and she waved me away, bending over the bowl again, one hand plucking the pale petals from a blossom of hawk's beard and sprinkling in a handful.

In my room, I opened the cloth bag. The bag smelled slightly of fresh hay, and inside it were Patrick's barn clothes. Stripping out of my pajamas, I pulled them on hastily. Although Patrick was only six months older than I was, he was taller and broader. His clothes were big on me, and ill-fitting, but looking at myself in the hallway mirror I saw that I looked like a stable boy in them. I studied myself, considering, and decided that something was missing. Even in Patrick's musty clothes, even with the smell of hay and horses on my body, I still somehow looked too clean, didn't look quite convincing enough. From the hall, I ducked out the side door and into the kitchen garden. Poised over a ruffled edge of lettuce, her small nose twitching daintily, a rabbit looked up at me, first startled, and then quizzical. I bent down next to a neat row of tomatoes and dug my fingers into the moist soil, smearing some of it over one cheek. The rabbit observed this small transformation and returned to her breakfast. I entered the cottage through the kitchen door, ready to see Tiege bent over the oven, but the kitchen was empty and warm and smelled of baking muffins. There was no sign of the bowl of chocolate batter, but a bowl of new eggs sat on the table, and the pink flowers I had cut still lay by the sink waiting for water. I peered into the small mirror below the clock: I would pass for a stable boy. Staring at my reflection, I took a deep breath, reassured.

Tiege appeared soundlessly, smiling at me in the mirror. "Just one more thing." She placed a battered cap on my head and pulled it securely over my dark curls. "Now you look perfect."

I took another deep breath and turned to face her. "You think so?"

Tiege nodded, then her brow wrinkled with worry. "If you don't feel comfortable with this, you must not go."

I shook my head and smiled at her. "I'll go."

Tiege nodded, "Well, then let's get some breakfast into

you." She moved toward the oven and peered inside, checking on the baking muffins, then she filled a pot with water and lit the stove beneath it to boil. I went to the drawer and pulled out napkins and silverware, and began setting the table. Although I had always eaten most of my meals at the palace, each weekend I ate breakfast with Tiege, and this had been our breakfast routine for as long as I could remember: Tiege baking fresh muffins and boiling soft eggs while I readied the table. Tiege hummed as she cooked, and now she turned and gave me one of her special smiles, the one meant only for me. Except for the stable clothes, and the stiff stripe of mud across my cheek, it might have been any morning.

Then Amelia entered the kitchen, nervous as a cat and pale, destroying any illusion that this was a regular morning.

❧

Her breakfast almost untouched on the table, Amelia paced the room, walking it up and down in tight circles, anxious. "I should be doing this," she said, and glared at me.

I ignored her and reached for another muffin. We'd had this conversation three times already, and the plan was still the same. I was to slip into the palace, up the back stairs, and into the queen's library. There, I would find the book Merrill had described to Amelia and escape with it. If I was caught, I was to say that I was looking for an equestrian book that Queen Charlotte had allowed me to borrow before. Not that I meant to get caught.

"Punishment could be severe," Tiege had warned the

night before. "There are only a handful of children still on the palace grounds, and the count has had them whipped for everything from not running quickly enough to being too weak to hold that beast of a horse he has."

"I'm not afraid," I had lied, staring into the ends of the fire.

In the fireplace, the logs cracked and burned, and for a long moment the room was quiet. Then Tiege had smiled gently. "There's no shame in being frightened when there is something to fear."

I had stretched then and grinned at her, admitting, "I'm a little afraid."

Tiege grinned back at me. "Good boy!"

But Amelia hadn't smiled. Instead she said soberly, "I'm very afraid. *Very. Very.* And I don't think you should do it."

But I was doing it. And now, as we had planned so carefully, I walked casually into the palace kitchen. The kitchen was empty, and I felt a flash of relief, not quite ready to use the prepared lie. Then, moving quickly, I crossed through the narrow pantry and crept up the back stairs of the palace. They were servants' stairs, but Amelia and I had used them often, for from our classroom they were the most direct route to the kitchen, which we had frequently raided during lesson breaks. Wary of Cook's wrath, and never certain whether she would be in the kitchen or not, we knew the stairs well, knew how to avoid every creak and groan. Now I went up them soundlessly. I reached the top of the staircase, and opened the door quietly, slipping into the hallway. We had agreed that if I seemed to be at all uncomfortable, seemed at all guilty, that it would raise immediate suspicion. So I walked as confidently and slowly as I could down the long, long hall to Queen Charlotte's library.

The palace seemed deserted, unnaturally quiet. Always before there had been the bustling of servants, the clatter of pots and pans from the kitchen, the singing of the maids as they moved from room to room dusting, and the light sound of running feet as the pages ran up and down the stairs with messages. A palace like a beehive—alive and humming. Now it was too quiet.

I walked as silently as I could without actually tiptoeing, my feet padding softly on the floor. It wasn't my feet that would give me away, I thought grimly to myself, it would be the sound of my heart, which was pounding so loudly that I was sure it would betray me. I imagined guards rushing from their stations, searching for the boy whose heart beat like an escaped tennis ball, bouncing and bouncing through the marble halls.

In the library, I walked directly to the left corner. There— I knew—was a small collection of horse books. They were mostly picture books, wide books of illustrations and photographs, and they hadn't been touched in years and years, not since the six-year-old twins had transferred their love of horses to ballet. Yet the queen had kept them still and now I chose one quickly. I selected a tall, thick book that pictured a rearing stallion on its cover, his muscled legs mahogany and the mountains green behind him. Having safely secured a decoy book, I began to search for the book that Merrill had once seen. My eyes scanned the room—the walls were practically wallpapered with bookshelves. The book could be anywhere. I closed my eyes and tried to imagine where such a book would be kept. And then I knew: Queen Charlotte would have hidden the book in plain sight, but where it would be overlooked by most adults.

I crossed the room quickly, my feet silent on the blue rug. The room held four window seats, and under each were the picture books the princesses had read with their mother when they were very young. They were a mottled collection of books, and only a mother would have thought to save them, for these much-loved books held torn pages smudged by jelly and small dirty fingers, they had been colored in and left in the rain, they had missing pages and covers that had long ago been lost. I crouched down in front of the window seat Merrill had favored and began to search. I ran my fingers over the spines of those books she had read: tall books, skinny books, books with no covers, ripped bindings, and then—there between two books of fairy tales was a book with a pale red leather binding. My heart quickened, and I pulled it out. The book cover was the same dull red, and there was no jacket cover. I flipped the book open and saw narrow script. And as I did, I heard footsteps in the hall.

I stuffed the red book swiftly between my belt and stomach, praying that the belt would hold. Then I stood and stepped quickly into the room's center, the horse book clutched in my hands just as a guard pushed the door open.

The guard was a young man in a black uniform. He had

a thick brutish face, his skin pockmarked and his eyes too small. He had greasy, coarse black hair, and when he smiled a slow mean smile at me, he revealed missing teeth. A large stick hung from his belt.

"Looking for something?" he growled.

CHAPTER 20

Caught

Amelia

Tiege's tiny kitchen was warm with heat from the oven and streaming sunlight. Even with both the windows and the door to the garden open, the smell of baking chocolate was strong. I sighed and looked again at the clock. Henry had been gone for thirty-four minutes. In eleven minutes, we were to assume that something had gone wrong.

Tiege pulled another batch of cookies from the oven, and with practiced hands, began to transfer them onto a cooling rack.

"Amelia." She turned to me, smiling. "Won't you please line one of those baskets with a napkin?"

I nodded, and wordlessly went to the back porch where baskets of all shapes hung on colored ribbon from the ceiling. I lifted one down and carried it back to the kitchen, where I lined the basket with a pink cloth napkin. Forcing myself not to look at the clock.

Tiege carried the cooling racks to the table and smiled at me. "Now let's get some of these cookies into the basket."

Together we packed the basket with warm cookies and when it was filled, Tiege pulled a yellow checked napkin over the top, tucking the edges in neatly. Then she stepped back and smiled again, admiring her work. "Perfect!"

Tiege took off her apron, hanging it neatly on the hook before going to the sink and rinsing her floured hands with water. She glanced distractedly at her reflection in the mirror, ran one hand over her dark hair to smooth it before turning to me and smiling, "I'm off!" Then she lifted the basket, tucked the handle under her arm, and walked toward the door.

"Where are you going?" I asked, my voice rusty with fear. I stood up and followed her from the kitchen.

Tiege stepped onto the porch. "To the palace, of course. I'm going to deliver some cookies." She winked at me and walked out into her wild garden.

I followed her down the winding path, almost running to keep up with her. "Shouldn't I go instead?"

Tiege didn't stop walking or even turn to look at me. "Don't be foolish, Amelia," she said mildly, though her voice held a slight edge. Then she slowed, and looked over her shoulder at me and her voice softened, "And don't worry, we'll be back before you know it. Now, go back to the cottage and wait for us there."

With nothing else to do, I went back to the cottage. I walked into the bright empty kitchen and looked at the clock. Henry had been gone for forty-six minutes. I wiped the counters down with a sponge, carefully washed the cookie sheets, and then dried them until they shone. Finding a stiff broom, I swept the floor, and then when the kitchen sparkled and there was nothing left to clean, I went out into the kitchen garden and sat on the steps. I could hear the clock in the kitchen ticking steadily on, each second building to a minute, and each minute turning into another minute where Henry didn't come home. Fear sat, heavy as lead, in my stomach.

The garden was quiet. I watched as a snail made its slow way across the curving dirt path, leaving a silver train behind it like a bride. A small green snake was curled up on a warm stone, sleeping. In the kitchen, the clock ticked another minute. From the edge of lettuce patch a small rabbit gazed solemnly at me and seemed to ask the question that kept running again and again though my head: *What if he doesn't come back?*

"I don't know what I'll do," I said aloud to the garden.

And the trees around me, rustling in the wind, seemed to bob their heads in agreement.

Henry

The guard grabbed me roughly by the neck, his other hand like a paw against my throat. "Drop the book, boy!"

I dropped it. The book fell to the floor with a thump, and the guard glanced down at it, his eyes taking in the horse and the mountain. "Stealing from King Raven is a crime," he growled.

I made my eyes wide, innocent. "I—I wasn't stealing, sir. Queen Charlotte always let me look at the horse books."

The guard looked around slowly. "I don't see anyone named Queen Charlotte here. Do you?"

"No sir."

"Maybe I don't see very well." He was enjoying himself now. He loosened his grip on my throat and pretended to look behind a love seat. "Oh, Queen Charlotte!" he called. "Are you there?" He cupped one hand around his ear, as if listening for an answer. Hearing none, he turned back to me, his mouth curled into an angry smile. "I guess she's not here anymore. Remember this, boy: the only royalty in Gossling is King Raven."

I bobbed my head down, as if with respect. "Long live King Raven!" The words burned my tongue, but the guard was pacified.

"Idiot boy. Only now you remember your king!" He snorted, but his tone was less murderous. He lifted the horse book from the floor and gestured to the walls surrounding us. "This all belongs to King Raven now. Any arrangement you had with Queen Charlotte is as dead as she is. Understood?"

I nodded.

The man put his face close to mine. His breath was rotten, and his beady eyes were small and bright. "You'll remember all right! You'll remember because you're going to be sorry you ever stepped one dirty foot into this palace. I'm about to teach you a lesson you won't soon forget!"

The guard grabbed my arm roughly, and half dragged me

from the library, then—his hand still a tight steel band around my arm, he guided me down the servants' steps. I could feel sweat beading along my forehead, and under the cap, my hair was suddenly wet with fear. The guard marched me through the small pantry, and into the large kitchen, where I almost wept with relief, for there stood Tiege.

She stood in the center of the kitchen, a basket of chocolate cookies over her arm, the smell of them making the room warm and cozy. Her face held a befuddled expression, as if she were confused about where to place her gift, or whom to give it to. When she saw the guard, her face became reverent and respectful, as if she recognized that he was a man who could give an order.

The guard sniffed the air like a feral animal, and smiled indulgently at Tiege. "You brought food, old woman?"

Tiege curtsied low before him. "Yes, General. I thought that with the kitchen staff reduced, the guards and officers might wish for snacks and find none."

The guard puffed a little at the idea that he'd been mistaken for a general, and his grip on me loosened. Tiege curtsied again. "The previous queen especially fancied these cookies."

His fingers still around my arm, the guard reached out one rude hand and snatched a handful of cookies. He stuffed them greedily into his mouth. "Good!" he exclaimed, his mouth full.

Tiege looked at me as if she were just seeing me, and her voice turned sharp, scolding. "The blacksmith is here, boy! You should have been down in the stables ten minutes ago!"

The guard growled, as if just remembering that I was there. "Making all sorts of mistakes this morning, lad!"

Tiege nodded as if this came as no surprise to her. Her eyes narrowed. "You're sure to get beat within inches of your life. I'm sure half the stable is searching for you."

The guard grunted, and then laughed, his mouth full of cookies. "I'll leave the beating to them then—save me the trouble." He roughly shoved me toward the door. "Get out of here—and don't let your boots muddy the halls again or I'll beat you until you're no use to anyone in the stables."

He took the basket from Tiege, and stuffed another fistful of cookies into his mouth, smiling. "Thank you kindly for these." He grunted, and then grinned, his teeth covered with chocolate. "I'll be sure to share with the others, if I don't eat them all. Who shall I say brought them, and what are these perfect cookies called?"

Tiege smiled her lovely smile. "Why, they're called the Queen's Favor, General."

The guard grinned again and dug into the basket for another handful of cookies. "Favor indeed! Delicious!" Then the man glared at me. "Still here, boy? I ordered you gone! Want that beating now? If not, then go!"

I left the kitchen on a run, letting the door slam behind me, ran across the lawn and down past the old apple orchard as if heading to the stables, ran like the wind, but then, on the edge of the wood, I doubled back and ran towards the far wall of Tiege's garden. There I slid through an almost invisible door covered with climbing ivy. I shut the gate behind me with a hard click and stood panting, Tiege's garden blossoming around me. A rabbit twitched his ears at me in welcome, and I realized with a start that I was safe. I sank to my knees, my legs quivering, and my heart beating hard against my ribs. I lifted my shirt and took out the queen's book.

CHAPTER 21

The Wrong Book

Amelia

It was a medium-sized book, the size of a large journal, nondescript and faded red with slender leather ties that could bind the book closed. Nothing extraordinary. Yet the pages were not the ordinary paper pages usually found in books; they were heavier—almost like canvas—as though the bookbinder had wanted them to last forever without the danger of turning to yellowed, brittle pages that could crumble at the touch.

Sitting together at the kitchen table, Henry opened the book carefully; turning first one page and then another. He looked at me, disappointment written on his face. "It's not the Book of Magic."

"What is it then?" I gently slid the book closer to me, and looked at it curiously. I opened to the first page. "It looks like a kind of diary or journal." I read the first page aloud, a page of curling script, each letter carefully formed and round as ripe plums.

225

5 December

Every day the baby grows heavier in me. The royal doctors are sure that the baby is a boy, and Father—still hoping for a male heir—agrees. I keep my counsel to myself, yet I know that this child is a girl, and that I shall name her Charlotte Claire. Dori, Lia, and I have dreamed her, and we, all of us, believe that she will be the only heir of Gossling. Poor Father, we do not see any male heirs in Gossling's future—there shall be no grandsons to run and hunt with, no boy to set a crown upon. No matter, though. Gossling has always been a kingdom of queens, and I rather think Father prefers girls anyway, whether he knows it or not. And Father need not worry if my sisters bear no children, for the line will continue—this unborn child shall have her own children. I see them in my mind's eye: sisters in a garden, running almost too fast to count them all: one, two, three, and, I think, perhaps a fourth.

Henry interrupted my reading, his words tripping over themselves in his excitement. "Amelia, your grandmother wrote that when she was pregnant with your mother! Don't you see? That unborn baby, Charlotte Claire, grows up to be your mother, Queen Charlotte! And it means that those girls in the garden are Merrill, Lily, Rose, and you!"

I nodded, my eyes still moving slowly across the page. "Listen," I ordered.

For five nights in a row I have had the same terrible dream: the kingdom of Gossling torn by war, with only a child to save it. And each night I have woken up sweating and shivering, because the dream ends before the fate of the kingdom is determined. Still, all day the dream follows me. A dream like a shadow on my mind: Dori, Lia, and I discussed it for hours today, but we cannot make sense of it. It's frustrating because always when I wake, the dream is slipping away, and I am left only with the memory of blood and fire and flashing silver. Left only with the image of two children by the village fountain. That's all— then I wake up, feel the infant stirring in my stomach, feel my body near rigid with fear, the taste of steel in my mouth, my spine tingling, as if it had been striped with the dull blade of a sword. Warning me.

I sit up in the darkened room and drink the cool water next to my bed. Water does little to calm my racing heart, but then I touch one hand to my stomach and feel her—the baby strong and kicking below my hand.

Lia, whose powers are stronger than my own, does not believe the dream to be a warning; she believes it to be a premonition, a picture of what is to come for Gossling. As such, she says we must prepare, must arm ourselves with whatever knowledge we can gather, for should that dark night come when two children crouch next to a village fountain, waiting to save the kingdom or not, they must have every gift, every lesson, every power we can give them.

7 December

The dream did not come last night, but another one did—a different one—one I shall not share with Dori or Lia. I do not believe that both the baby and I can survive her birth. In my dream I saw that there was a choice: that only one life could live, not both. Tomorrow at first light I shall travel to the witch of the Night Forest and I shall beg her for her magic, beg her for owl clover, that pink flower that, when eaten, shall allow the baby to pass unharmed into this world, even as the mother leaves it.

Dori and Lia would never allow for such a sacrifice, but neither of them has carried a child, warm as a winter dove, under their hearts. Neither of them have felt the flutter of another heartbeat beating in their bodies, nor felt the rush of small feet drumming against their stomach walls. They could not understand what it would mean to die for someone whose face you have only seen in dreams. And they could not allow me to die, any more than I could ever allow them to. No, I shall not tell them this dream.

We all believe that this baby is the only baby

that shall be born of us three, that there shall be no other. And so this is the other reason that this child must live—she is the child who shall grow up to bear those sisters dreamed of in a bright garden. And one of those sisters, I believe, shall be the girl by the fountain, the child who shall fight to save the kingdom.

I set the book down gently on the wooden table and looked with full eyes at Henry. He looked somberly back at me. "She chose to die so your mother could live."

I nodded, and glanced down at the open book again, wondering at the sacrifice made by a grandmother I never knew. A woman who would not live to know her daughter, knew only that she wanted her daughter to live so much that she would die for her. For her and for Gossling.

"Do you think all parents are like that?" I asked Henry.

He pushed his hair back from his forehead. "I think so," he said slowly. "Maybe not all, but probably most."

I thought of Henry's mother, and wondered if she had made a similar sacrifice in the moments when he was born, choosing his life over her own. "I think so too," I said. "I wonder if her sisters ever found out what she was planning." I turned to the next page, but Elizabeth had written nothing more.

However, hers was not the book's last entry. On the next page the handwriting had changed; it was now the neat, small print that I recognized as Dori's.

1 February

All the kingdom weeps. As she knew she would,
Elizabeth died this morning in childbirth. The
baby, Charlotte Claire, is a healthy one, and her
gray eyes are the eyes of her mother. As of this
writing, Father has refused to see the child, as he
blames her for Elizabeth's death. But the infant
was blameless, only Elizabeth could choose, and
it was never a choice: she would not allow the
baby to die. This child shall be queen, as
Elizabeth was meant to be queen. When Father
is no longer able to rule, then Lia and I shall rule
Gossling for her until the day that she is old
enough to rule the kingdom herself. Charlotte
Claire. Princess Charlotte. Queen Charlotte.
May she be fair and kind. May she have
confidence and mercy. Strength and pity.
Intelligence and love.

I stopped reading and swallowed hard, thinking to myself that all the traits Dori and Lia had wished for Mother,
she had been blessed with. All those traits and so many
more.

"Is that all Dori wrote?" Henry peered over my shoulder.
Carefully, I turned the book's pages. "No."

The entries went on and on, although the handwriting al-
ternated, written sometimes in Dori's tight, neat print and
sometimes in Lia's loose, rambling script. The journal was a
record of their lives and of the kingdom, a braid that could no

more be separated than a queen and her people. The pages were full: there were finance charts, detailed accounts about fall harvests, and carefully recorded statistics about water levels. There were entire entries devoted to baby Charlotte's food intake, and to the charming things she said and did; how she was the apple of her grandfather's eye. There were funny sketches of a child who looked like Mother turning somersaults in the sunken garden. There were silly drawings of this same child sitting with a tame fox on a bench in the statue garden. There was a long entry about the country's 800th birthday celebration, which we learned was celebrated by the entire kingdom, with the tower lights that nestled on the four mountaintops lit, orchestras playing until their strings broke. Everyone danced and danced, the chefs made the fountains run with chocolate, a cake-decorating contest was held and bakers from all over the country came to showcase their work, and the children of the palace were given the job of sampling them all. We read with sadness about the old king's illness and death. Page after page detailing the daily life of an extraordinary kingdom doing ordinary things. Time passed, and on the day of Mother's coronation as queen of Gossling, Lia had written only:

This is a day of great joy, not only for Charlotte and for all of our kingdom, but selfishly, a day of quieter joy for me and for Dori, for we were never meant to be burdened with a crown or a kingdom. We pass that delicate circlet of gold happily to Charlotte, that thin crown that weighs so heavily on me shall be light on her head.

On a fresh page, nearly twenty-five years later, Mother had written her first entry in this book of histories.

3 April
The plague continues and now I am certain that some evil is behind it. Caused by something—someone—unknown and unseen, but remembered still. We shall fight it until it kills us, though I believe we shall kill it first.

I looked at Henry numbly, unable to continue, those words echoing terribly in my head: *we shall fight it until it kills us . . .*

Henry slid the book in front of him and read quickly, his eyes skimming across sentence after sentence, paragraph after paragraph, page after page, that detailed the long accounts of the plague's progression across Gossling. There was a hastily drawn map that charted the spread of the disease, and a terrible record of the lives lost to the plague. Page after page after page of names. I flipped to the journal's last page, and as I read I sucked in my breath hard.

Amelia, if you are reading this, then I am dead.

My eyes filled with tears, and I could hear my mother's voice speaking to me, reading what she had written.

You were my last child, Amelia, my final daughter and so great a gift. In many ways you have been my greatest challenge and my greatest joy, and it pains me that I will not be there to watch you grow up as I once imagined I would. But I am always with you, Amelia.

I know that if you have found this book, then you are looking for the Book of Spells. We destroyed it, and it would not have helped you anyway. What power you have, lies within you.

I am ill now, and with death so near I am free to imagine the lives of you all. There is so much I wanted to tell you, to teach you—be respectful and kind. Be brave—find courage in doing what is right, even if you act alone. Be as truthful and as true to yourself as you are able. Merrill, I write this advice to you too, but for you—my first child—the choices of your life were not spread so widely before you. For you were born to be queen. Born to it. Not every first child is. Your father was the youngest of five boys, and it was his middle brother who was meant to rule Sarao, not the oldest. This is not true for Gossling: it is you.

Fight for this, all of you.

Henry read her last sentence aloud:

Five times over: Love. Love. Love. Love. Love.

"Is that all?" I wondered.

Henry turned the page. "No, there's something else, but I don't know what it is."

233

We studied the strange seal together—made of red wax and copper, it seemed to show a picture, but of what, it was hard to tell. I closed the book gently.

I sighed. "I'll tell Merrill we couldn't find it."

Henry sighed too and looked sorry. "Maybe I should go back into the palace tomorrow."

I shook my head. "It's too risky, and besides, the book is gone—Mother wrote it had been destroyed."

Henry leaned back in his chair, his face stubborn. "Maybe she wrote that so that if the wrong person found this book they would stop searching for the Book of Spells. But I think the Book of Spells is in the library, that I didn't look in the right place."

In my head I knew it was too dangerous for Henry to go back into the palace, after all, he had just barely escaped. I also knew that telling him he couldn't go would make him all the more determined to, so instead I shrugged. "Let me ask Merrill first. She might have thought of another place it could be hidden."

Henry nodded unhappily. "Okay, but you should probably go see her now, before it gets too dark."

I looked around in surprise and realized that the shadows in the kitchen had moved, and the clock said five o'clock.

CHAPTER 22

The Book of Histories

I SLIPPED OUT THE BACK GATE and ran down to the Lake of Swans, the book clutched in my hands. The afternoon seemed oddly quiet, only the honking of the swans and the rustling of tree branches lent any noise to the day. I crossed the lawn as quickly as I could, running.

"We didn't find it," I said breathlessly, reaching my sister.

Merrill sighed and the slender branches around me quivered and sighed with her. "I didn't think you would, but I hoped," her voice barely contained her disappointment. "It was brave of Henry to try." Then her voice became curious, sharper, as if she were suddenly focused. "What book do you have in your hands?"

I looked blankly down at the red journal, for a moment forgetting that I had carried it with me. "It's some kind of history—a journal kept by Dori and our grandmother and Lia and Mother, but that's all it is."

Merrill sounded excited. "It looks like the book I told you about."

I shrugged. "I know, that's why Henry took it—he thought it was the book, but it's not. See?" I flipped open the book to the first page. As it had before, my grandmother's sloping handwriting filled the page, then I turned to the next page, and then the next.

"Stop!" Merrill cried. "Don't you see it?"

"See what?" I looked down at the page before me. There was a journal entry there, and nothing more.

"Turn the page," Merrill ordered.

I turned the page obediently. The back of the page was blank, just like the back of every journal entry, as if someone had been afraid that ink on both sides of a page would leak through and smear its message. The page opposite it was filled with my grandmother's script.

"Amelia," Merrill spoke slowly, "don't you see what's on the page in front of you?"

"See what? A blank page?" It was hard not to sound impatient.

"The spell," Merrill said.

I peered down at the heavy blank page again, and for one moment I saw a flash of color, a bright winking of something silver and shiny, but then it was gone.

"I can't see it," I said miserably, shutting the book gently.

Wind raced across the lake, stirring up waves, their tiny whitecaps tossed toward the sky, spraying the shore. I turned toward the lake, and Merrill's branches swayed in the sudden breeze. In the breath of wind, the swans rose up on the water, as if ballerinas rising to their toes; they trumpeted a long honking sound. Whether it was one of triumph or warning I did not know, but I shivered, goose bumps running up my arms, and realized that the afternoon was growing darker, the sun slipping away. In the palace, lights were being lit, and the ravens that waited restlessly on the windowsills stirred—screeching and whining.

Merrill lowered her voice, "It's the Book of Spells. Amelia, you found the book!"

"But what does it matter if I can't even see the spells?"

Merrill's voice grew still quieter. "But I can see them, Amelia, and in learning them, I can help you."

"How?" I wondered.

"I don't know," Merrill said slowly, "but I know I can."

The light was leaving the afternoon quickly now, and dusk was all around us. It wrapped the weak sun in her deep cloak, and the evening became dipped in dusty gray. The wind whispered something across the lawn, and the grass bowed before its message, the trees leaned in to hear it. Merrill seemed to quiver, listening to something unheard. Her voice became strangely urgent. "Go back to Tiege's cottage, Amelia, and for now take the book with you. Should anyone try to take it from you, you must toss it into fire or water. Do you understand?"

I nodded. "I understand. But won't that ruin it forever?"

"It might," Merrill said. "But a book like this is better destroyed than in the hands of one who wishes to use its magic for something evil."

"But then we wouldn't know any of the magic." My voice was thick with frustration.

"We would find another way then," Merrill said quietly. "Magic is not all we have."

There was another burst of wind, and again the swans on the lake rose up honking and crying, this time their cries high and strained. From far across the lawn there was a sudden faint sound from the palace as the heavy doors were swung open. Again the wind rushed around me, and this time I heard its quiet whisper: *Go!* I ran.

❧

"It is the right book," I told Henry and Tiege over dinner.

"But where are the spells and pictures?" Henry asked, confused.

"Only Merrill can see them," I said miserably.

Henry put down his fork and looked miserable too. But Tiege smiled and said what she had said before, "Maybe they are only meant for Merrill to see."

"But why?" I wondered.

Tiege shrugged. "I don't know, Amelia. But I do know that you two need to finish your dinner. There is still much to be resolved on the grounds of Gossling Palace, and better to do it on a full stomach rather than an empty one."

That night I slept poorly. As I slept, I dreamed of a book that I could step into. I dreamed of Count Raven—a man I had never seen—and watched as he transformed into a cruel bird. I dreamed of a panther locked in an amber coffin. I dreamed of my sisters trapped forever as tree and swans. I dreamed our country burned.

I woke up late in the morning, the room filled with light, the covers twisted around me. Woke up feeling impatient, with a headache and a sense that we had to leave. I spent the day in Tiege's garden, restless and waiting for the late afternoon to come, that lazy hour before dinner when the palace slowed, the ravens that filled the sky rested, and the grounds were quiet and empty of people. Waited impatiently for that hour to come, for then I could visit Merrill, and there were questions I needed to ask her.

When the clock read four thirty, I collected the gardening hat and pruning shears and headed down to the lake. I bent down next to Merrill, as if I were planting. "I don't know what to do next."

Merrill was quiet a long moment before speaking. "Amelia, you'll have to find a way to reach Dori in the Western Valleys, and then you will have to find a way to lead."

I looked out over the quiet water, at the trees and gardens behind them, and tried to imagine them in ruins. Saw the image from my dream—the country burned. I turned back to Merrill. "I can't lead. I can't do anything! A first princess is born to lead, not a fourth!"

"Amelia," Merrill said, her voice serious, "people are not born *to* lead or born *not to* lead. Leading is a choice. Anyone—everyone—has the ability to lead."

"Except ordinary people," I said, my voice petulant, tears tickling my eyes.

"*Everyone*," Merrill said firmly. "All it takes is belief in yourself. There is no one telling you that you can't except yourself."

"But I can't; even Mother wrote that it was to be you . . . ," I began again, frustrated that she wasn't listening to me.

"Amelia." Merrill's voice was suddenly stern, the same voice she had used in the classroom, "you *can* lead, and you *must*. You are the only one who can!"

"What should I do?"

"I don't know," Merrill said in a tired voice. "I've thought and thought, but I think that just the way I'm the only one who can read the spells, that you're the only one who will be able to know for certain how to lead the people of Gossling, and the only person who can free us from Raven's spell."

I felt panic rise inside me. "Tell me what to do! I don't know what to do! I don't know!"

"You'll know." Merrill's voice was confident. "I know you'll know what to do once you've thought about it." She sounded steady and sure.

By the palace there was a movement in the trees, a flutter of black wings. Merrill's voice became quieter, concerned. "You should go, Amelia."

"But I want to stay with you." I felt tears prick my eyes.

"You can't, it's not safe," Merrill whispered.

I stood up reluctantly, but her voice stopped me. "Wait," Merrill said. "Amelia, I'm sorry that it's not me. It should be me, not you, trying to solve all of this."

I nodded miserably.

Merrill's voice was gentle. "I know you can do it!"

Across the lawn the ravens lifted off their branches, and in the lake beyond us, the swans began screaming and hissing, rising up off the lake: a distraction.

"Run!" Merrill whispered.

And I did.

CHAPTER 23

❧

The New Direction

BACK IN THE SAFETY of Tiege's garden, I collapsed into a rocking chair next to Henry, who was reading a book at the tea table. Breathing heavily, I scooped Snowy up into my lap.

Henry flipped the book closed, one finger holding his place. "What did Merrill say?"

I shrugged. "Nothing really."

He glanced at me, his face curious, but said nothing, waiting.

I smoothed down Snowy's soft hair. "She said we should go to Dori in the Western Valleys."

Henry sounded impatient. "We know that already, but what did she say we should *do*?"

"She said *lead*," I said helplessly, trying not to cry. "She said I'd figure out what to do." Snowy licked my hand sympathetically.

"That's all she said?" Henry said indignantly.

I nodded my head, and felt my eyes fill with tears again.

I bent over Snowy, as if inspecting something in his fur, so Henry wouldn't see me cry.

There was a long silence, and Henry pretended to read his book while I continued to pet Snowy. I thought about who might have answers on how to lead, listed them in my head: Mother, Father, Merrill, George, Dori, and Lia. Thought bitterly that two of the people on my list were dead, one had no answer, one was imprisoned, and the other two were in hiding.

"I think it's time that we found Dori and Lia in the Western Valleys," I said decisively.

Henry nodded. "So, tomorrow we'll begin to prepare—create a map and a plan on how to reach them, then we can leave in two days' time."

"No." I shook my head, suddenly anxious to be doing something, anxious to be gone. "We'll leave tomorrow."

"Why not wait until we're totally ready?" Henry's forehead wrinkled in confusion and he ran a quick hand through his hair, making the curls stand up on end.

I glared at him. "It doesn't take two days to get ready, and besides, I don't think we should stay here anymore. We're wasting time."

"It's a bigger waste of time if we leave without a plan, and then end up lost because we didn't take a day to figure out where we need to go," Henry retorted testily.

"That's what you think," I shot back. Snowy shifted uneasily in my lap, and then hopped to the ground before disappearing into the bushes.

Henry slammed his book down on the table, and his mouth was tight with anger. "That is what I think. And I also think you're rushing to leave here because you don't know what to do and you want to feel like you're doing something!"

I felt my face flush pink. "Well, you're wrong, I *do* know what to do, and I say we leave tomorrow. And if you don't want to come, then *don't!*" I practically spat the last word, and, without waiting for a reply, stalked away from the table.

❧

At dinner that night we barely spoke and Tiege watched us with troubled eyes. I had told her earlier in the afternoon that I was leaving the next morning for the Western Valleys, with or without Henry. She had nodded, her face neutral, and had continued to slice carrots without comment. When Henry had slammed through the kitchen soon after, his face was stony and he said nothing, though a few hours later he had unceremoniously dumped a small packed bag by the door, which I took as a sign that he was joining me. Even though I was still angry, I was also relieved: I wasn't really prepared to travel alone.

After the dishes were done, Tiege began to roll out dough to make bread with, then with deft hands she transferred it into loaf pans before taking out chocolate, sugar, eggs, and cookie sheets. She hummed under her breath as she began to whisk her ingredients together. "For your trip," she said cheerfully. "You'll need to have some food to take with you. You can't eat like rabbits for too many days! You need more nourishment than that—you two were skinny as scarecrows when you arrived, and you're just barely plumping up again now!"

The kitchen was warm with the heat of the oven, and

filled with the cozy smell of baking cookies. Watching the three loaves begin to plump and rise, I began to feel sleepy, and Tiege smiled at me. "I think you should get some sleep, Amelia. Tomorrow is going to be a long day."

Stifling a yawn, I nodded, then kissed her good night and headed to my bedroom. In the kitchen I had been close to falling asleep, but suddenly in my soft bed, I felt wide-awake and anxious. I tossed back and forth, my mind racing with questions I had no answers to. *What if Henry was right and it was too soon to leave? We already knew that the ravens were dangerous: they had bitten Meg, and they were somehow responsible for the fire that had almost killed us. What if I was leading us into danger?* It was hours before I fell into a restless sleep, and it seemed that I had only just fallen asleep when Tiege was leaning over me, and shaking me gently awake.

&

It was barely dawn when I crawled out of bed, my body tired and stiff from lack of sleep. I dressed quickly and then carried my small pack to the doorway, setting it down next to Henry's. Tiege fed us eggs on toast and tea sweet with thick honey. Henry sat, only half awake, at the long wooden table, his fork moving slowly between his bowl and mouth, while I sketched a map to the Western Valleys as best as I could remember.

"Eat," Tiege ordered, and I put my pencil down and dutifully picked up my spoon.

Henry scraped the last bite from the bowl and cleared his throat, as if finally waking up. "Tiege," he said suddenly. "Do you think we should leave for the Western Valleys today?"

I stopped sketching, feeling suddenly defensive. Tiege's face was unreadable. "What do you think?" she asked in a quiet tone.

"I think it's too soon—I think we should wait and make an actual plan. *Think* before we leave!" Henry glared at me across the table.

"Yes, and you've already made your opinion quite clear." I slapped my pencil down on the table. "I think we should leave today, and it's my decision!"

"Oh yes, Your Majesty, whatever you think is best, Your Highness," Henry said mockingly. He grabbed his bowl from the table and dumped it noisily into the sink.

I felt my face grow hot with anger and embarrassment. "What do you think?" I turned to Tiege.

Tiege looked thoughtful and her tone was measured. "There are merits to both arguments: there is something to be said for action, but there is also something to be said for creating a clear plan."

"That's your advice?" I could hear the rudeness in my voice, and saw Henry's face shocked and furious—I had never spoken to Tiege like that before.

Tiege acted as if she hadn't heard the rudeness, and said mildly, "Still, what do I know? I'm an old woman, and this journey is not mine to take."

I glared at my glass of milk, *You are old,* I thought meanly, *and you weren't born a princess and you couldn't understand the burden of leading.*

From the corner of my eye, I could see Tiege watching me closely, as if she could read my thoughts, and I felt myself blushing again. After a long moment, she turned to Henry. "Run to the orchard and pick some cherries to take on your trip today. There's a bowl for collecting them by the sink."

"But . . . ," Henry began.

"Go!" She shooed him off. "Be sure they're ripe."

In the silence of the kitchen we could hear Henry's bare feet padding along the stone path. Tiege rose and lifted our empty plates from the table. I stared at the table and listened as she gently set them in the sink. The kettle on the stove whistled and Tiege poured herself a cup of tea, and slowly stirred in cream. Then, unrushed, she sat down again at the table.

"Amelia, you're right to feel angry—you are looking to be told what to do, and no one can tell you. Then when you make a decision, you feel like it's being challenged, and you're not even convinced it was the best decision to start with."

She was right and it startled me; I nodded warily.

Tiege smiled slightly. "My advice to you won't sound helpful, but it is: don't doubt yourself if your belief is true." I nodded, but she wasn't through. "However, no matter how sure you are, it's always worth weighing the words and opinions of those you trust. These choices are yours and so is the journey, but others can have different perspectives, and these also are worth considering." She paused and looked at me as if deciding to share a secret. "You're wrong about me. I too have known the burden of a crown. I'm an old woman now, but"—she lowered her voice, and she suddenly sounded almost painfully gentle—"I know the choices you make are not easy ones—I once was a young princess far from here."

I looked up in surprise and she nodded. "Let it remain our secret, though."

Henry burst through the door, the blue bowl in his hands heavy with cherries, a ring of red berry stain around his mouth.

"What?" he asked as Tiege and I began to laugh.

"Wash your mouth!" Tiege smiled, and glancing in the mirror at himself, Henry grinned back and headed toward the sink.

❧

We left Tiege as the sun began to spread through the veiled mist of the morning, driving away all memories of the night. She kissed us both, and hugged Henry extra hard.

"Be careful," she said simply. She stood in the doorway of her little cottage until we could see her no more through the blossoming trees.

The journey out of the castle grounds was much more difficult than our journey in. Fierce armed guards patrolled the periphery of the grounds, their steps measured and crisp, and ravens flew in dark clouds above the palace, crying and shrieking as they flew.

As we crept slowly from the castle grounds, I felt a flicker of doubt at what we were doing. I turned to Henry.

"I was wrong—," I began.

Henry interrupted me. "I was too. I didn't mean to get so angry."

"And I didn't mean to be rude." I took a deep breath,

"And also, you were right about me just wanting to leave so that we could be doing something."

Henry grinned. "I know."

I smiled back. "I'm sorry."

"Me too. Anyway, leaving today isn't the worst plan—we don't have much time before the Raven's spells on your sisters become permanent."

I shivered, chilled by the reminder, then quickened my step.

Safely outside the palace grounds, Henry pulled our swords from their hiding place under the lilac bush. Then, with my compass tight in my hand, we began to walk toward the Western Valleys.

CHAPTER 24

Danger

WE WERE CAUTIOUS TRAVELERS. Outside the safety of Tiege's garden, I felt exposed—every sound in the forest seemed a threat, every noise or rustle seemed to be an indication of danger. For days we had traveled west through the woods beyond the palace, carefully following the map I had made—a close copy of the one we had once studied in the map room. On the fourth day we walked for nearly thirteen hours; when we finally stopped, it was night and the forest was dark.

Henry slowly built a fire for cooking the fish we had caught in a nearby lake, and blurry eyed I fried them. We ate without speaking, both of us so tired we could barely chew. Henry's feet were covered with blisters and mine were nearly raw. Still, we had gone far in our days of travel and I was confident that we would be in the Western Valleys soon.

"I just thought of something." Henry looked troubled as he put out the small campfire we'd made, covering it with damp soil.

"What?" I was making beds for us under two huge flowering bushes, carefully spreading our blankets out, while trying to avoid shaking the branches.

Henry brushed the ashes off his hands and headed toward his makeshift bed. "Dori and Lia don't know when we're coming. We have to find a way to tell them, otherwise they won't know to look for us."

I paused, thinking. "How?"

"I don't know." Henry crawled under the bush and pulled his blanket up around him, his eyes already drowsing shut. "We can think about it more in the morning."

But I was troubled. Long after my bed was made I lay awake thinking, until finally I could think no more, and I fell into a deep sleep. In my dream I saw Tiege in her garden: *Remember, the animals of Gossling are your friends.* Then I head Lia, laughing, *I made the spells rhyme so I could remember them.* Then my mother's voice, calm and steady, said, *You can write a message spell, Amelia. Send it, and I promise you it will arrive.*

I woke up with a start, the night black around me and my head swirled with fragments of the dream. I lay back again, and tried to think. Then suddenly the spell was clear to me, as clear as if I were reading it from a book.

> *Whisper bright, whisper light*
> *Send a message on this night.*
> *Compass rose reads due west,*
> *Amelia and Henry on this quest.*
> *Listen close, animals fair,*
> *Two days from now, we will be there.*

I spoke softly, and when I was finished, the night seemed somehow more awake, there was the sound of snapping twigs nearby and far above me, an owl hooted, and on the lake, the loons let out their long, soulful cries. Secure in the knowledge that the message had been sent, I lay back again and soon fell into a dreamless sleep.

In the morning, as Henry and I sat eating Tiege's sweet cinnamon bread, I told Henry about the dream and the spell. He looked hopeful. "This could be a good sign—maybe you're getting your magic!" He took a huge bite of the bread, munching it happily.

I considered this, and then shook my head, dismissing the idea. "Maybe I'm getting a *little* of my magic, but," I sighed, "I'm not thirteen yet, and Mother said no White Queen gets her magic until thirteen."

Henry shrugged. "Oh, well. A little magic is better than no magic at all."

❧

Henry was certain that there were ravens in the air. All morning long, he had turned anxious eyes to the empty sky above us; looking.

We stopped for lunch by a narrow stream, dipping our metal cups into the cool water and sitting down heavily on our packs. The morning was very quiet. "I think we'll be at the Jeweled Mountains by tomorrow," I said. I looked over my shoulder, but the sparse trees behind us seemed empty, innocent.

Henry looked too, and then shook his head as if to convince himself that there was nothing there. He bit into one of the ripe pears we had picked the day before. "Maybe even tonight if we move quickly."

Although the morning was quiet, I felt it again, the tickling sense that we were being watched. I stood up. "Let's go now."

Henry stood too, and lifted his pack. "Don't you want a break?"

"No." I looked over my shoulder again at the thinning forest. "I think we should keep going."

Like me, Henry turned to look at the trees behind us. "Me too."

By nightfall we were almost in the shadow of the Jeweled Mountains, and I felt my body relax slightly; if the ravens were searching for us, the mountains would offer some shelter from the wide blue sky.

But we would go no farther that night, because suddenly, from far above us, came a triumphant cry, a sort of scream. Frightened, we looked up and saw the sky filled with hundreds of dark birds.

"Ravens!" Henry cried. "Run!"

Henry and I ran for the thin cover of nearby trees as birds swooped down at us; their bodies hard black bullets with sharp, open beaks. They dove at us again and again with shrill, high screams, their wide wings flapping before our faces, their long scraping feet grabbing at my arms. I covered my eyes and ducked my head down, swatting at the birds as they closed in on us, closer and closer and closer.

"Say the spell," Henry cried.

I closed my eyes, squeezed them shut, and grasped Henry's hand hard in my own.

Wind of east
Wind of west
Wind of sea and shoreline's breast
Lean in close, lean in near,
Make this White Queen disappear!

The wind roared in, a howling sound as if the wind rode on the backs of wolves. And there was darkness.

CHAPTER 25

The Jeweled Mountains of Nylorac

I AWOKE INSIDE A BLUE ROOM, blue and rounded, as if I were inside a jewel, or inside the egg of a robin. Groggily I rubbed at my eyes, trying to focus them, trying to make sense of what I was seeing. I tried to sit up but couldn't, and looking down I saw that I was in a bed covered with a thick down quilt. I turned my head, and saw Henry on a bed across from me.

"Henry, wake up," I hissed at him. "We've been captured."

"Not captured," a deep voice laughed, "*rescued!* Welcome to the Jeweled Mountains of Nylorac, Princess Amelia."

I turned, and there sat a huge man, his face half covered in a heavy brown beard and his eyes almost buried beneath his curling hair. I gulped.

"Do not be afraid," his deep voice continued. "You have been in our mountains for two days now. The boy was hurt, but he is getting well, and soon you shall both be strong enough to continue your journey."

"What happened to Henry?" My heart began to pound, and I sat up as much as I could on the bed.

"Sit back, Princess, you've just awakened after a long rest and should not move so quickly yet. A raven with a poisoned beak bit your friend. A serious injury, but he shall fully recover."

"How did you know where to find us?"

The man leaned back in his chair. "We knew you were coming. The bats from the Night Forest told us that there were two children traveling toward the basin of the deserted mines. They told us the story of Count Raven and of the princesses transformed into tree and swans. They told us of the courage of those traveling."

"Bats?" I echoed weakly, confused. Suddenly exhausted, I sank back on the bed. "You know the witch of the Night Forest?"

The man nodded kindly. "Yes, and she knows that we are friends of the White Queens. You see, years ago, when we first came to these Jeweled Mountains, we were a gentle people, and our leader had a warm friendship with the young White Queen Charlotte."

"My mother."

The man smiled. "Yes. Yet despite our friendships, living alone in these mountains, surrounded by the deep mines of gold and silver, we forgot what kind of people we had been, living only for jewels and gold. The jewels made us greedy, and living high in the mountains made us isolated; few people made the journey to see us. As we became further absorbed with mining the mountains, we turned the few friends that visited us away. Years passed and our lives focused only on pulling gold from the mines.

"In our obsession, we forgot almost everything about ourselves. We forgot our songs and our stories, forgot our traditions and customs, forgot how to cook our special foods, and forgot our laws. We lived for the dark mines and the treasures buried deep within the blackest bellies of the mountains. And so it happened that one year spring came with all its birds and flowers and new life, and we were blind to it, woke early each morning and descended deep into the mines, coming out long after nightfall. Summer too; we did not see the mountainsides blossom with flowers and sunshine, we did not feel the warm sweet breeze sweep through our valleys or smell the fragrant air at sunset. When autumn came again, we missed the season, did not see the valleys filled with racing wild ponies, we did not see the mountains' trees change from green to gold and red. Did not wake up to see the sun spread her thin arms around those trees in a tight embrace so that for a few moments the mountains seemed to burn with fire. And when winter finally came, and the air was filled with a thousand sparkling snowflakes, and long icicles hung from the gray rocks, and the mountains were blanketed with snow, we did not see that either. We saw only jewels; we saw only the dark tunnels of the mine. We paid no attention to our homes; we ate little, and slept less. And because we paid no attention to that which was around us, we did not maintain the mighty dams that held back the rushing water that comes when the winter snow melts and spring arrives. For a few years these strong dams held, but there came a year when a flood poured through the mountains. The winter had brought heavy snows, and when spring came and this snow melted to water, it roared through the valleys with terrible force.

"Although we were in great danger, we would not leave the diamond mines, would not leave behind the jewels, not even to save ourselves. As the waters poured into the mountains, the White Queen Charlotte risked herself to travel to us; she came to save us. Although we had refused her friendship for many years, she would not let us drown in our deep mines of gold.

"When we would not leave, she threatened to destroy the mountains herself, for she believed that the gold and diamonds of these hills had corrupted us. But she did not do this; instead, she and our leader spent six days locked in the diamond room. For five days she told him the story of our people, sang him the old songs, reminded him of his kindness and his friendship, and all the while the flood waters came closer and closer to the mines where we now all but lived.

"On the sixth day, our leader walked from the room and led us out of the mountains and into the faraway safety of the Night Forest. We stayed there for five years, and in that dark, peaceful forest we remembered again who we were, and when we finally returned to the Jeweled Mountains we returned because we loved their beauty, not because we wished to hoard and exploit their treasures.

"This was nearly a lifetime ago. We haven't returned to the world beyond the mountains, but we remember who we were—remember to love our beautiful mountains; remember to care for each other. And, of course, we have never forgotten the kindness of our great friend—your mother. We were very saddened by news of her death, but remain eager to repay the queen's kindness."

"But how did you know that we needed help?" I wondered aloud.

"A stag saw you attacked, and ran to us with the news. We stormed the quarry and threw rocks at the ravens, driving them away, but there was still no sign of you or the boy. We were getting ready to extend our search, frightened that you both had been captured, when you were found together in a small cave. We carried you deep into our mountains." The man paused and his face looked troubled. "There was another child hidden along the ridge, a strange dark-haired girl. Although the bats had not mentioned a third child, it is rare for us to see an unknown child wandering so far into the mountains. We thought perhaps she was with you, and tried to rescue her too, but in the confusion we lost her." The deep voice grew concerned. "Is that child in danger?"

I sighed. "Yes and no. Meg began this journey with us. However, she was bitten by a raven, and it changed her. She became dangerous—like the ravens." A thought bounced through my head. "Will the bite change Henry too?" I couldn't keep the fear out of my voice.

"No." The man's voice grew thoughtful. "We cleaned the wound well and removed the poison. I doubt that the poison would have affected him as it affected this other child, for the deep anger of the ravens can only poison those who are willing to take such poison into their heart."

I nodded, considering this. It seemed true—if any heart could withstand poisoning, it was Henry's. However, I couldn't help but wonder if I would have been able to withstand it—for although I try to be good, I know I'm not as good as Henry. I don't have the same gentleness and I don't have the same patience.

"Come, let us leave your friend asleep; we shall go to the kitchens. You have not eaten in nearly two days," the man said.

"Two days?" I asked as I sat up again.

He smiled, showing white teeth through his dark beard. "You've been very tired! You've been sleeping here since your arrival."

"But where are we, exactly?" I asked.

"You're in the Palace of Nylorac, which is so large that it sprawls all through the mountains. Specifically though, you're in the healing room."

"But who—" I stopped, felt suddenly shy asking this man, whom I had spoken to for so long, what his name was.

"Who am I?" The man smiled. "I'm Lucien, a physician. I've cared for you along with many others." He gestured toward Henry and I saw that another man sat at the head of his bed.

"Thank you," I said shyly.

"It's been a pleasure," Lucien said warmly. "Now, shall we go and find some food?"

I nodded, and Lucien lifted me effortlessly from the bed.

Quietly we left the room and walked out into a cool hallway painted a soft gold. The hallway was long and winding, and as we twisted around corner after corner, I tried to count the doors, losing count after twenty. "Is this all part of the palace?"

"Yes, it's part of the main palace," Lucien answered, "but you'll see that there are many, many levels—all of our people live in the palace, making it more like a small city. We are on the top level, but lower levels contain museums and gardens, a river, a bird sanctuary, oh, and so much more!"

"The top level?"

Lucien laughed. "It's hard to explain. Here." He stopped before double doors and then pushed them open, stepping onto a large stone terrace.

I caught my breath. We were on the very top of the high Jeweled Mountains. "It's like being in a ship's lookout," I said to Lucien, turning north, east, south, and west. "I can see everything! Look!" I pointed above us, where clouds hung like white balloons at a birthday party, so close that I could almost touch them. "We're in the clouds!"

Lucien nodded. I looked around again. "It's beautiful," I said quietly.

"I thought you would think so," Lucien said, and smiled. "However, there is plenty of time to admire our view after you've eaten. Come, let's go to the kitchen—it's just a little farther down the hall."

I heard the kitchen before I saw it. Heard the loud clattering of saucepans and silverware, and the cheerful hum of cooking. As we grew closer, the hallway seemed to warm with good smells, and I realized I was hungry.

In the bright kitchen at least fifteen chefs were cooking busily, hurrying back and forth with dishes and tasting spoons.

"The child is awake!" exclaimed one chef carrying a huge pot. He came to a dead stop in front of us, and stared at me with open curiosity.

"Not just *any* child, a White Queen," Lucien said sharply. "And don't stare."

The man looked down in embarrassment. "Pardon, White Queen."

Lucien shook his head and smiled. "No, I'm sorry to be so sharp, Michael. We came to the kitchen to find some food for her." He set me down on a coral countertop. "Now," he continued briskly, looking at me, "let's find some."

Another chef came toward us, plump in a bright blue apron, with round cheeks that were as red as the cherries of Tiege's orchard. "Little Queen, what would you like to eat?"

I hesitated. "Could I have ice cream?" I asked slowly.

The woman beamed at me. "Of course, and what a delicious choice!"

In a moment she was back with a heaping bowl of ice cream. As I began to eat, the woman turned to Lucien, and her tinkling voice was almost somber. "How is the other child?"

"He's doing well, though he continues to sleep," Lucien said. "Still, I believe he shall wake up today or tomorrow."

"But he'll be okay, right?" I asked anxiously, my spoon stopped in midair.

"Yes," Lucien said reassuringly, "he'll be fine."

Lucien turned back to the woman. "Priscilla, do you wish

to join me in showing the little queen some of our mountain palace?"

Priscilla smiled. "I do, but before I can, I must finish a soup I've been preparing."

Lucien nodded. "Then we shall meet you on the central balcony whenever you are able." He turned to me, "You've been inside for two days, I think the air would be good for you. Come."

I slid off the high counter, and taking his hand, followed Lucien back into the hallway. I thought that we would return to the lookout terrace, but instead Lucien strode down the hall in a different direction, stopping before a large set of doors. He flung them open ceremoniously, and I found myself standing on a glorious balcony. The floor was made of solid gold, a pattern of blue sapphires and green emeralds running through it, it was more elegant even than the ballroom at home.

Lucien looked at me staring at the floor. "I imagine you can guess why this is called the Golden Terrace."

"It's lovely."

Lucien shrugged, "It's only a floor. We made it during the time when we were consumed with gold—though the artist's design *is* beautiful. Now come over here; I want to ask you something." He walked toward the edge of the terrace, and I followed him tentatively. When I reached the railing, I looked down over it cautiously.

"What's wrong?" Lucien asked, smiling. "Are you frightened to be up so high?"

"No," I said truthfully. Then I asked hesitantly, "It's just that, is it safe for me to be out here? I mean, couldn't the ravens—"

Lucien smiled nicely. "No raven could fly this high, the air is too thin for them. It's safe."

"Oh." I felt relief bubble in my stomach; no raven could spot me here among the clouds and mountaintops. "What did you want to ask me?"

"I wanted to ask you where you planned to go. Is it to the Western Valleys?"

I nodded, and Lucien nodded back, as if this was something he already knew. "I want to show you something." Lucien reached down below a nearby bench and pulled out a telescope. "Look through here," he instructed.

I peered through the telescope, and Lucien turned my shoulders gently until I faced west. "Do you see the valleys?" he asked.

"I see them!" I exclaimed in surprise. "We're so close! I didn't know we were so close!" I let the telescope drop from my eye.

"You're *very* close," Lucien agreed. "And when Henry is well enough, we shall lead you down through the mountains and out an old and nearly forgotten exit that shall put you right on the path to the Western Valleys."

I sighed. "I wish we were already there."

"Patience," Lucien said, and smiled. "Every journey has its share of stops and each one serves some purpose."

CHAPTER 26

The Western Valleys

ANOTHER DAY PASSED before Henry woke up, and during that time I explored the interior of the mountains with Lucien and Priscilla. And then, finally—

"You're awake!" I cried as I ran through the door. I jumped onto the bottom of Henry's bed. "How do you feel?"

Henry brushed my question aside and asked impatiently, "Amelia, do you know that we've been here for *three* days?"

I nodded. "Of course I know that. Do you know that you were bitten by one of the ravens?"

Henry nodded distractedly and pointed to a man standing next to his bed, "He told me." Henry then turned to Lucien. "Are you in charge?"

Lucien smiled slightly. "You could say that."

Henry didn't smile in return. "We have to leave now. You can't keep us here."

I rolled my eyes. "No one is keeping us here—you were sick and sleeping."

Henry blushed slightly. "Well, I'm not sleeping now, and we have to leave."

"What's wrong with you?" I glared at Henry and slid off the bottom of the bed. "They saved you! You should at least *pretend* to be grateful."

"I am grateful. I mean, thank you," Henry said stiffly to Lucien.

Lucien smiled. "You're very welcome. And I do understand that you want to continue on your journey. We know the importance of your quest."

"There isn't much time." Henry's voice was strained. "We have to get to Lia and Dori in the Western Valleys. If we wait much longer, Count Raven's spell against the princesses will be final and his armies shall destroy Gossling. We have to get back! Amelia has to lead the people against Count Raven!"

Lucien sighed. "You're not ready to travel. You've only been awake for forty minutes, Henry."

"And I feel fine," Henry said testily. "I felt fine in the first ten minutes, and in the second, and in the third, and in the fourth—"

Lucien held up his hand. "I understand, but you still need rest."

"You *don't* understand," Henry said in frustration, struggling to get out of bed.

"I *do*," Lucien said adamantly, pushing him back gently. "And as a doctor, I also understand that your body needs to rest. Yet I do understand why you must leave." Lucien sighed again. "And so, provided you rest today, we will leave here in the morning."

Henry looked surprised to have won his battle so easily. "Really?" he asked suspiciously.

"Against my better judgment, yes, really." Lucien smiled slightly. "But you must spend the rest of today eating and resting. And doing absolutely *nothing* else."

"I promise," Henry said heartily. Then he looked around curiously. "Where are we?"

☙

We left at dawn the next morning.

Lucien woke us gently. "Come," he said, "it's time to go." We dressed soundlessly and quickly, following Lucien into the hallway.

Priscilla waited for us there, a picnic basket and four lanterns next to her.

"We shouldn't carry lights," Henry said immediately. "The ravens could spot us."

Priscilla smiled at him. "We're not going outside right now."

"But . . ." Henry's face flushed angrily, and he turned to Lucien.

Lucien held up his hand before Henry could speak. "We *are* going to the Western Valleys, we're just going to take a shortcut. Follow me."

Lucien led us down the hallway to an elevator. Stepping in, he slipped a small gold key into a lock under the elevator buttons. "Why do you need to use a key?" I asked.

Lucien looked at me and his eyes were steady and kind. "Because we're going to a place that is considered dangerous."

"Dangerous?" Henry asked.

Lucien nodded. "Yes, but hopefully not so to you."

❧

We exited the elevator and stood in a foyer, empty except for a tiny door. Lucien bent down and inserted a key into the door, he turned the doorknob and slowly the door creaked open. There was nothing but darkness inside. Priscilla lifted a lantern and shone it into the doorway, yet the dark was so great that it practically swallowed the light.

Lucien crouched down and slid his large body through the doorway. Taking a lantern from Priscilla, he turned to us. "Don't be frightened—it's dark in the tunnels, but there is nothing to fear."

"I thought you said it was dangerous," Henry muttered.

I glared at him. "Come on," I hissed. I followed Lucien through the doorway and down a long narrow stone staircase. Henry followed a moment later, and then Priscilla. I heard her lock the door behind us.

"Where are we going?" I asked. My voice bounced back crazily in the darkness.

"To the mines," Lucien answered over his shoulder.

Even with the lanterns, the light was dim, and I held the railing tightly. As we descended lower and lower into the mine, the air changed—became thin and wet. Finally, the staircase ended and we were in front of a huge stone door. Lucien inserted a key into this door too, turning it twice to unlock it.

The huge door slowly slid open, and Lucien lifted his lantern high. Light flooded the cavern before us, and the whole room seemed to suddenly shimmer. I caught my breath, for the cavern was filled with gold.

Lucien turned to me and smiled in the eerie gold light. "Don't look so surprised. Remember: these mountains are filled with it."

A thought crossed my mind, worrying me. "But doesn't it—" I stopped.

"Tempt me?" Lucien finished my sentence gently. "No, gold is just a metal, just an abnormality of stone."

"It's beautiful," I said tentatively, now truly looking at the cavern—its floors stacked with piles of gold.

"It is, but then many things are," Lucien said dismissively. He began to move through the cavern, weaving along a path between the gold.

"Didn't you say that where we're going is dangerous?" Henry asked, following him, and turning in wonderment to look at the gold around him.

"Dangerous to some," Lucien corrected. "It's not the mines that are dangerous, it's what they contain. I doubt there are any who would care to return to the life we once lived, but it is not a chance we wish to take. That's why there's a key."

Behind me, I heard Priscilla lock the door and test it to be sure.

❧

We traveled all day, weaving through caverns and caverns of diamonds and jewels, through countless mines of gold and silver, until I became weary of it—hardly saw it as precious. I thought of Lucien's words: *dangerous to some*. And I grinned, knowing that I was not in the group that would find this dangerous.

Finally we stopped. Lucien set down his lantern and the picnic basket. "We are now just ten minutes from the western exit of the Jeweled Mountains."

Henry looked around. "Where is it?"

Lucien lifted his hand. "Up!" he laughed. "Tonight we shall sleep here, and then at early dawn you two shall continue your journey. Once you've exited the mine, you are only a day's walk from the Western Valleys, but," he cautioned when he saw the excitement on our faces, "you are only safe to travel at dawn, so your journey shall probably take three days, maybe two if you travel quickly."

"It will take us two," Henry said firmly. "We only have three days left to break the spell!"

That night I had a restless sleep. I dreamed I was lost in a maze of gold—that my pockets and gowns were weighted down with jewels and silver, trapping me with their finery. I woke up to Priscilla's tinkling voice, "Wake up, little queen, dawn is almost here!"

Lucien and Priscilla led us up a spiral staircase, away from the cavern that we had slept in, higher and higher until the gold of the walls faded away to hard stone, until finally we reached a very narrow opening and I saw the weak gray of morning peaking across the sky.

Lucien bent down and looked at us seriously. "Beware! Just days ago you were spotted in this area by ravens. By now they

269

have reported what they have seen to the count, and I am certain that thousands of birds search for you. Remember to move only in the early mornings—ravens hate the dawn of new days."

Priscilla hugged us both. "We will be praying for your safe journey."

எ

Henry and I stepped through the narrow opening and into the cold air of the new morning. Instinctively I looked up to the sky and felt a rush of relief that it was empty of dark birds. We traveled quickly for close to three hours, and although Henry was still tired from the poison of the raven and his face was still pale under his sunburn, he was determined too. When finally the sun began to tease the edge of the sky, we reluctantly began to search for a place to hide. Sliding into a long hollow log on the edge of a crowded wood, we slept.

I awoke suddenly to the sound of fast-beating wings. My body tightened with fear, and I could hear Henry wake up too, his breath ragged. Ravens flew above where we hid, their piercing cries ripping through the darkness as they searched for us. They left, but we did not fall back to sleep; instead we lay silently until dawn again crept into the sky.

"If we hurry, we can reach the Western Valleys this morning," Henry said, fumbling in the dark to button his thin jacket.

"Maybe," I said.

"We can," Henry said.

❧

And we did, but just barely. We were close to the Western Valleys when the sun seemed to appear suddenly, and Henry and I had just enough time to duck down into the brush when we heard ravens in the sky.

"If we move slowly," Henry whispered, "I think we can make it. We just need to stay completely hidden."

We moved slowly, soundlessly, hardly daring to breathe. Moving inch by inch by inch until we were on the edge of the Western Valleys. Then, suddenly, the ravens that had cried and shrieked as they searched for us abruptly turned northward, as if responding to a signal of some kind.

Safely in the valley, and without the threat of ravens above us, I stopped and pulled out from my pocket the compass that George had given me and studied it. "I think we're in the right place."

"Now what?" Henry dropped his pack onto the ground, and flung himself down on it. "Should we keep going or stay here?"

I looked around uncertainly. I had been so sure that as soon as we reached the fairy hollow on the edge of the Western Valleys that we would immediately find Dori or Lia or Theo or the twins. And while it was true that the skies were free of black birds there was also no sign of anyone.

Suddenly the sound of low honking filled the air. Henry

looked up into the dusty blue sky of morning and pointed. "Look! A swan!" He jumped up and down, waving.

I looked up as a second swan appeared; two delicate silhouettes above us. "Lillianrose?" I whispered, and hugged my arms around my body.

Henry shaded his eyes with his hand, and his voice broke with relief. "It's them."

❧

Lily and Rose led us to the campsite. As they did, they described how for close to a week they had flown back and forth over the valley, searching for us. With the ravens heavy in the sky, it hadn't been safe for them to go beyond the borders of the fairy hollow, whose magic prevented the ravens from flying over the valley, and yet they hesitated not to, for they feared something terrible had happened to us. How they dreaded returning each night to the little group around the campfire, hated to report to them that we were still missing. That there was no sign of us.

When we finally stumbled into the campsite, it was nighttime. The campsite was little more than a cleaning in the woods, and through the darkness I could make out three figures sitting around a high-burning fire. Lily called out to them, and suddenly the figures came to life—racing over to where we stood.

"Thank goodness!" Lia said over and over again, as we took turns being buried in Dori's warm arms.

"We were so worried!" Theo cried, taking Henry's pack

from him and ruffling his hair, as the twins interrupted each other describing how they found us.

"Stop!" Lia said suddenly. "They're shivering, and I would guess they're hungry too."

Dori wiped at her eyes. "Well then, let's get you warm! Then you can tell us where you've been." Dori half-dragged us over to the roaring fire, and happily we collapsed on the warm ground.

"How's Merrill?" Theo asked anxiously.

Lily's voice was cross. "We all want to hear what they've been doing, but if you don't mind, some of us have been flying all day and are starving for dinner!"

After dinner, filled with soup and warm from the fire, we exchanged stories. Henry and I learned that the five of them had been in the Western Valleys for over a week, and when each day we still didn't arrive, they had grown nearly sick with worry—believed the worst had happened. Dori had sent word through the animals to look for us but none had seen us. First because we had been deep within the Jeweled Mountains, and later because we had hidden ourselves so carefully.

Before coming to the Western Valleys, the twins had spent weeks on Fox Lake, one of Gossling's great lakes. There, they had become friends with the hundreds of swans that lived on that huge lake. They had also borne witness to the destruction brought by the count's army—and watched helplessly as they burned fields heavy with unharvested crops, robbed and looted houses, and beaten those who tried to fight them. It was the twins who had been the first to arrive in the Western Valleys, and they had flown concealed within the protective anonymity of two hundred swans. Two days later, Theo, Lia, and Dori had arrived with their own stories of the count's destruction. For, before coming to the Western Valley, Lia, Dori, and Theo had fought to escape the count's armies in Central Gossling.

"The cities and towns are all but destroyed there," Lia said soberly.

Dori nodded and her face looked pained. "The Golden City was burned a week ago, and the destruction has been devastating. Thousands are without homes, there is no running water, no food . . ."

"Are the people fighting Count Raven's armies?" Henry's face was hopeful.

Lia shook her head. "No."

We were all quiet around the fire for a moment. Dori sighed a long, tired sigh. "These are sad days for Gossling."

Lia stirred the fire, and looked up at the sliver of moon and the bright stars. "There have been sadder days, sister. Think of the country of Reede—there, no one had hope; no one had the will to fight. In Gossling, at least, there is still some hope." She gestured to us.

"I don't understand!" I burst out, my face flushed with frustration. "Why are the people in Central Gossling allowing Raven's army to burn their homes and destroy their farms? I don't understand."

"People are frightened," Theo said simply.

"But there are thousands of us! Thousands!" I said

hotly. "Surely, if everyone fought together we would defeat them. Surely the count's magic is not so strong!"

Dori stroked my hair. "It's not that easy; it never is. The people have lost faith in themselves. They've lost themselves in fear."

"How?" Henry's hands were clenched in tight fists, and I could tell he was trying not to cry.

"How?" Dori was thoughtful. "The way we all do. Do you remember when you were very small, and you believed you could do anything?"

We nodded.

"Do you believe that now?"

Slowly I shook my head. "No."

Dori smiled sadly. "You lost faith in yourself. But the ability—your ability to do anything, to be anything, has never faded. Only your belief has. Now the people believe they can fight only after three signs have come."

"So we have to make the three signs come true," Henry said.

"We can't," I said flatly. "We can't fulfill those."

"You're not listening to Dori." Henry glared at me. "Believe we can, and we can. Do you want your sisters to spend their lives as swans and a tree? And what about the people of Gossling? If we don't fight, then they die. We'll fight until they are strong enough to fight with us, and if they need a sign to believe in themselves, then we have to make that sign happen! We have to!"

I was about to answer, to tell him again that this was

impossible. But before I could, Lily said evenly, "Tell us the three signs again."

Henry cleared his throat and recited. "First, the rivers of Gossling will be crossed without bridge or boat or ice; second, a halo of light will crown the mountains; and finally, a night sky will turn white."

"And what if we somehow fulfill the three signs and no one rises to fight?" Rose asked.

"Then we fight alone." Dori's face was grave.

"It won't happen," Henry said firmly. "The people of Gossling will rise up!"

"The people of Reede didn't—when the Amber Queen seized power they never fought against her. Even when her reign ended, the people remained half-asleep—paralyzed by inaction, and ashamed of their cowardice. They remain that way," Rose said flatly.

And we were quiet, remembering my mother's frustration with Reede's old king. "I don't understand!" I remembered my mother saying angrily to my father. "We can help them rebuild their country! Help them ignite their people! We will come to their aid." And Father's face had become troubled. "We cannot give aid if it is unasked for, or unwanted."

"We're not Reede," I said stubbornly. "We're Gossling, and we'll be different."

"The people of Gossling will rise up," Henry said again. "I know they will. They have to."

Lia nodded curtly. "Well, it won't be tonight, and if it's to be tomorrow, then it would be best if everyone went to sleep."

Theo nodded in agreement and stood up. "I'll make up beds for Henry and Amelia."

Theo made the beds so they circled the fire, and I quickly crawled into mine, snuggling down under the warm blankets. I could hear Theo's deep voice talking in low tones to Henry and the quiet sounds of birds settling into the branches.

Dori came over to me and sat down. "What are you thinking about?" she asked softly.

"Meg," I answered.

If Dori was surprised, she didn't show it. "What about Meg?"

"Well, Henry was bitten by a raven too, but the doctor in Nylorac thought that even if the bite had gone untreated, it still wouldn't have had the same effect on him as it did on Meg." I spoke haltingly, trying to make sense of what had happened.

Dori listened carefully, but said nothing.

I settled under my blankets. "I guess it's because Henry is good and Meg is bad."

Dori looked thoughtful. "It's rarely so clear-cut, Amelia. Rarely so simple—people are not all bad or all good."

"You're all good," I said loyally.

Dori smiled. "No." She said it so simply that I knew it was true. "I'm not good all the time, Amelia. No one can be. I grow impatient, I think unkind thoughts, I lose my temper. Minor crimes. But bigger ones too. For example, I wished my stepmother Dixon would suffer the way she had made so many others suffer. And regardless of how bad my stepmother was, my thoughts were cruel."

"You're still good, though," I said.

"I am," Dori said, and chuckled. "I am more good than bad. Just as perhaps Meg is more bad than good. Yet still, good lives within her, and that can't be dismissed."

I sat up a little and looked across the fire to where the firelight danced across Henry's face as he slept. "But she'll never be as good as you or Henry."

"Lie down, Amelia," Dori said softly. "She might not ever be *as good*, but people have different strengths. Also, Meg's parents are kind, and she was raised with love—that always helps . . . And yet"—Dori's voice was sad—"it's more likely that the raven's bite will always leave a mark on her."

"So she'd never have a chance to change?"

"Maybe not," Dori said.

I sat up suddenly. "Dori, I want to use one of my wishes from the witch of the Night Forest for Meg. Do you think that's a waste of a wish?"

Dori shook her head and smiled. "I think it's a very, very good use for a wish. But you have to wish carefully—you can't wish that Meg's personality be changed, for she must do that herself—the witch's magic cannot do it for her. However, you can wish that the raven's bite doesn't poison her. Then Meg will have her own choice—change or remain the same."

In the dying light of the fire, I dug through my pack, searching for the three stones. I took one out and held it tightly in my hand and wished for Meg.

CHAPTER 27

❧◈❧

The Longest Days

IT WAS STILL NIGHT when Dori woke us, and the coals of the fire burned low. Nearby, Lia packed the bags and blankets, and Theo heaped dirt over the last burning embers of the fire.

"Time to wake up and get dressed," Dori said gently, shaking me out of a dream. Half asleep and stumbling, Henry and I pulled on our clothes. When we were all dressed, and the last of the camp was packed up, we gathered together by the dark fire pit, eating Theo's burned berry porridge.

Her porridge finished, Dori spoke quietly. "It is time. We have little more than forty-eight hours before Raven's spell on the princesses becomes permanent."

"Then we need an action plan," Theo said in his most professorial voice. "Let's start with the halo of fire because it seems the most challenging."

"Fine," Lily said irritably. "How?"

"On top of each of the four mountains, there are stone watchtowers. They were built more as message centers than as

279

watchtowers—a halfway point for the rulers of Gossling and her neighboring countries to communicate."

"What do you mean?" Rose looked confused.

"A messenger from Gossling's queen or king would bring a message to the tower. When the fire was lit, the other country would know there was a message for them."

"Sometimes"—Dori's forehead wrinkled, remembering—"the fire was a warning or a signal of some kind."

"Either way," Theo continued, "each tower has a fire pit. Light each of the four fires, and the mountains of Gossling are crowned with haloes of light."

"But one person cannot possibly light them all," Henry cried out, his face strained with worry. "The space between the mountains is too great, and there isn't time!"

Everyone was quiet, thinking about the time it would take to climb to the tops of such large mountains. "I have an idea," I blurted out suddenly. "The twins could fly to the two farthest mountains."

Rose sat up and arched her long neck. "I could fly east."

Lily nodded. "I could go south."

"Good." Lia smiled. "And then Theo shall go north, and Henry and Amelia will together take the tallest and closest of the mountains, behind us to the west."

"But what about the other prophecies?" Lily asked.

"Never mind. First," Lia said, "let us concentrate on crowning the mountains with light, then in thirty-six hours we shall meet again at Gossling Palace, by that time we will have a plan to fulfill the other prophecies. Today, though, we separate. Dori and I shall go to Central Gossling, where Raven's armies continue to destroy the fields and cities. We shall use our own magic to fight his. And girls,"—she looked at Lily, Rose, and me—"Friday morning you must be at the Lake of Swans before dawn. Join Merrill and Amelia there. At first light, the spell is permanent—the twins will forever remain as swans and Merrill as a tree."

We were all silent as we ate the last of our porridge. Finished, I went to stand up, but Lia pushed me down again gently. "I've got to cut your hair, Amelia. Since the attack in the Jeweled Mountains, there is now a description of what you look like. The woods and cities of this country are filled with ravens. They'll be looking for a young girl with long red curls. They won't be looking for a boy."

"No!" Lily jumped up, knocking over her bowl. "You can't cut it!"

Rose said softly. "Mother would hate that."

Mother had loved my hair long. Long, long hair like a flame with ripples and curls and gold. Although I hated it and could never be patient for long, Mother would sit down to brush it each day, smoothing it, and tying ribbons in it to tame it.

"It has to be done," Lia said gently. "The risk is too great."

"Your mother would understand," Theo said kindly, "and it's just hair. It will grow back."

They nodded, but Lily and Rose still turned their faces away as Lia cut.

❧

When Lia was finally finished my neck felt cool. I reached up my hand and felt the empty area where my hair had

281

been. Lia gently blew on my neck, blowing away any stray strands that remained. I turned and looked at the pile of hair behind me and gave a long whistle. "Wow!"

"Wow, indeed," Lia said. She called for Henry and ordered him to give me a set of pants and shirt. "Put these on now, no dresses while you climb mountains, and certainly no petticoats."

The air was chilly, and I quickly slipped on Henry's clothes. When I was dressed, Lia eyed me closely; her eyes narrowed in thought and she nodded, satisfied. "Like a shorn sheep."

Coming up beside me, Dori's eyes filled with tears and she fingered what was left of my curls. "My Lord, you look like a boy."

"Good," Lia said briskly. "Then she'll never be spotted." She picked up handfuls of my long hair from the ground and threw them into the wind, laughing when a sparrow swooped down and picked up a long strand, carrying it off for nest building, hair trailing behind him like a red banner.

The sun, a thin gold disk, slipped into the sky and lightness began a slow spread across the eastern horizon. We stood together, a small group, watching the day begin.

"It's dawn," Theo observed.

"We will see you at daybreak in two days' time," Lia said, lifting her light pack from the ground.

Dori turned to Henry and me. "Be careful," she warned, "this won't be an easy fight."

"The people will rise up," Henry said, as he had said so often.

Lia's face clouded with worry. "Even if no one else shall fight, we will. Freedom will not be forgotten by everyone."

We were all quiet. A small sparrow alighted upon a branch by Henry, and he moved toward her, turning away from us. I watched as her delicate feathered head tilted from side to side before she rose into the air and flew south toward Gossling Palace.

I watched the bird fly in the direction of my home. "The people will rise up," I said, my voice husky.

Henry looked at me in surprise and then nodded.

"They will," Lily said.

"They will," Rose echoed.

"Long live Gossling," Theo said, low and quiet.

Then, with the dawn of the thirty-eighth day breaking, we set off, heading north, south, east, and west.

CHAPTER 28

The Rivers of Gossling Will Be Crossed

Tiege

There was a whisper in the tiny ear of a sparrow, a message. The smallest soldier of the White Queens' army, the sparrow climbed onto the back of the wind and rode it east from the Western Mountains. Ravens were thick in the air, still searching Central Gossling for the fourth princess, and for sport the huge black birds dove cruelly at the small sparrow. They did not know that she carried a message from the White Queens, for if they had known, they would have killed her. The sparrow flew as fast as she could. When she could travel no farther, she whispered her message to a bold running stag. When the stag finally came to rest on the banks of Gossling River, he gave the message to a strong beaver that swam miles and miles downstream, before passing the message to a rabbit that crouched on the shore. The rabbit ran and ran and ran until she reached a very small white dog on the edge of the palace grounds. The last messenger of Henry's whispered message, Snowy brought the message to Tiege.

In her cozy cottage Tiege took out all of her baking tins and ten bricks of chocolate, then, with Snowy at her heels, she went into her garden and clipped some pirate's beard, that delicate pink flower that could make a grown man sleep for hours. It was almost noon and the sun was high in the sky, and the day seemed ordinary. The garden was filled with rustling animals, and Tiege smiled at them, and then with the pirate's beard tightly in her hand, she went back to her kitchen and began to bake a special treat for Count Raven's guards.

❧

It's a good thing to ask for help when you need it, and even better to ask for help from a person that you trust. Standing on the edge of the campground, as everyone readied to travel up the mountains, that is just what Henry did: he asked for help from the person he knew would always give it.

Henry knew a secret about his godmother, Tiege, that few others knew. Like Amelia, he knew that Tiege was a princess, but he also knew that just like Dori and Lia, Tiege held her own powers. And Henry was practical, maybe the most practical member of the group that stood in the Western Valleys at dawn—he knew that for Gossling to have a chance of defeating Count Raven that within the next forty-eight hours three prophecies needed to be completed. And he knew that wasn't very much time.

&

Tiege was born on Turtle Island, a tiny peaceful kingdom far away from Gossling, on the warm southern seas. Turtles had been her first friends, and when Tiege first heard of the prophecies, she remembered swimming on the backs of those giant turtles, their shells knocking against each other in the waves, their bodies creating slow traffic in the warm blue water. Turtle Island, where the rivers could be crossed without bridges or boat or ice.

With the chocolate cookies baking in the kitchen and Henry's call for help in her ear, Tiege stepped out to the garden. She raised her warm dark hands and called the southern wind to her, whispered the story of the princesses and the raven, explained the story of the prophecy, and she, too, asked for help. Twelve hours after the small, determined group left the Western Valleys, that gentle wind took Tiege's message to her old friends, called it out in the rivers and lakes and ponds and creeks, whispered it to the mountain's streams and the wild oceans. And just as she had asked them to, the turtles came. Hundreds and hundreds. Their large, solid bodies slid into the Gossling River until it appeared to be filled with slick stones.

"The prophecy!" a fisherman cried out, his boat suddenly locked in place by turtles. "The prophecy!" And the people flocked to the river, ran to see it: a river that could be crossed without bridge or boat or ice.

෨෧

Dusk came to Gossling Palace, and there was electricity in the air, a strange energy. It was as if the earth itself was holding its breath, for the first prophecy had proved true and there was a chance that the other two would be as well. In the village of Gossling, people peered at the sky, hoping to see the crown of light ring the mountains, but they saw nothing—the mountains were merely mountains.

And the next day too, the mountains were just mountains, there were no haloes of lights to define them. *Nothing*. It seemed to me a terrible math equation: it had been twenty-four hours since we had begun to travel to the mountaintops, and nearly twelve hours had passed since the fulfillment of the first prophecy. So then, that left how many hours before Raven's spell was forever sealed, and my sisters were trapped forever? *Twelve*. There were only twelve hours until the dawn of the fortieth day.

In the palace, Count Raven's soldiers mocked the people of Gossling, and laughed at the idea that one of the princesses would return. Laughed at the idea that a prophecy could destroy Count Raven's power, or that a child's magic could be greater than Count Raven's.

Two soldiers sauntered into the dungeon where George and the rest of Queen Charlotte's advisors were being held. They looked through the bars at them and smirked. "Your country is filled with hopeful idiots! The princesses are long dead!" one taunted, his beady eyes filled with hate. The other gave a short, mirthless laugh and spat on the floor. "Long live King Raven!" The soldiers kicked at the barely filled dinner plates that were meant to feed the advisors, overturning them. "Eat up," one said over his shoulder as he stamped his boots through the spilled food. "Wouldn't want you to get too thin." Laughing, the men left the dungeon.

Unlike the soldiers, the men who guarded the advisors had once been the queen's own guards, and although they were now forced to work for Count Raven, they were still loyal to the queen. When the footsteps of the soldiers finally died away, one of the guards whispered to the advisors, "They're agitated for a reason: yesterday the first prophecy proved true."

George felt a flicker of hope. While he didn't believe in superstitions, he did believe in magic. He had seen it with his own eyes.

❧

Far from the dungeon, in the palace's bright kitchen, the soldiers who guarded the palace toasted each other and their king, Count Raven. Their cups were filled with ale, and they ate cookie after chocolate cookie from a heaping basket that sat on the center of the kitchen's table. It was a basket with a pink liner, and the small note attached with ribbon read in curling script the name of the cookie: *The Queen's Favor*. The men ate and ate, until they could eat no more.

CHAPTER 29

A Halo of Light Will Crown
the Mountain

Lily

Two sisters and two towers. Two fires to light—one to the east and one to the south. For a day we flew almost without speaking; watched the sky change above us from the pink of morning to the bright blue of midday to the gray-blue of dusk. Felt the air cool as the sun fell from the sky, the air cold on our bodies, the night became a deep velvet black; until even the stars were hidden.

Exhausted, we rested in a field in the southeastern corner of the country. We had not seen the twinkling lights of a town or city for miles and miles. Foreign and quiet, the field was filled with high grass and crickets; their song a lullaby around us.

We had flown with necklaces of yarn around our necks, and tied to the yarn was a box of matches. Rose shook the yarn from her neck and looked down at the matchbox grimly. "How do we light a fire when we have no hands?" she asked.

I stared at her and then at the matches and felt despair wash over me; we hadn't thought of this. "We can't," I said helplessly.

"But there must be a way." Rose's voice was low and determined.

The night was still, even the crickets' fiddles and the *click-click* of the blowing grass grew quiet.

Rose lifted her head. "What about the magic?"

"The magic?" I said slowly.

"Yes," Rose looked hard at the book of matches on the dark ground in front of her. The matches lay motionless and then suddenly lifted into the air. One match struck against a rock, and a flame jumped to life.

I laughed, and blew it out.

"Magic," Rose said.

Magic.

❧

We did not rest long. The towers were still miles beyond us and there were not very many hours left.

"I'll see you in the city of Gossling." Rose flung herself into the air, and for a moment there she was—a snowflake in the dark. Then she was gone—her body covered with the soot of the night sky.

I flew too, muscles straining hard against the wind until I reached the dark tower. I stared at the matches, lifting them with my mind until they struck the kindling in the fire drum of the tower and burst into flame. I stared to the east and saw that Rose's tower burned too.

Amelia

We were still hours from the top of the Western Mountains, struggling up the dark rocks, our hands cut and bleeding, and our knees scraped, when we stopped to rest. We sat on the edge of a sharp ridge and looked out into the night. The sky was very dark and I wondered if Tiege had fulfilled the first prophecy, if now the people of Gossling searched the sky as Henry and I did, seeking out that halo of light.

Then as we looked out into the darkness, we saw the very weakest of light burning on the top of the mountain to the north. At first it was nothing more than a small flickering light.

"Do you think the tower is lit?" I asked Henry.

He tugged on his lip and looked at the small light. "It could be. Or it could be someone walking with a lantern."

But then, as if to answer our question, the fire grew until its light was strong. Henry laughed with relief. "It's the tower! He made it! Theo made it!"

My eyes swung to the dark mountains of the east and south and as we watched, two towers were lit as if by one hand, fire that sprang to life in the south and east. *Lillianrose.* And with this gesture of light, the second prophecy was almost fulfilled.

Yet I was sure we were still half a night's journey from the top and there was little more than twelve hours before the spell became permanent. I looked at Henry. "Do you think the other prophecies have been filled?"

Henry shrugged. "I don't know, maybe, but the final fire must be lit, and there isn't much time. Look," he pointed, and in the darkness I could see that over the Northern Mountains, far, far away, but moving swiftly, was a darker tide, another army of black.

"We must light the fourth tower and quickly! Here." I pulled a white stone from my sack, held it tightly, squeezed my eyes closed, and wished.

I opened my eyes and before me stood a large white horse. I grinned with relief. "Get on, Henry," I said matter-of-factly, as if giant horses always sprang from white hard stones, "We're going to the top of the western tower."

෨෪

Here again was the unexpected: two hours before Henry and I completed the halo of light, to our northwest, a night guard of Reede saw Theo's light.

Long ago when King Chellgren's father was the young king of Reede, he had made a pact with his neighbor and friend the White Queen: should ever a distress signal be sent, the other would send aid. That king's son was now king himself, and an old king, but although the signal had never been used, it had not yet been forgotten.

In the palace a night guard saw the light. He rubbed at his eyes, for he was tired, and eyes can play tricks. He blinked again, and still he saw flames. Very distant, but flames still. Then the guard jumped from his chair, shouting and sounding the alarm. "It is the fire of Gossling! The signal is up!"

And the old king was roused from sleep. He stood at his window, and saw—far in the distance—the tower flames. He knew nothing of the raven or its prophecies, but when he saw the fire he remembered the old pact and believed that the people of Gossling were asking for help.

For forty years, the people of Reede had lived under the reign and fear of Raven's mother, Dixon. They had not asked for help. They had not fought for their freedom, they had simply surrendered, and when they had been freed of her rule, they had still slept. Acted without thought, seemed to live in a dusty world of dreams and inaction, and yet now something stirred in the king, something awoke in him as he stared at the fire that had once been a signal between two friendly countries, a signal that asked for help.

"Raise the army."

The steward had not heard him. "Sir?"

The king cleared his throat, cleared away the sleep and the indecision of fifty years. "Raise the army, we go to Gossling's aid."

That was four hours before. Now, it was close to one in the morning, and though our tower too was now lit, the magical horse that had appeared to take us to the tower had just as swiftly disappeared. And so Henry and I stumbled down the mountain, slipping on the rocks and roots below our feet. We stopped to rest for a moment on the edge of the third ridge.

Henry's voice was thick with wonder. "Look." He pointed, and following his eyes I saw, like a clear river of lanterns, the army of Reede moving swiftly toward us.

We ran to greet them, meeting them in a circled grove midway down the mountain.

The old king slid from his horse and walked toward us, his stewards and pages marching behind him.

"Your Highness," I said as I knelt before him. "We welcome you and your armies."

"Where is Queen Charlotte, child?"

"Our queen is dead, and so is our king." My voice broke.

"Who leads your armies?"

"The fourth princess of Gossling."

He nodded. "Can you bring me to her?"

"Yes." I stood before him as tall as I could. "I am the fourth princess of Gossling, Princess Amelia."

And the king was not angry, nor did he laugh, nor did he leave.

He knelt before me. "We honor the pact of your grandmother, the White Queen, and my father, King of Reede. We serve the people of Gossling; we fight with you."

I'm sorry to say that I cried, but I did, sat on the ground and wept. The king crouched beside me and placed his large warm hand on my head. "It has been a long road for such small children. But have faith, child, for there is still road ahead and war. There will be time for tears later, for now there is no time for fear or remorse, only courage. Rise, child, you are not the fourth princess any longer. Tonight you are Gossling's queen, and you shall lead your people to fight. I believe you shall win, but know that even in defeat, you shall find victory—for you have fought for freedom. And as for my own people, we despair of war, but we shall find pride in fighting for what is right, after so long ignoring what was wrong. Rise, Queen!"

And I stood.

CHAPTER 30

A Night Sky Will Turn White

KING CHELLGREN AND HIS ARMY began the steep descent to the valley, where they marched to meet Count Raven's winged army, and Henry looked at me. "We have to get back to Gossling City. You have to use the third stone, Amelia."

I pulled the stone from my sack and studied it. "We might need it later. What if the third sign never comes?"

Henry sighed. "The signs, the prophecies, they mean nothing! We both know that what matters is having someone to lead the people of Gossling. And that someone is you. But you can't lead from on top of a mountain! Do the transporting spell!"

"But—," I began. "I don't think my magic is strong enough to transport us both." I looked at him helplessly.

"It worked in the Jeweled Mountains," Henry said evenly.

"It *barely* worked, and it didn't transport us very far."

Henry tugged on his lip. "What if you used the Great Witch's wishing stone to help your magic? Together they should be enough to transport us to Gossling Palace, or at least closer than we are now."

I thought for a moment. "Okay, I'll try." Henry grabbed one of my hands, and in my other fist, I clenched the final stone hard, and closed my eyes.

Mountain treetops, far from home,
With help of magic wishing stone,
Swiftly travel, fast as light,
Bring us to Gossling on this night.

Nothing happened. Henry and I looked around us, it was still night, we were still on top of the Western Mountain.

"Say it again!" Henry urged. "Close your eyes and try again." We both closed our eyes, but before I had a chance something wonderful happened:

And when I opened my eyes, we were standing together in a field, Gossling Palace in the distance.

Henry opened his eyes and laughed. "Wow! I knew you could do it!"

Then we turned toward the nearby glowing lights of the city and started to walk.

On the edge of the city I began to feel sick, my stomach clenching and unclenching. I stopped and stood in the center of the dark road.

"What?" Henry demanded, stopping too.

"Nothing, I just . . . well, what if I can't? I mean, I don't know how to lead an army, or raise one . . . ," my voice trailed off miserably.

Henry glared at me. "Well, you're going to have to try. Because who else is going to do it, Amelia? Lily, Rose, Merrill? No! No one can, except for you!" He began walking, and then looked back at me. "Are you coming?"

I sighed. "I guess."

"That's the spirit," Henry said dryly.

Rose

The eastern tower lit, I began to fly for Gossling Palace. The night was velvet black and yet in the distance was a speck of white, a snowflake in the darkness. I called out, believing it was Lily, but a strange voice answered, a low honk.

I flew on, and saw another fleck of white, another snowflake—a swan. I called to it, and again a foreign voice answered, and as if in answer to that swan, a flurry of honks replied, and looking behind me I saw a long road of white, like the long train of a bride. Following me. Joining me. Our friends from the Great Lakes.

When we arrived at Gossling City it was two fifteen in the morning but the whole town was awake. It seemed almost every man, woman, and child was standing in their nightclothes gathered in the square, their heads raised to the four fires that burned on the mountains.

"It's the halo of light!" a woman breathed.

"The second prophecy has proved true."

"But what of the third?"

The swans we had traveled with looked troubled. Lily's

voice was sad. "Even with two prophecies fulfilled, the people have no faith."

Another swan nodded. "It's true. They would rather wait for a third sign, than fight for their freedom."

I remembered Henry's small, serious face and his words: "They will fight! They have to!"

"Then the third prophecy must be completed," Lily said slowly. "*A night sky will turn white.*" And although some say we think as one, I had no idea what she meant when she cried out, "How many swans can be called upon to join us?" Then she raised herself into the air, her white, white wings outstretched and milky against the night sky.

The swans began a low honking, but the ravens in the trees were not disturbed. They did not realize that the honks were cries for aid. Lazy, perhaps, they slept on.

Swans flew to the cities and towns of Gossling—thousands of swans. Lily raised her wings and rose up against the black night sky. Below her, there was a rustle of sound, a waving of feathered wings, as ten thousand swans lifted into the air and created a white sea in the darkness. With that the third and final prophecy was completed: *A night sky shall turn white.*

At the palace, the guards and advisors drowsed while the count's soldiers slept deeply, drugged as they were by Tiege's cookies. One of the queen's old guards was awakened by a dream of his country as it had once been.

When he awoke, he saw the white sky above him. "It's the final prophecy. The queen lives!" he cried out. His voice was weak, but it woke the other guards and they too turned their faces to the white sky, and then wept with joy. Then quietly, quietly, they crept to the dungeon, where they stole the keys off a drugged soldier from the Raven's army and soundlessly unlocked the door of the jails, freeing George and the other advisors. Then, still silent, they unlocked the gates of the palace and opened them wide, for they believed that the people of Gossling would now rise up, they believed that freedom was near, the hour soon upon them.

Amelia

We arrived at the city's center as the swans rose into the air, as the night sky slowly became white. Sitting on the edge of the square's fountain, we watched as the people rushed back and forth under the white corseted wings of feathers, pointing and laughing and weeping with relief that the final prophecy had been fulfilled. Henry and I stood by the stone fountain laughing and splashing each other with water.

"Where is the queen?" cried one man, looking around.

"It doesn't matter," a woman shouted above the noise of the beating swan wings. "She is among us; the third prophecy has proved true."

But it was too late. The crowd looked around them as if to find the queen in their midst, struck by the idea.

"Step forward," Henry hissed at me. "Amelia, step forward."

But I was frozen. I was not a queen. I was not even a proper princess, not the way my sisters were, I had neither grace nor charm nor wisdom nor even long golden hair. Who would believe that the queen they had waited for was me?

Small, firm hands pushed me forward so hard that I stumbled on the fountain's edge and almost fell. I turned to see who had pushed me and there stood Meg, her arms folded across her chest. Meg's hair was black, but there was still a streak of gold remaining, perhaps wider than before. She smirked at me, but her words were true and perhaps now even a bit kind. "You're the queen, Amelia. Act like it."

"It's her," I heard Henry cry from beside me. "The queen has returned," and then he fell to his knees.

CHAPTER 31

Battle

THERE WAS A HUSH, a sickening quiet, as the people looked at me. I'm sure I wasn't much to look at: my cropped red hair curling wildly, my nose burned, my cheeks smattered with freckles, both elbows scabbed, a long scratch down one cheek. I barely looked like a girl, no less a princess. Who knows what would have happened if a kind, familiar voice hadn't called out, "Amelia! It is the Princess Amelia! She lives, dear child!"

George, tattered and thin from his time in the palace dungeon, pushed through the crowd and hugged me. With a tear-streaked face, he turned to the people gathered on the square, before turning back to me, studying my face as if to memorize it. "My dear child, I thought all four sisters were lost, I thought I had failed your parents four times, and then the prophecies came true, and I had hoped and thought it impossible, but you live!"

"The queen lives!" a man yelled.

"Yes, yes!" The crowd shivered. "The queen lives!"

"Long live Gossling!" a voice cried, and then the crowd was quiet, waiting for me to lead them.

"A fourth princess isn't meant to lead, and an ordinary princess *can't!*" I heard my voice telling Merrill.

And her voice, steady and sure, "People aren't born to lead, they *choose* to. Make that choice, and you shall lead!"

"You can do it, Amelia," Henry whispered behind me.

And I began to speak.

"It is true that the prophecies have been fulfilled, but not all news is good. The armies of Raven march for the city and palace tonight. More armies have struck the northern ridge, and in the south there are reports that they come too. To the west, our allies from the kingdom of Reede have raised an army led by King Chellgren; they fight for our freedom in the Western Mountains. We have many allies. Many fight for our freedom. Only the people of Gossling do not fight. As of now, with your help, this will no longer be true.

"Now we must fight for our country. We fight for our valleys, our hills, our deep forests, our blue rivers, we fight for the children of our country, and we fight for our women and our men. We fight because we believe that our country and our freedom are worth fighting for.

"My mother and father detested war. But perhaps there must be war when there is injustice and violence that will not end. So I order, I implore you. Raise your weapons, whatever they may be: shovel, saucepan, or sword! I pray this battle will be a short one, I pray that we meet with victory, but if this fight is long, if we find defeat, let us know that we fought for what this country once was, and what it shall be again! *Free!*"

I lifted my sword. "Who fights with me?"

"I do!" It was Henry's lone voice, and then it was a chorus of voices, and then as we had dreamed they would, as Henry had always believed they would, the people raised their tools, their weapons, their voices, and stormed Gossling Palace and began to fight just as they could have done at any point during this story. The country of Gossling is small, but it does not lack bravery, only confidence.

❧

The palace battle was a fierce one, and one that I hesitate to tell about. I have always hated stories of war. In my father's library, men would often tell stories of battle—some true, many invented, all exaggerated. And these tales always told of heroism and bravery, but the blood and terror of true battle was always omitted.

Until now, our country had not really known war. In our battle against Raven, our armies were armies of civilians, not soldiers. Just ordinary people led by an ordinary princess. They were loosely organized and ill-equipped for battle, but they were brave and they fought hard. As my mother had said so long ago: ordinary people do extraordinary things every day. The count's armies were vicious with their small eyes and dark cloaks, and in their black armor they seemed almost invincible. Attacking the count's army in the palace, my small army of barely unarmed townspeople seemed almost silly in comparison.

Yet with the people of Gossling, we stormed the castle. George led the advisors to the sword room and those ancient swords were again drawn for battle. Tiege's cookies had left many of Count Raven's guards drugged and sleeping, and we bound them and dumped them into the very dungeon where they had kept our advisors hostage. Still, there were plenty who were not sleeping, and these were ready to fight.

Sword by sword by sword, we fought. Henry and I fought together on the long palace terrace that overlooked the Lake of Swans and I thought how my mother had said that she too would like to learn how to handle a sword so that she might protect her country. Each time I threw my sword toward another soldier in Raven's army, the man turned into a raven, and—crying—flew off into the sky, and was gone. Suddenly, I realized that the terrace was empty of the Raven's army, and that only Henry and I remained. Sweating, I grinned at Henry and he grinned back. He wiped his arm across his forehead and then his face grew pale and he grabbed my hand. "Look! It's almost daybreak."

I looked at the sky, and saw the first pink dusting of day across the fading night sky, but still I stared at him, not comprehending.

Henry's voice was urgent. "Remember the spell? Remember that on the fortieth morning the spell against the princesses would remain forever?"

I stared at him in horror, frozen.

"Come on!" He pulled my hand. "We have to get to the lake!"

CHAPTER 32

The Spell

WE FLEW DOWN the palace steps and across the lawn, which was damp with the dew of early morning. All around us the war continued: the men and women of Gossling fought the count's winged army on the steps, lawns, and gardens, and all along the sloping drive. But we could not stop to fight with them or give aid; we ran for the lake. When the ravens saw us racing toward the water, they cried out and flew to the palace.

"Hurry! Hurry!" Henry shouted. "They're going to get Count Raven."

The weeping willow tree that was my sister was listless, her leaves yellowing and limbs low. Lily and Rose sat in Merrill's branches, their bodies limp, feathers drifting from them like the softest snow.

"It's too late!" I started to cry, staring at them.

"You have to be in a circle," Henry said, shoving me next to Merrill. Ever so gently, he lifted the birds from their branches, placing Lily next to me and Rose next to Merrill so we stood in a circle.

Without warning, the wind rose, shrieking and crying around us, and black clouds spread over the dawn sky, blocking the weak beginning of light. Swooping toward us in this sudden darkness, the ravens screamed.

"Hurry," Henry cried, his voice almost lost in the wind. "There isn't much time before daylight, don't be fooled by the darkness!" Rain began to beat down on us. "Say the spell to free them, Amelia!"

The spell. I felt a cold fear spread through my body. This was a spell I knew no words to. I looked helplessly at Merrill, but she was unresponsive—exhausted and fading—and could offer no help.

"Say it!" Henry yelled and shook my shoulders. "You can do it! Hurry!"

But my mind was blank. I felt a flash of anger—Dori had said that when the time was right, I would know the words. So why didn't I?

And suddenly—strangely—I did:

Feathers of snow,
Roots of tree,
Double in childbirth,
Sisters, three.

I stopped for a moment, my body thrown back by the wind. "I don't know the rest," I said, a sob caught in my throat, but over the wind and rain and crying ravens, Henry couldn't hear me.

"You do know, Amelia. This is your own magic—this is

your own power, and you've had it all the time," my mother's voice was very calm in my ear. "Focus now."

I squeezed my eyes closed tight and cried out:

Free from soil,
Free from flight,
Four White Queens rule this night!

There was silence. Nothing. No sound of wind. No screams of ravens. No sound of rain. Just quiet.

I felt my mother's breath on my cheek, smelled her perfume. "I'm so proud of you," she said. And then she was gone. I opened my eyes, and blinked in the sudden sunlight.

"You did it!" Henry shouted, and threw his arms around me. I looked around, and where there had been a tree, Merrill stood grinning and stretching, and where there had been two swans, the twins stood hugging each other and squealing. His sword deserted, Theo came running across the grass toward us, and he and Merrill kissed and kissed, until Henry threatened to be sick if they didn't stop.

"He's right," Merrill said, her voice suddenly serious. "There is still a war to fight."

"No," I said simply, suddenly realizing what I had known all along. "Once the spell was broken, so was Count Raven's power. His armies have been turned to ash. The war is over. Gossling is free."

We all turned to the palace, as shouts of surprise and wonder rang out and the citizens and armies of Gossling realized that their enemy had turned to nothing more than dust.

"Let's return to the palace," Merrill said, straightening her gown. "There is much to do." She stepped forward and then she stopped, her face turning a sick shade of white. She gasped, staring over my shoulder.

I turned.

The man was as I had imagined him to be. Tall and aged, his pale, wrinkled skin taut against his skull and his dark cloak flapping behind him. He smiled at me. "So then, this is the fourth princess." His voice was sugared and sweet. "How I have searched for you! Dear child, did you think you could escape the Raven?" His voice turned cold as ice. "No."

He looked at us each in turn, and his thin lips twisted into a tight sneer. "When you stand in the presence of darkness, you bow before me! Bow!" A terrible jolt of fear spread through my stomach and made my body cold and heavy with dread.

"Bow, Amelia!" the count ordered. "Your sisters are safe, that's true, and perhaps that shall give you comfort in your last minutes, for I intend to kill you now."

Lily cried out, but the man did not turn toward her. He looked only at me and said in a low, measured voice, "I'm going to kill you, Amelia. I'm going to kill you, and your sisters shall watch your death and suffer that they are powerless to stop it."

He smiled; a slow, crooked, sinister smile.

"No, you're not!" Henry yelled, stepping forward. The motion distracted the count for a moment, and in that moment Merrill ordered, "Quick! Grab hands!" and we did.

Count Raven stepped back a bit, wary, but his face still

wore the same sickly smile. "Come, children, you don't believe that you have any power! You haven't been taught the spells of your great-aunts, of your mother! If you had, surely you'd have used them by now."

Merrill's chin lifted a tiny bit, and I felt my body relax slightly. Merrill knew something that the count did not, I was sure of it. And suddenly I knew: Merrill had read the Book of Spells. I gripped her hand tighter, as she said quietly:

Call to the mountains,
Call to the sea,
Call White Queens,
I call three!

And before I could remind her that there were four of us, Dori, Lia, and Tiege appeared in the circle's center.

"You!" Count Raven's smile curled into an angry sneer and his hands clenched into tight fists by his side.

"Yes," Dori said pleasantly. "Dear stepbrother, it has been too long! Do not worry about the girls' experience. Any that is lacking, we shall provide. After all, we have had seventy years to strengthen ours."

The count looked startled for a moment, but then his brow smoothed again. "Yet without your sister Elizabeth, you are only two White Queens, and your power is weakened."

Tiege drew herself up, and her small dark body seemed to glow and shake with light; she smiled ever so slightly.

The count stepped backward again, and a flicker of something like fear passed over his face.

Lia smiled a small, secret smile. "Raven, you have misjudged the power of three women bound with love for these children. You have caused sickness, sadness, death, and war! Everywhere you go, you leave evil behind you like the long, sticky trail of a snail." She strode through our circle, breaking through our hands and stepping before him. "We should have done this years ago."

The count moved, and in that movement, I saw his shape transform into a raven.

"He's going to fly!" I shouted, but it was too late for him.

Lia and Dori raised their hands high above them, and Tiege smiled as they chanted:

Black is rain, black is night,
All that is evil, turn to light!
Shell of crab, hair of doe,
Amber red, white as snow,
Dark of feather, and rabbit pale,
Change that with wings into snail—

Once said, forever sealed!

And the man-bird was gone. But in Lia's hand was a very small dark snail.

"You turned him into a snail?" Theo wondered, peering to look at the sticky creature.

Dori sighed. "Yes, and he'll probably end up making half the trees in the garden sick, but he'll be a snail all his days."

"He might be eaten by a bird," Lia said.

"That he might," Tiege said thoughtfully.

Lia placed the snail on the edge of the lake. "Go with gentleness, Raven."

He did not go far, however, for a moment later he was snatched into the beak of a mockingbird who swallowed him as a bitter meal.

CHAPTER 33

Gossling's Queen

BY NIGHTFALL all the country knew that freedom was ours. Fireworks exploded over the palace, and the kingdom shook with music and laughter and merriment. Early the next day, the armies of Reede moved through the countryside toward the palace, and they were greeted with confetti and cheering. Indeed, George mistook the visiting army as a parade because of the excitement and welcome it received. But a guardsman raced into the dining room announcing that King Chellgren advanced.

Forgetting breakfast, I ran down the palace steps and down the long road to the gates where the army of Reede marched toward the palace. Once again the old king slid from his horse. "The night was long, White Queen, but this morning is bright and clear."

He smiled down at me and I smiled back and then bowed before him. "I give you the thanks of my kingdom. Our people are in your debt for your kindness and aid."

"Friends are not indebted to each other, Queen. The

313

country of Reede considers the country of Gossling a friend. We know that had we asked so many years ago, your people would have fought with us, and I believe our histories would have been much different. The cost of freedom is very dear, and we have learned that well. We will not forget again." He smiled broadly and suddenly looked young.

I grinned back at him. "Can you stay for a while? Allow your armies and horses to rest before you begin the journey home?"

The old king nodded. "We would welcome breakfast, and water for our horses, but we are anxious to return home. There is much to do in the country of Reede. Still, travel and work are best done on a full stomach."

"And it's pancakes," I added.

"Even better!" King Chellgren crossed the long lawn to the palace with me.

❧

I had been queen for three days when I realized that I did not want the responsibility of being queen. You might think that after a war has ended in victory that all is well again in a country. This is not true. Count Raven had destroyed fields and crops, slaughtered animals, closed schools, burned mills, stolen from the museums, and bombed public buildings. Merrill was right: there was much to do.

And I was not the person to do it. After all, a twelve-year-old fourth princess is not ready to be queen. I had no idea how to reshape the school systems, how to fertilize the fields, how to rehabilitate the economy, or even how to rebuild the museums and arts centers. Perhaps I had been able to lead us in war, but I was not prepared to lead us in peace. Nor did I want to.

The morning I decided this, I strode into the library where Merrill, Theo, and George sat with the advisors. "I don't want to be queen anymore," I said loudly and dramatically, and then marched right out the door.

George caught up with me in the hallway and slipped his large hand into my own. "Come, let's go for a walk."

Bundled in my fall coat, my hands warm inside my gray gloves, I walked in the large main garden with George, pleased to be with him. We walked in silence, looking around us. Autumn was almost over and the garden was dying now, only the very last of the fall flowers remained, the red and yellow marigolds, the stubborn white pom-poms, and a few hearty goldenrod.

I sighed, and George looked at me. "Somehow it's rather sad here, isn't it? Let's go see how the pumpkins are growing."

We crossed into a kitchen garden that still hummed with life. Gardeners crouched in vegetable patches pulling up carrots, and digging up potatoes, while others were busy pruning fruit trees and tying down the summer's tomato plants. Large orange pumpkins knelt pregnant and round on the dark soil, and yellow and green squash waited on their tangled vines to be picked. George and I walked slowly along the stone path.

"I'm not going to be queen anymore," I said to George defiantly.

George stopped walking and crouched down so that our eyes were level. "Amelia," he said kindly, "you wouldn't have stayed queen even if you had wanted to. First of all, you're too young to rule Gossling, and second, third, and fourth of all, there are three princesses ahead of you who have the right to rule, should they choose to."

With a rush of embarrassment, I felt my face get hot. It was one thing to refuse to be queen and quite another to be told that you weren't allowed to be. "Well, I didn't want to be queen anyway," I said, drawing myself up as tall as I could.

"That's a shame," George said, standing again and wrapping his big hand around my little one. "Because someday, somewhere, you'll be the very finest kind of queen. After all, you already have been." He smiled at me, and I couldn't help it, I smiled back.

❧

The "transfer of the crown" as George named it, was to take place the following Sunday on Merrill's eighteenth birthday. As my mother and father had promised so long ago, there was to be a huge celebration that the entire kingdom would celebrate. However, it was not only Merrill's birthday and crowning we would celebrate, it was also her wedding.

Merrill had proposed to Theo four mornings after the battle had been won. It happened when we were sitting at breakfast. Theo was musing about starting our lessons again that afternoon, Lily and Rose chattered excitably about their afternoon ballet class, while George munched on his third pastry and flipped through the newspaper. Dori was explaining to Lia the rather tedious cleaning schedule she had designed for the palace's maids and housekeepers, though she shot a dark look at my sisters and me. "Everyone is responsible for cleaning her own room, mind you."

Henry looked anxious. "Does Amelia have to clean her room right after breakfast? We were going to play Dragon Slayer in the garden with the palace children."

Dori frowned, mentally rearranging her cleaning schedule.

"Please," Henry and I begged in one voice.

Dori smiled at us, relenting. "You can do it after lunch then, but it had better be spotless."

"It will be," I promised.

An ordinary breakfast, made extraordinary because of the weeks we had just lived through. Ordinary. Then, unexpectedly, Merrill turned to Theo and said, "I love you and I want to marry you."

Lily choked on a bite of bacon, and George thumped her hard on the back. Rose's hand stopped midair, reaching for a muffin, and a maid transferring a fresh platter of new eggs to the table froze. Henry and I grinned at each other, and Dori and Lia exchanged a look that was impossible to read.

"Marry me," Merrill said, and she smiled at Theo, a smile so bright that it could have lit the sky.

Theo smiled back with that same smile. "I love you too— love you more than words can say!" Then his smile disappeared, and his face lost all color, turning a strange shade of gray. "But I cannot marry a queen . . . I'm not a king, I'm a scholar! And what about the council? It says in the constitution: *A queen must marry a king or prince.* And I am neither."

Merrill looked annoyed for a moment. "What qualities does one need to be king that you do not possess? You are loyal, kind, smart, and my best friend! On top of that, we're in love, which is the most important quality of all! It would be an honor for you to be my king, and to rule beside me." Her voice was defiant, though it quavered slightly.

Theo looked down miserably at his porridge. "It can't be, Merrill. I'm sorry."

Merrill—steady, unflappable Merrill—burst into tears. She threw her napkin down on the table and pushed her chair back so fast that it toppled over, then she fled from the dining room.

"Merrill!" Theo jumped up and ran after her.

❧

The room unfroze. Lily started crying and Rose stared wretchedly down at the table. Henry frowned into his orange juice and I scowled, my eyes looking out the wide window to the Lake of Swans, where Theo stood talking to Merrill, both his hands in hers.

"Well," George took off his spectacles and pinched the bridge of his nose, "certainly *something* can be done, don't you think?" He glanced at Dori and Lia, and they nodded briefly, though their faces were tight and sad.

"Come now." George looked around the table at all of us. "Let's not look so glum yet! Things aren't so bad that they can't be fixed." He smiled his wonderful smile. "Now, I'm going to excuse myself, as I have some business to do."

❧

In addition to being my father's chief advisor, George also served as the head of the Gossling Council. The people of Gossling elected each member of the council. Now George called an emergency meeting; he wished to introduce an amendment to the Gossling Constitution.

Generally the council met in the Court Building in the heart of Gossling City, but Count Raven had damaged it, so the meeting was to take place in the palace's large ballroom. It was a ragged group that filed into the ballroom, and their faces were quizzical—as if wondering what new emergency had occurred to prompt such as a meeting. Yet, although in some ways it was an emergency, George's constitutional amendment had nothing to do with war or invaders or farming or fields; it had to do with marriage. To Henry and me, listening outside the door, the meeting seemed to drag on forever, but really it was quite brief and the decision unanimous. In the end, the council voted that George's amendment be passed, and so it was added to the Gossling Constitution: *A queen or a king could marry whomever they love, citizen or royalty.* As one council member wisely said, "Love cannot be dictated by law."

CHAPTER 34

The Extra-Ordinary Princess Amelia

THE NIGHT BEFORE Merrill's birthday and marriage celebration we girls all slept together for one last time in the nursery.

Lily looked around my bedroom and her face grew sad. "It's strange that only a few months ago Mother was standing here with us."

Rose stopped brushing her hair and looked around too, as if she half-expected Mother to walk in. "Has it only been a few months? It feels like years—so much has changed."

Flopping down on my bed, I nodded. "You both changed a lot!" I grinned at the twins and made the sound of a honking swan.

"Funny!" Lily yelped, and her face lost its somber expression. She lifted up her pink pillow and threw it at me, laughing.

"Don't kill the messenger. Except for a little haircut, I didn't change!" I threw the pillow back at her.

Rose put her brush neatly on the bedside table, and then slid under her covers, arranging them carefully around her. She looked thoughtful. "Actually, I think you changed the most."

Lily nodded, and fluffed her pillow before lying back on it. "Even if you didn't change much on the outside, you're different, Amelia."

"Sure," I said, rolling my eyes.

But Lily shook her head. "I'm not teasing, you have changed. I can't explain it, but it's there."

Rose yawned and rolled over. "We should go to sleep. Tomorrow everything is going to change again."

Merrill smiled. "Hopefully for the good!"

"It will be very good," Lily said sleepily.

"Very," Rose murmured, already half asleep.

✤

I couldn't sleep. I watched as the fire began to burn down and the moon's shadows grew longer, and I thought about all the things that had changed in the weeks since Raven had lost his power. Without Count Raven, without war, and without my parents, life settled into a new kind of ordinary. In some ways it was all different: outside the palace walls, the country struggled to rebuild homes and public buildings, new crops were planted, schools resumed their schedules, and shop owners opened their stores again for business.

Inside the palace, life was different too: without my parents, the palace sometimes felt lonely. The dining room, even when filled with Lia's laughter or George's funny stories, still felt empty, as if the room too waited for them to sweep in and pull chairs to the table, apologizing for being late, and entertaining us with stories of what they had seen and adventures they'd had.

In other ways, life was as it had been before. Henry and I took lessons from Theo every morning, and every afternoon I suffered through all the lessons and indignities of making me a more graceful princess, and after I was done, Henry and I waited for the palace children to return from school, and we played with them until dinner. Meg continued to annoy me, as no doubt I continued to annoy her, but there was a small difference between us; not quite a friendship, but something. And sometimes Meg seemed nicer, and it was true that her hair—although still streaked with black—grew blonder and blonder each day, and I thought about what Dori had said about choices. Dori continued to scold and spoil us. She and Tiege and Lia spent hours in Tiege's bright kitchen laughing and eating cookies, and Tiege and Lia spent much of their days tending to the jungle of flowers that Tiege called her garden. Merrill and Theo were hopelessly in love, and hopelessly busy—working into the early hours of the morning to figure out ways to help Gossling rebuild. Lily and Rose continued dancing lessons, and continued to speak and act like one, but something was different, something I couldn't quite pinpoint, somehow they weren't quite so similar. For the first time in their lives, people could tell them apart. Lily looked like Lily, and Rose looked like Rose, and the nickname Lillianrose faded away, forgotten.

❧

The nursery was quiet, and across the room I heard the deep even breathing of the twins as they slept. I turned over in bed, finally tired. Far in the distance, the tower bell rang midnight. "Happy birthday," I said sleepily to Merrill.

"Thank you," she whispered. Merrill got out of bed and stirred the fire, quietly replacing the poker; then she came and sat on the edge of my bed. "Amelia, are you still awake?"

I nodded, yawning.

The tower bells began to chime again—this time eighteen chimes, to mark the birthday of Gossling's soon-to-be queen. In the morning there would be a coronation and a wedding, and at night there would be a thousand fireworks and two giant cakes and a huge party, celebrated across Gossling.

"You're going to be queen tomorrow," I said to Merrill.

"It already is tomorrow," Merrill said, smiling a little.

I rolled my eyes at her, "Okay, you're going to be queen *today*."

Merrill laughed, but then her face became grave. "Gossling wouldn't have a queen today without the fourth princess. I don't know if you've heard, but my ordinary, not-so-special, not-very-remarkable, very regular little sister saved Gossling," she said softly, mocking me, and I could hear the smile in her voice. Then her voice changed and became serious. "The twins

323

are right, you know: you are the most changed. But they're wrong too, because you're also just the same Amelia."

I looked up at her and grinned. "Ordinary."

She smiled back. "Just ordinary Amelia. Some might even say *extra-ordinary*! But I'll settle for ordinary, because if this is ordinary, then I hope you stay ordinary forever and ever."

And I did.

ACKNOWLEDGMENTS

I'd like to thank my father, Kenneth C. Ebbitt, the best story-teller I know. I'd also like to thank my brother, Kenny, who listened to my first stories. Thanks also to Jennifer, Cooper, and Ryan Ebbitt; Robert Russo, for my writing room; the Geduld family: Buzzy, Victoria, Amanda, Nancy, and Brammy; Barbara Vlak, Aimee Sherman, Bree Andrews, Claire Williams, Thu Van Dinh, Sue Lipani, Amy Wilensky, Matt O'Keefe, Leah Stewart, Bryant Palmer, M. B. Gruber, and to my very patient agent, Richard Abate. Thanks to my favorite student readers: Flip and Sari Biddelman and Emily and Lauren Capkanis. And above all, a huge thanks to my editor and best friend, Victoria Wells Arms, who has been editing me since I was fourteen.

CAROLYN Q. EBBITT

received her MFA in creative writing from
Columbia University. She is a teacher and
reading specialist, and she lives in New York
City. This is her first novel.

www.carolynqebbitt.com